Secrets of the Forest:

Calling Up the Flame
~ The Creation and Sustenance of Fire ~

and

Feeding the Spirit

~ Storytelling and Ceremony ~

Volume 2
Secrets of the Forest Series

Written and illustrated by Mark Warren

WALDENHOUSE PUBLISHERS, INC.
WALDEN, TENNESSEE

Secrets of the Forest: Calling Up the Flame and Feeding the Spirit
Copyright ©2015 Mark Bazemore Warren, 1947. All rights reserved. No part of this book may be reproduced in any form, or by any means, electronic or mechanical, including photocopying, recording, or any information browsing, storage, or retrieval system, without permission from the author.
Illustrations by Mark Warren.
Photographs by Bard Wrisley, Adam Nash, Betty Litsey, and Susan Warren.
ISBN 13: 978-1-935186-89-2   ISBN 10: 1-935186-89-2
Library of Congress Control Number: 2017907476
"Calling up the Flame: the art of fire-creation, pyre-building, wood selection, being match-savvy, sustaining a fire, fire-by-friction using the hand-drill, bow-drill, and fire-saw; and Feeding the Spirit: storytelling and ceremony. Over 100 original hands-on activities; 309 illustrations." -- Provided by publisher
EDU029000 EDUCATION / Teaching Methods & Materials / General
REF031000 REFERENCE / Survival & Emergency Preparedness
OCC000000 BODY, MIND & SPIRIT / General
SPO009000 SPORTS & RECREATION / Camping
Published by Waldenhouse Publishers, Inc.
100 Clegg Street, Signal Mountain, Tennessee 37377 USA
888-222-9229   www.waldenhouse.com
Printed by We SP Corporation, Seoul Korea   05/25/2017   79402

Dedication

To Herb Barks, my friend
For all our days on the river ... and all the days in between

Secrets of the Forest

Learning Nature through the adventure of primitive survival skills
... and teaching it to your children

VOLUME 2.

Calling Up the Flame

Everything you need to know about FIRE: pyre-building, wood selection, being match-savvy,
sustaining a fire, fire-by-friction using the hand-drill, bow-drill, and fire-saw

and

Feeding the Spirit

Storytelling and ceremony

 over 100 original hands-on activities

Photography by Bard Wrisley,
Adam Nash, Betty Litsey, and Susan Warren

The SECRETS OF THE FOREST Series
~ The Books of Medicine Bow ~

Volume 1:

<u>*The Magic and Mystery of Plants*</u> (Identifying and using wild plants for food, medicine, and craft) **and** <u>*The Lore of Survival*</u> (Shelter, water, rabbit stick, hunting, tools, insect repellents, cooking, traps & snares, food, and medicines)

Volume 2:

<u>*Calling up the Flame*</u> (Everything you need to know about FIRE: pyre-building, wood selection, being match-savvy, sustaining a fire, fire-by-friction using the hand drill, bow drill, and fire saw) **and** <u>*Feeding the Spirit*</u> (Ceremony and storytelling with purpose)

Volume 3:

<u>*Eye to Eye with the Animals of the Wild*</u> (Stalking, tracking, hide-tanning, and snake lore) **and** <u>*At Play in the Wild*</u> (Games: academic, adventurous, and around the fire)

Volume 4:

<u>*Projectiles*</u> (Making bows and arrows, the art of archery, throwing spear, knife & tomahawk; the atlatl) **and** <u>*The Blessed Path of Water*</u> (Whitewater canoeing: from lake to river)

TABLE OF CONTENTS

Foreword

Most of my thirty-four years of teaching at Minnetonka High School in Minnesota was spent working with "at-risk" youth in an alternative school setting. We called this school within a school "the Mini-School Program." One of the main components of Mini-School was its "trips" program, in which instructors led groups of eight to ten students on one to three week wilderness canoe trips, backpack trips, and winter camping trips. The main objectives of the trips were to promote goal-setting, cooperation, accountability, and discipline in a challenging environment. Our hope was that these lessons would then transfer to the students' daily lives back in their urban setting.

I was fortunate to meet Mark Warren in 1986 on, of all places, Isle Royale in Lake Superior, where I had brought a group of students for a seven-day outing and he had come to experience wolves. From our brief conversation, I was prescient enough to realize that the lessons and activities he used with students at his wilderness school, Medicine Bow, could add a dimension to the work I did with my students.

Thus began a seventeen-year relationship where Mark came to Minnesota for a week every October and engaged my students in the activities outlined in "Secrets of the Forest." The effect on my students was profound. The kids found the games, the crafts, the knowledge and survival skills imparted – stalking, tracking, cordage, shelter, fire, and more – fun and enjoyably challenging. Most important, however, was that these exercises fostered in my students an awareness, a consciousness, of how they fit in, not just in a natural setting, but in their daily lives at school. They exhibited confidence and self-assurance after a week participating in many of the activities Mark outlines in "Secrets of the Forest" that was not evident before. These lessons struck home with these teens in large part, I believe, because of his use of ceremony.

So, I say to fellow teachers, parents, and grandparents – immerse yourself in the activities Mark outlines in these volumes and get your kids outside. You and your kids will find the lessons engaging and fun. But most importantly, these activities impart Mark's overriding philosophy – that we are connected to and part of the natural (REAL) world. This awareness is essential to our well-being in an increasingly technological world.

~ Doug Berg, Minnetonka teacher and outdoor adventure leader

Author's Note

As it was once phrased within some native mythologies, certain trees "swallowed fire in the olden days." These words might seem to evoke a fabulous image, like a lightning bolt searing into wood, but this "swallowing" process was not so dramatic an affair. It was silent and invisible, however, no less profound. It was done on a second-by-second basis during the daylight hours. We now call the phenomenon "photosynthesis."

I suspect that – on an instinctive level to which we are not privy today – the people of earlier times innately understood the fundamental role of green plants in capturing the sun's energy. That understanding might explain – at least in part – why the Cherokee in my area once paid tribute to plants through ritual, prayer, and gift-giving. Among the many utilitarian uses of plants was knowing how to recapture some of that soaked-up solar energy for the purpose of producing a flame. But which species of trees provided the best material?

The answer to that question may have been obvious to native tribes, who lived their lives so integrated with the natural world. Any Cherokee child probably could have cited a list of good fire-making wood. In my lifetime that special cadre of trees had to be discovered through trial and error experiments.

Of course, all trees experience photosynthesis, and all will release their stored solar energy when burned as fuel. But only select trees will deliver up a flame from the heat of human-made friction, and they will surrender that fire only to the hands of one who knows the proper technique for releasing it.

Revisiting this ancient skill is like rounding the curve of a historic circle, one that can enrich us by the reconnection to history alone. The special value of fire-making is not solely in producing a flame. It is re-entering the forest in a frame of mind that sees the natural world as *the real world*. It is re-assessing the forest, elevating it from the scenic but prosaic backdrop of our days to a vibrant and living storehouse brimming with the essential gifts of life.

To create fire by friction you will be collecting *select* dead wood for a fire kit. Remember, not just any tree will do. The density, texture, porosity, grain, resin retention, and hardness (or softness) of some species of wood preclude the feasibility – if not the possibility – of creating fire by friction. The limiting factor is human strength.

Even the most problematic woods might be used successfully to create fire with the aid of high-speed machinery. As an example, I have, on occasion, inadvertently created fire in sawdust with a chainsaw while sectioning a dead scarlet oak, a tree generally considered (by practitioners of woods-lore) *not* to have "swallowed fire."

Likewise, certain plants offer fine material of leaf, bark, pith, wood fiber, or seed down that can be worked into tinder (the combustible material which can easily burst into flame) … while others do not. As in all the survival skills, a fire-maker who has invested time in plant study has a distinct advantage over

someone who approaches the skill as a "sporting event" isolated from Nature. (Botany, in my opinion, is the foundation of virtually every survival course I teach … even tracking, archery, and stalking.)

In this book we will dive headlong into the adventure of accumulating these botanical details, understanding the relationship between plants and fire, and mastering the ancient techniques of drawing a flame from dead wood.

There is a swell of satisfaction that fills a student of survival skills at every milestone of his journey: to sink his teeth into the surprising taste of a plant that he has positively identified for food-harvest … to creep within a few yards of a deer or turkey or squirrel to observe its habits … to curl up under a dry, self-made, primitive shelter as winter rain hammers the earth all around. Each accomplishment feels monumental. But creating fire is special.

Producing a flame makes a seismic shift deep in the soul of the fire-maker. To walk into a forest knowing that you can produce a flame with your bare hands using the simple materials of the woods (and knowing that this flame will take care of so many of your needs) engenders an indigenous pride of self-sufficiency and self-esteem. A successful fire-creator belongs to a larger picture of life on Earth – one that includes a more intimate connection to the past, a more pragmatic immersion into the present, and a more hopeful confidence in the future. Such a fire-maker, past or present, touches the heart of the Earth and feels its heat.

The Standing People – as the Cherokees called the trees – do literally "swallow" fire. When we create a flame from grating two pieces of wood together, we release that celestial energy. We are like apprentices to the Maker of All Things, understudy-authors of a pyretic genesis, creating a tiny "sun" of our own … that is, a bright ember. We feed it, use it, and then, at the end of the day, sit back and gaze into its mystery.

What are these orange, yellow, blue, and sometimes copper-green flames that dance and twist so fluidly, embrace us with warmth, cook our food, temper our tools, and shed light upon the moment? A fire is the hearth of the world. Wherever you happen to be as you sit before your self-made flames, you have come home.

PART 1

~ Calling Up the Flame ~

"Torches of seasoned pine knots are much in use among the Cherokee for lighting up the way on journeys along the difficult mountain trails by night. Owing to the accumulation of resin in the knots they burn with a bright and enduring flame, far surpassing the cloudy glow of a lantern."

~ James Mooney, History, Myths and Sacred Formulas of the Cherokees

CHAPTER 1
Striking Out
~ the match, for better or for worse ~

One morning after a heavy rain my fifth-grade wilderness campers peeked out from their tents with defeat in their sleepy eyes. The forest was soaked, and last night's campfire was in black and sodden ruin. The students knew that a fire was needed for our breakfast, but their hunger did not want to wait.

Their biggest disappointment, I think, was that, instead of remedying our fire-less situation, I sat by the creek reading a book. On the day before, we had hiked for miles cross-country through the mountains to get to this creek, whose beauty, I had promised, would be worth every step of the way. And it was … until now. To the children the increased roar of the rapids seemed only to emphasize how the rain had sabotaged our trip.

For my students, the dawn portrait of a rain-christened forest was less scenic than daunting. Fire was *their* job and they knew this, but no one appeared motivated. After a time of watching them mill about – no doubt waiting for a rescue (a secret backpack filled with dry wood?) – I gathered them together and asked a question.

"If you consider all the dead wood available in this rain-drenched forest, how much of it, would you say, is dry?"

You can imagine their expressions. Nothing in sight was dry.

"None of it," someone finally said.

They were surprised to hear me say, "The answer is ... except for the rotten wood embedded in the leaf litter ... *most* of it is dry!"

I let that statement hang in the air for several seconds. Then I continued.

"Only the outside is wet. Inside each wet stick there is lots of dry wood waiting to be revealed by our knives."

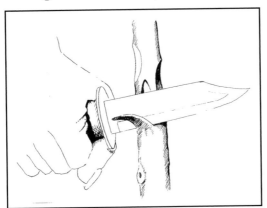

This simple exercise dominated our early morning. Without it we could not have achieved a successful fire.

We spent the next hour stripping off wet bark (thumbnails work well on kindling-sized pieces) and shaving away the wet exterior of dead wood. In the process we collected a large pile of dry, curly slivers from the interior of white pine, hemlock, and tulip magnolia – all fast-burning woods which would throw off a lot of heat for drying out sticks that we hadn't carved.

The shavings were thin, like narrow potato chips. So much surface area (compared to total mass) offered quick exposure of wood to air and heat for ignition. More importantly, they were dry ... cut from the interior of outwardly wet sticks.

As our premium insurance for success, we also carved shavings off a dead Virginia pine – known in these Southern Appalachian Mountains variably as "lighter-wood," "fat-wood," "fat-lighter," or simply "lighter'd." (We will cover the uses of lighter-wood later.)

On previous gatherings with me, this class had spent a lot of time learning about fire-building, but we had never undertaken the challenge in such wet conditions. Now they had created (earned) every piece of fuel to be used for the initial kindling. Using their shavings the children carefully composed a pyre – stacking sticks in a logical progression that would allow a match flame to grow to a larger flame and travel upward without prematurely confronting a piece of wood too large to ignite. With patience and lots of knife-work, we achieved a roaring fire that boosted spirits and cooked our breakfast.

Drench a Stick and Burn it

– Select a pine tree with dead branches low enough to be reached from the ground. Break off a limb at least as thick as a man's thumb. Anchor a 12"-long section of this stick underwater in a stream for an hour. Later, retrieve it, and, using a rock or a metal tool, scrape away any bark that might be present. Dry your hands with a towel and feel the wood to get a sense of the stick's dampness on the surface. Using a knife, carve away the outer layer into a pile of shavings on a dry surface. Holding one of these chips with forceps or a pinch-stick (see illustration), try to ignite it with a match. If it does not light, carve away more thin slivers

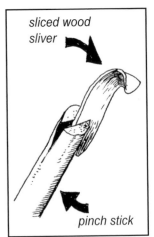

sliced wood sliver

pinch stick

closer to the core. Once you have found dry wood at the interior, carve lots more and pile these shavings together like a wooden igloo, poke a doorway with your finger and try lighting with a match inside the doorway.

If I were to suggest one survival skill as mandatory for people of all ages, it would be fire-making. It's not that I would expect everyone to embrace the old ways of *creating* fire – as impressive as that skill is – but I think that everyone ought to know how to get a fire going with a single match … and sustain it without the use of flammable chemicals or paper … both of which might not be available in a needy scenario. The fact is: most people can't.

To most adults with whom I have discussed this, their typical efforts at getting a fire started include using a flammable chemical fluid. And, indeed, whenever I happen to be in a public campground, that is exactly what I see.

In my experience as an observer, it is almost always a man in charge of the fire. He throws sticks into a pile and on top of that squirts a good portion of a can of some flammable liquid that I can smell from thirty yards away. He strikes a match, steps back, and tosses the match in an arc to the evaporating liquid.

Phwump!

There are usually wide-eyed children standing close by, watching the conflagration, constantly being told to get back. From the looks on their faces, this appearance of a flame might be the most exciting part of their day … and with good reason. Fire is magical. You can't *not* look at a fire. It is too alluring, compelling. I suspect that fire has always held this fascination for all ages.

I suppose there is nothing too very wrong about the use of lighter fluid. There is the air pollution factor, of course, but we who love open fires might have a difficult time winning any argument about rationalizing our contribution to air pollution. But this dousing and lighting method simply shows no finesse. It's a crude manner of engaging in one of man's oldest survival tasks. Its weak point is the man's dependence on the chemical. Without it, he might go through quite a few matches before achieving a sustainable flame. In fact, I've seen people use a full box of matches as kindling – that is, throwing the full box into a struggling pile of smoldering sticks.

I make these assessments of modern-day fire-building incompetence with a fair amount of certainty, because I hold adult fire-making classes at my wilderness school. The first task I give my "fire students" is to clear a space, gather sticks (only) and build a structure (the pyre) that they are to light <u>with a single match</u>. Very few can do it. Those who fail are often surprised. Even if I expand their arsenal to two matches, the result is the usually the same – namely, because the original mistakes made in the building of the pyre are not corrected.

The success/failure ratio in my classes averages out to 1.5 successful one-match fires out of thirteen attempts. That's 11.5% of the class. Then, after so many first-try failures, I take the students through a detailed demonstration of building

a well-thought-out pyre. Their second attempts at the one-match fire challenge usually enjoy a 100% success rate. Interestingly, near the end of the class – after the lessons on creating fire by friction (without a match) – the success rate is encouragingly high. On the average, eight out of thirteen students produce a flame. But making a pyre and creating a fire are two different things, and mastering the former should most definitely be a prerequisite to the latter.

Most people who have blundered into or been thrown headlong into a survival situation usually have a good many assets already at hand. Even in an airplane crash – if some of the fuselage is intact – there is shelter from rain or snow. A motorist in remote country with his car broken down does still have his car, which is a good wind-proof and water-proof compartment. Hikers usually have a tent or tarp.

In each of those cases there is also probably some kind of blanket or other insulation available, a container for catching rainwater, and more than likely some food – even if it's just a bag of chips or a candy bar. (Hunger, though one of the early concerns people fret over in a survival situation, is not life-threatening until about two weeks.)

Hypothermia is a deceptive enemy. It stalks in, ambushes, and debilitates, rendering its victim helpless faster than he might expect.

If the mishap occurs in winter, the most pressing need might very well be heat; for right up there with panic and dehydration on the list of fatal factors in a survival situation lurks hypothermia. In cold (and, especially, wet) weather, the dropping of body temperature is the nemesis of anyone stranded away from help. Knowing how to get a fire going fast – and how to keep it going – could mean the difference between being able to perform the tasks required of you and being helpless. In other words, it draws the line separating life and death. Fingers – our most important tools – are usually the first body parts to go numb and useless.

Hypothermia is a deceptive enemy. It stalks in, ambushes, and debilitates, rendering its victim helpless faster than he might expect. Once in its clutches, there is no letting go. A hypothermic person can no longer fend for himself. He needs the help of another person to provide external heat (a fire, heated rocks, a warm body) or internal warmth (hot drinks).

The chances are good that someone in one of the aforementioned scenarios would be a smoker with matches or a lighter. The motorist would have a built-in lighter on his dash – assuming the battery works. Presumably, the hiker would have packed matches. Each of these victims might even have access to a flammable liquid: airplane fuel, gas from the car's tank, and fuel for a camp stove. But maybe not. The plane's fuel tank could have ruptured. Perhaps the car ran out of gas. The hiker's fuel supply would be limited.

Once again, knowing about fire-building would prove essential … and not just for warming the body. Fire can also be used to purify stream water and to cook something that good fortune or successful hunting might afford.

Some teachers of survival skills place fire rather low on the list of priorities. I rate it high. There is comfort in fire, both physical and psychological. In Southern Appalachia – where I live – winter cold is exacerbated by humidity. 25° Fahrenheit in north Georgia can feel like 12° in Colorado. Even in the spring and early summer (and well into summer during a rainstorm), Appalachian nights can be dangerously chilling for the unprotected.

Furthermore, the South has a unique pest in the chigger – a mite, also called a "red bug." In summer, a person nestling into leaves to stay warm is fairly offering himself up as a human sacrifice to chiggers. All people do not react to chigger bites adversely, but for those who do, chigger bites are maddening, demoralizing, and the source of prolonged misery. The swelling at each bite results from an overreaction by the immune system, and the bump itches mercilessly. The chigger adds just one more dimension to the need for fire, for the heat of fire can replace the need to burrow into chigger-infested leaves for the purpose of retaining body heat.

Fire is used in making tools, fire-hardening weapon points, tempering stone for flaking edges, burning out bowls and spoons and canoes, cooking, purifying water, tanning hides, providing insect repellency, heating stones for boiling in wooden or animal containers, smoking meat, holding predators at bay, roasting seeds for grinding into flour, drying clothing, making medicines, thickening glue, reshaping wood, coaxing dyes from plants, clearing land, taking the bite out of a harsh winter … and the list goes on. Though often disguised as a light switch, thermostat, oven, or other modern electric device, fire continues to be one of the most prominent threads that runs through human history.

Lighter-wood

Some species of pines – after they are dead – transform into wonderful sources of highly flammable kindling, both for spreading fire into a pyre and for providing light (at night) or smoke (for hide-tanning and insect repellency). The Cherokees made much use of this gift of the pine as torches, especially for the illumination of interior rooms as well as lighting the way along a mountain trail at night.

A number of species of pines produce lighter-wood, but in Southern Appalachia the primary maker of lighter-wood is Virginia pine (*Pinus virginiana*). On the coastal plain – where Virginia pine does not grow – longleaf pine (*Pinus palustris*) is the main source.

All pines make flammable terpenes – the chemical basis of turpentine – which is why pine forest fires demonstrate such blistering conflagrations, but all dead pines do not become lighter-wood. Virginia pine, rather than rotting at its core as so many trees do after they have died, rots from the outside and concentrates its highly flammable resin into a glassy, amber "semi-petrifaction" at the center of trunk and limbs. This resin solidifies and resists bacterial decomposition, thereby preserving itself for fire-makers. One resin-rich splinter of lighter-wood can burn upright like a candle for many minutes, drawing up fuel by a wicking action. No *other* piece of dead wood in Southern Appalachia will burn very long upright with a flame at its top, not even a store-bought matchstick.

Virginia pine lighter-wood

Because finding lighter-wood involves identifying wood that has been dead for a long time, the challenge might seem intimidating, but there are some excellent clues to help you recognize it. First, locate a section of forest with living Virginia pines. (Look for pines with very rough, flaky bark in plates no larger than a credit card. Needles are sheathed in pairs, not 3's or 5's. Each needle is approximately 3"long and twisted like a corkscrew.) There you are likely to find dead specimens, which may exhibit a spine-like appearance as the surviving "backbone" of a rotted tree. The nubs of limb remnants appear as "vertebrae," to these hardened spines.

Look for parallel swirl-lines that flow around the base of the limbs where they join the trunk. These lines somewhat resemble the threads of a wood screw. Sometimes these limb remnants have disengaged from the trunk and are lying loose on the forest floor in the approximate shape of thick, wooden spikes. The swollen base of such an isolated, free-lying limb usually shows the aforementioned swirl lines ("screw threads.")

With your knife, carve into any firm part of the wood and look for streaks of amber-colored, concentrated resin. You'll find it in layers giving off the strong odor of *Pine-Sol* bathroom cleanser. The easiest clue for identification of lighter-wood lies in this aroma. When burned, the wood emits a black, acrid smoke and audibly sizzles and bubbles a little like fat in a frying pan – hence, the name "fat-wood."

The Wonder of Lighter-wood – Locate a dead Virginia pine and cut slivers until you expose a richly aromatic section of wood. Cut one more sliver and mount it on a pinch-stick. From a dead dry limb of any other type of tree, carve a sliver of equal size and mount it separately so that the two flakes hover side by side several inches apart. Using 2 matches light both flakes at the same time and compare the burn-time.

The Lighter-wood Candle – With a hatchet or axe (adults only, please) free up a hefty stick of lighter-wood, 8"long, 2"thick at one end, and tapered to a point at the other end.

Split the thick end 3"deep and then split again perpendicular to the first. These two cuts have now quartered the cross-section of the thick end. Wedge these quarters apart from one another using small pieces of rock or hardwood so as to achieve maximum surface area of the splits. When night settles in, stick the sharp end of the candle into a safely cleared area of ground and light the top for a reading candle.

It is often said and written that lighter-wood forms only at the base of pine trunks, but I suspect this misinformation comes from those who have harvested exclusively from the stumps left behind after pines have been cut down and hauled away. In fact, lighter-wood is produced along the full-length of a fallen tree, though it may take decades to develop.

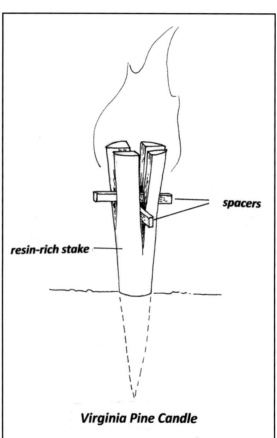

spacers

resin-rich stake

Virginia Pine Candle

Don't Get Spoiled by Lighter-wood

The lighter-wood that my rain-soaked campers used in the story that opened this chapter was not a necessity, but it was a tremendous asset. To prove your competence as a pyre-maker, I recommend that you **not** use lighter-wood in a pyre in the early days of your fire education. Once you become a skilled pyre-maker, you'll probably enjoy using it for the time it can save in your camp chores. But throughout your career as a pyre-builder, construct occasional pyres without lighter-wood so that you will remain confident about pyre-building should you find yourself in an area without such a pine.

I suggest the same for students of the northern and western states who rely on birch bark, which contains methyl-salicylate and provides a fire-builder with something akin to a flame-thrower for getting things started, wet or dry. This also applies to river birch (*Betula nigra*) on floodplains of the Southeast. One day an important fire might be needed in a birch-less woods.

The Pyre

A *pyre* is a pile of sticks that one intends to light for a campfire. A *good* pyre is a carefully thought-out arrangement of sticks designed to ensure that a small flame can climb upward through the pyre's architecture and sustain itself. The initial flame must encounter and consume successively larger sticks, thereby allowing the flame to grow in size until it can ignite the largest pieces of firewood. In addition, it is all-important to arrange this flame's growing-direction as *upward*, simply because heat rises.

Knowing how to create fire without knowing how to build a good pyre is like having a spirited horse in the corral but no rope to catch it; therefore, pyre-building ought to be a prerequisite for learning fire-by-friction.

Whenever I have taken adult students at their word that they were already competent at putting sticks together for a pyre, I discovered later that usually they really knew little about it. So now, when I hold an adult class on the hand-drill or bow-drill, I begin with a pyre-challenge that involves using a single match per person.

 <u>The Uneducated One-Match Fire, Part A</u> – Choose a safe area and challenge each student to construct a pyre (without any instruction) that will be consumed after being lighted by one match. (For students under 12 years-old, allow two matches.) There are a few arbitrary rules: No matter how much care goes into preparations, no matter what misfortune might occur due to wind or water or mishandling, no extra matches are afforded the student. The fuel must be comprised only of gathered dead wood, no leaves (this includes pine needles and grasses), no loose inner bark.

Leaves are generally not a good idea, because they can smother a flame like a blanket or choke it with smoke or steam. If leaves burn out in a flash, a useless cavity is left behind in the pyre. Or worse, smoldering leaf material can sail away on the wind to start an unwanted fire elsewhere!

No inner bark can be used in this activity unless it is naturally attached to a stick in its form-fitting layer. No paper or other manmade materials. The actual lighting with the match must be done with the forearm (of the hand holding the match) *flat on the ground.*

The goal is to have the flame build and climb up the structure and sustain itself without assistance from anyone until it can ignite a 3"X 3"piece of newsprint. This square of paper will be positioned over the pyre at the height of your knee by sharpening a 3'-long stick at both ends, sticking the paper on the top end, and jamming the bottom point into the ground.

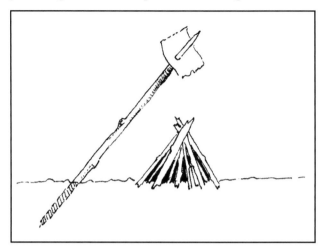

While you give the students 45 minutes to collect materials and construct their pyres, bring a large container of water to the site for safety. At the end of that time, gather the entire group to visit one of the pyres for the show-and-tell moment of truth. Just before the lighting attempt is made, ask all participants to study the pyre to note this particular architect's method. Impale the stick into the ground so that the paper hovers above the pyre at knee-height. To allow for wind direction, ask the pyre-builder to dictate exactly where the paper is to be positioned laterally. Be forewarned: Very few students succeed at burning the paper.

Each pyre will be visited by all and the attempt witnessed by all. Discussions about success or failure should follow each attempt. But before handing over a match and a scratch strip for that first pyre, this is a perfect time for a lesson on match use.

Everything You Need to Know About a Match

Many children approach their first hands-on experience with a match with anxiety, even fear. Because of an innate sense of caution, they might be tempted to grip a match as far from the head as possible. Such a grip invites breaking the matchstick during the striking. This results in an even more intimidating scenario: using a shortened match that puts the fingers closer to the flame!

By pinching the base-end of the match with thumb and long-finger, then swiveling the match like a gate toward the index, one can place the free index fingertip just below the match head as a fulcrum.

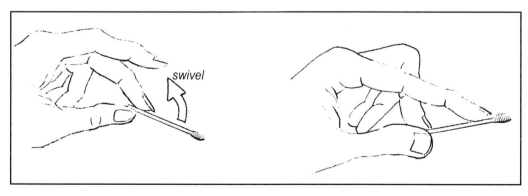

Using this fulcrum requires a backward-twist of the wrist that positions the index to *push* the match along the scratch strip. Such a grip and strike prevents breakage.

A box of "strike-on-box-only" matches is useless if its striking surfaces are in bad shape, so protect the box's scratch strips from moisture and dirt with these rules: No fingers should contact these strips. No setting the box on the ground.

A good rule for safety is to strike a match away from your body. Though it is not a guarantee, this directional stroke minimizes the chance of sending a "match-head meteorite" toward your clothing or hair. (It's always a good idea to tie back long, loose hair before dealing with fire.)

Before striking, determine wind direction by grinding a handful of dry dead leaves, dust, and duff between your palms. Watch which way the smallest falling particles drift. Repeat while facing in other directions to be sure that an eddy current created by your body did not cause you to misread the wind.

 Getting to Know a Match – Before introducing your students to a match, spend time on your own, striking matches over a cleared area of ground with a bucket of water centered in your work space. Drop all spent matches into the water for safety. If ever you or your students get flustered with a burning match and can't decide the best course of action, drop the burning match into the bucket. (This back-up plan will be very appealing to first-time match-strikers in the next exercise.)

This solo practice with matches will serve you well in preparing you for the problems your wards will encounter when they learn the skill from you. You will better understand how to address their particular problems or challenges with matches. You should expect both mental and physical challenges with students. Handling fire is a big step for some young ones.

Once the wind direction is known, place your back to the wind, strike a match close to your body, set the box aside on a dry surface, and immediately protect the surging flame with the free hand cupped around it as you hold the match head downward at a 45° angle.

Sometimes a flame might struggle because of a cross-wind. If this happens it is necessary to invert the match temporarily, giving the ebbing flame as much exposure

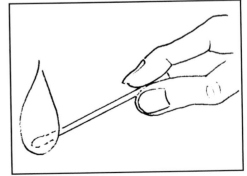

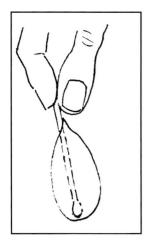

as possible to the uncharred wood of the stick. This puts the reduced flame below the fingers, so stay alert! As soon as the flame begins to grow, return the stick to the 45° angle to protect yourself from a burn. (The second purpose of the bucket is for plunging a hand into water in case of a singe.)

When the flame settles to a steady teardrop shape, turn the match vertically with the flame at top and watch the flame diminish, struggle, and then extinguish due to lack of fuel above it. A sudden puff of smoke signals the death of the flame. (If the flame does not die in this position, you may have chosen a brand of matches with flammable chemicals embedded in the stick. If so, choose another brand.)

A match held vertically (with the flame at the top) "goes out" because heat rises. Or more accurately, because gravity causes colder, heavier air to fall and displace the lighter hot air. Therefore, since a flame seeks an upward route, it needs fuel above itself to stay alive. This is why the angle at which a burning match is held turns out to be important. Before encountering a pyre, the only fuel available to a match flame (after combusting chemicals in the match head) is the matchstick itself. The flame must climb the gradient of the stick to stay alive. If, however, the angle is too severe (close to vertical with the flame at the bottom) and the flame climbs too quickly, a burned finger and dropped match usually result. (Time to plunge!)

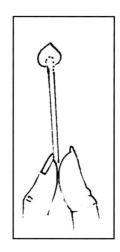

Controlling a Match – Provide a box of 2"wooden kitchen matches to be used by your students in a practice session before lighting their experimental pyres. With a bucket of water sitting on cleared ground, demonstrate the proper technique for striking. Cover safety precautions for loose hair, wind protection, grip and wrist position, strike-direction, cupping the flame, and the proper 45° angle for a burning matchstick. Then, before the flame approaches the halfway point on the matchstick, hold the stick vertically, flame at the top, again cupping it from the wind if necessary. Let your wards see and believe that the flame will go out by itself in this upright position.

Let each young student who is new to the use of matches practice striking a match, establishing a steady flame, and showing that she can control the flame by holding the stick vertically to watch the flame abate and die. Use as many matches as necessary until each student experiences this automatic death of the flame.

Some fearful first-timers may need hands-on-hands help from the teacher. No matter how much forewarning you provide, there may be some who panic when the match ignites. In this panic mode they forget the proper angle to hold the stick and consequently burn themselves by holding the match vertically, flame-down. (Douse those singed fingers in the bucket of water.) With fears such as these – which can be difficult to allay – repeat the exercise as many times as the student

is willing until he gains confidence. It is not advisable to force a reluctant student to strike a match. Wait for a time that he chooses. It is always best if the decision to strike is the student's. Eventually, each wary one will usually come around. **Warning: Before a student strikes a match, be sure that any loose or frizzy hair is held back by a hat, ribbon or headband! Hair (especially loose and frizzy) can catch fire quickly! Certain clothing, too.**

The Hot Spot

Now that the students are prepared to light their "uneducated" pyres, give them this last jewel of kitchen-match physics. Ask the group a question:

"Where is the hottest part of the match flame?"

You'll likely get a variety of answers. The tip-top of the flame (the sharp point of the teardrop) is the point of convergence of all the heat rising from the flame. It is similar to the concentration of heat in a tiny bead of sunlight funneled down by a magnifying glass. (Remember when you discovered as a child how to make a dead leaf combust with a lens? Bring outside a magnifier and let your students experience this O-so-safe way to handle fire.) Impress upon the students that they need to touch that flame's *tip* to <u>the very piece of wood they first intend to ignite</u>. Name this twig or shaving "the fuse" and define it so, in order that the actual lighting of the fire is never a haphazard exercise built upon hope rather than on confidence. To light the fuse accurately – to see the flame-tip touch the fuse – the lighter must crouch or lie down to position his eyes low to the ground for a reasonable view.

<u>Advanced Match-Handling</u>

– Some students will already possess a savvy and relaxed relationship with a burning match in hand. They will need more of a challenge to keep them interested in the match-handling lessons. Once they have struck a match and established a steady flame, right away instruct them to hold the match vertically, flame-up. When the flame shrinks to the size of a blueberry, ask the student to rescue the flame by inverting it 180°. (If he moves the match too fast, the "wind of relativity" can snuff out the flame.) If he successfully revives the flame, he must reposition the stick (to 45°) before getting burned. Then, like all the other members of the class, he angles the stick vertically, flame-up, and allows it to die, proving that he had control over the fire.

Though this exercise is not feasible for all, it is instructive for all to see it performed by one of their peers.

<u>The Uneducated One-Match Fire, Part B</u>

– Now it's time for the lighting of the experimental pyres, one by one, as all the class spectates. Encourage predictions. If someone voices a deliberate opinion, ask that person to explain her hunch based upon what she can point out in the pyre.

If the newsprint ignites above the pyre, remove the impaled stick immediately and dunk the paper in the water to prevent any burning pieces from going airborne. Whether a pyre is a success or failure, do not leave that pyre-site before dousing it with water and thoroughly crushing all remains into the earth with boot soles.

First Pyre Critique

After each pyre-lighting attempt that fails, you'll have the surviving structure of the pyre to use as a lesson for what went wrong. Point out which flaw in the making of the pyre contributed to its failure. The following are the most common mistakes of failed pyres:

1. The match breaks due to an improper grip. The now-shortened matchstick is intimidating for a second strike and forces more mistakes.

2. The match goes out from improper handling even before any of the pyre can be lighted. This includes holding the match at an improper angle, dropping it, or hastily moving the match through the air (tantamount to a brisk wind) before it has had time to establish a steady teardrop shape on the matchstick.

3. No space was allowed for the lighted match to enter the pyre *below* the kindling, and so the flame is snuffed out when pushed into the pile of wood.

4. The initial kindling section near the bottom of the pyre burns out before the surrounding structure can catch, leaving a charred outer skeleton of sticks surrounding a smoking cavity. This often happens when a pyre-builder feels compelled to build a wooden tipi *first* (usually a fragilely balanced tripod or cone of sticks). Such an outer-structure makes it difficult to then add an interior of kindling because the tipi is in the way!

5. With no cavity beneath the kindling, the pyre-builder tries to light the top of the pile of kindling, but the heat cannot travel downward.

6. The lighted match is held below a stick too thick to ignite. This is often the result of the pyre-builder not getting his head low to see where his match flame is positioned.

7. Because he did not plan a "fuse," the pyre-builder tries to ignite different sticks of kindling rather than devoting the limited burn of the match flame to one point.

Thinking Like a Flame

In teaching how to build a pyre, I like to tell a student, "Think of your match flame as a newborn. Babies cannot eat big chunks of solid food. They must begin with tiny pieces. As they grow they can tackle larger pieces, but the progression must be patient and logical. A 'child-flame' simply cannot chew up an 'adult-flame' meal."

Because it must climb, a match flame's array of meals (collectively, the pyre) is like a ladder whose rungs get successively thicker. The larger the flame grows, the thicker rung it can consume. The best way to arrange a successful architecture for a pyre is to "think like a flame." Imagine yourself as that newborn flame on the match head. What size meal would you want first to encounter? And once you have consumed it, what size should your next meal be? Where should it be waiting? Visualize the actual climbing path of the flame and build the pyre accordingly.

A Problematic Wind

A strong wind is difficult to contend with, and it might be best to wait patiently for a lull before striking. If you don't have that luxury, get very serious about

> **The best way to arrange a successful architecture for a pyre is to "think like a flame."**

using your body as a protective wall. If you kneel when striking the match, seal your thighs together to prevent a draft there. Better yet, lie on one side and let that side of your body seal against the earth. (The best fire-maker students always end up with the dirtiest clothes.)

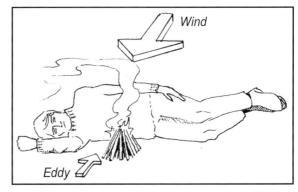

In a group exercise, lots of friends can make a barrier wall. But this wall of bodies must be tightly pressed together. Arms and elbows must be jammed into cracks between torsos – like the chinking between logs in a cabin. It's a memorable bonding experience, everyone helping one pyre-builder to be successful in his effort.

The Fuse

A smart pyre-builder carefully plans which piece of wood she will first ignite with the match. I call this piece "the fuse." There must be no doubt that the fuse will take the flame, so plan for it to be thin, light (porous), dry, and easily reached inside the pyre. Define this twig or wood sliver *while you are building* your pyre, not later as an afterthought.

Though we are purposely abstaining from lighter-wood at this point, do take note that on a wet or rainy day your best choice for a fuse is a sliver of dead, resin-rich Virginia pine. The longevity of its flame assists in drying out the neighboring kindling.

One more advantage of using a fuse in a match-lit pyre lies in its downward protruding position beneath the shelf.

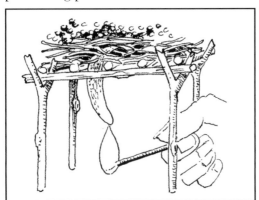

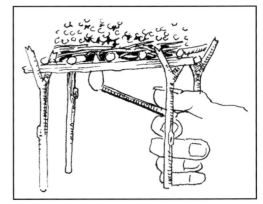

If the pyre-maker has laid kindling a few inches above ground on a shelf of some kind (an excellent idea!) he is forced to angle the match head up in order to touch the flame to the kindling lying atop the shelf. At such an angle the flame on the matchstick suffers and can go out. A fuse allows the lighter to hold the matchstick at its proper angle, so that the flame can burn up the matchstick.

Making a Fuzz Stick

– Many pyre-builders like to use a single, thick stick of soft wood (like pine or tulip tree) as their fuse. To prepare it for the match flame, slice your knife blade into it as if you are going to shave away a sliver; but, rather than completing the cut, let the sliver remain firmly attached to the stick like a curled barb.

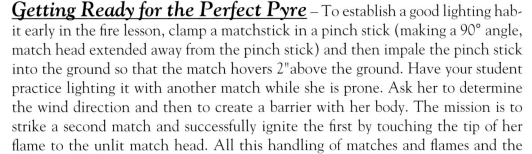

Repeat this all around the same end of the stick as many times as possible without carving away any of the previously made slivers. Position the fuzz stick in the pyre under the bulk of kindling where it can be easily accessed by the match.

fuzz stick

Getting Ready for the Perfect Pyre

– To establish a good lighting habit early in the fire lesson, clamp a matchstick in a pinch stick (making a 90° angle, match head extended away from the pinch stick) and then impale the pinch stick into the ground so that the match hovers 2"above the ground. Have your student practice lighting it with another match while she is prone. Ask her to determine the wind direction and then to create a barrier with her body. The mission is to strike a second match and successfully ignite the first by touching the tip of her flame to the unlit match head. All this handling of matches and flames and the practice of lying down on the ground help a child along on the path to efficient and safe fire skills.

"The Indian keeps warm with a small fire. The white man keeps warm running around to gather wood for a huge fire."   ~ *Traditional camp adage, author unknown*

CHAPTER 2
"Thinking Like a Flame!"
~ *master pyre building* ~

Now that your students have tried their hand at pyres of their own invention, it is time to share with them the details of a pyre-design that will never fail them. Let's review a few fire-related laws of physics that need to be understood in learning the skill.

1. Heat rises.

2. An initial flame needs a reasonable graduation of stick-sizes in order to grow. That is, don't expect a burning stick the size of a pencil to ignite a stick thick as a baseball bat. Some children assume that, just because a flame can touch the larger stick, the flame will transfer to the heftier piece.

3. Wood burns best when its surface area greatly exceeds its mass. In other words, a stick shaved into slivers ignites much more easily than the stick before it was sliced. (It's the same amount of wood, but slivers create more surface area per given volume of wood.)

4. Fast-growing, porous wood and pines with terpenes burn hot and fast, but they make poor coals.

5. Dense hardwoods are slower to catch but sustain a flame longer and make lasting coals.

Building the Fail-proof Pyre

There are many ways to begin the dry stacking of sticks (the *pyre*) for a fire, but all of the best methods take into consideration this concept: The initial fuel to be lighted must be positioned high enough above the ground so that the match (or other flame source) can be inserted *underneath* it. Laying a lighted match on top of a pile of sticks is defying the forces of physics, yet I see it all the time – even from adult students. The design outlined below is a good one to use on an earthen site where the ground is soft enough to puncture with a pointed stick.

Site Preparation

If you are in a new or remote camping site, it is preferable to dig up a big "bowl-full" of dirt and set it aside to be replaced later in the cooled concavity before you depart the area. That temporarily removed topsoil is full of earth-friendly microorganisms. When you return them to their original place, you cover your signs of having been there – an admirable code by which to live.

A pit dug about the size of a bathroom sink lowers your lighting area from the windy zone; and paradoxically, on a windless day, it actually draws air to assist your flame. The slopes of the pit help to contain hot coals and keep burning logs from rolling into dry leaves. These pit slopes also reflect heat toward the sitting areas around the pit, keeping folks warmer on a winter's night.

If you are choosing a new fire site, look up to see what path the smoke can take. A summer fire needs a good "chimney" route through the trees, or else smoke will choke leaves to death. By keeping your fire small – "Indian-style" – you'll minimize that kind of damage to the Standing People.

Rake away any leaf litter from your proposed fire site. A safety margin of 3' to 4' feet of bare earth should surround your fire pit like a protective "moat" to prevent the spread of fire to the forest.

The Pyre Base and Shelf

The first phase entails constructing a shelf that will elevate the kindling, allowing a space beneath it for your match, lighter, or burning tinder bundle. There are several ways to achieve this. Most young students enjoy the scaffold-construction, so we'll cover that first. Gather dead hardwood branches (oak, sourwood, dogwood, etc.) and from them break four, firm, pencil-thick sticks 5"-7"long, each with a small Y-shaped fork at one end. As you break them to size, crude points might be created on the forkless ends. If not, carve a point so that you can push each stick into the dirt, making a 5"X 5"square of uprights to support a shelf that will look like a miniature Plains Indian burial scaffold.

This is the time to determine the direction of the wind. Decide which two poles will define your doorway, through which your match and fingers will eventually enter for lighting the pyre. (As you will soon see, the other three sides of the scaffold will be closed off by a tipi of sticks.) If a mild breeze is blowing, your doorway should face the wind. If the wind is strong enough to endanger the match flame and the initial flame that catches in your pyre, position the square of poles so that the wind comes through the door at a 45° angle.

With this orientation of the wind and the door in mind, push the forked poles vertically into the ground until each pole's Y-crotch is 2 ½"above the ground. Orient all the Y's to face in the same direction.

If the ground is firm, you might need to twist each stick back and forth like a drill to sink it into the dirt. While doing this be careful to keep that stick vertical. If you don't, you'll widen the hole you are creating and loosen the soil. As a result the stick will not stand firmly enough to support the weight it must bear.

Lay two parallel *primary rafters* (pencil-thick hardwood) into the Y's on two opposing sides of the square. Across these *primary rafters* lay *5 cross rafters* perpendicular to the primaries. There must be ¼" to ½" spaces between the cross rafters.

Up to this point all wood used should be dense, slow-burning hardwoods. You'll want this infrastructure to last even when your fire has been ablaze for several minutes.

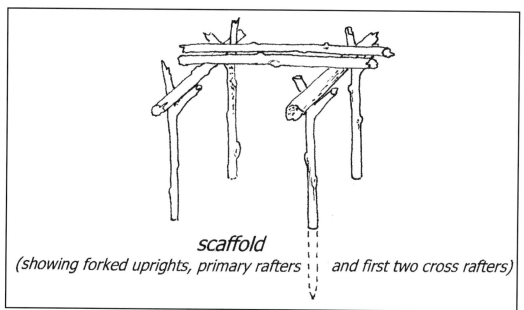

scaffold
(showing forked uprights, primary rafters and first two cross rafters)

If the ground is too hard to penetrate with forked sticks, simply use 2 short, thick sections of dead branches laid parallel to serve as primary rafters. (Even rotten wood, stones, or linear mounds of earth will suffice.) Consider branch pieces 2" thick and 5" long. Because these limbs are rounded, they should be chocked on either side with pebbles to prevent rolling. Across these two supports lay down the 5 cross rafters.

Thinking Outside the Tinder Box – Give your students the challenge of thinking up another way to elevate a kindling shelf. Who can invent another support for the shelf that does not involve rocks, wood, plants, manmade objects, or piling up dirt?

The answer: Dig a small trough in the dirt and lay 5 cross rafters across it like the beginning phase of a miniature bridge construction.

 Building a Scaffold for Strength – Using 4, pencil-thick, Y-shaped sticks as supports, students can individually build the scaffold just described. To test the sturdiness of each construction, place the same fist-sized rock on top of each finished structure. All whose shelves stand up to this weight prove themselves to be architects of a reliable foundation for a pyre.

 Variations on the Pyre – Each time you hold a session on pyre-making, ask for a different foundation from you students. After the Y-pole scaffold, try using other supports: thick sticks laid parallel; chunks of rotten wood; flattish rocks; linear, parallel mounds of dirt; and the shoulders of earth beside a small, hand-dug trench.

Kindling

Now comes the all-important selection of kindling. In dry weather, many kinds of dead wood can be used, but the best are very thin and light (porous, fast-growing) or rich in natural flammable chemicals. In the Appalachians the tiniest branchlets come from the eastern hemlock tree. A dead needle-less limb, reachable but high enough to stay dry (away from ground moisture), divides and subdivides into a web of deliquescent branching so thin as to appear almost threadlike.

Taking the time to gather these smallest twigs in individual, non-branching pieces can guarantee success for the initial lighting of your fire … *but only if the twigs are dry.* Hemlock's slender dead branchlets hold onto minutely convoluted bark (which can hold moisture) long after they are dead, so if the weather is wet (or even humid) you would do well to pass by hemlock. Bark holds water both in its complicated texture as well as beneath its sleeve-like sheath. Moisture content might not be detected by touch. There is a clue that suggests dampness: when dead twigs do not snap easily but instead do a lot of bending, the kindling will probably disappoint you. I have seen many barely-moist piles of hemlock kindling resist bursting into flame even as they glow red like hot wires when exposed to a match flame.

On a rainy day, lighter-wood is your ultimate kindling gift from the Standing People, for its chemicals burn even when water is present. Shaving off curls with your knife produces a fuel with unparalleled flammability and with surprising longevity. However, remember that we don't want to teach novices a dependency on lighter-wood. Reserve its use for rainy conditions. At this point in your fire education, let's not propel you and your students into the advanced challenge of making fire in moist conditions. That skill will come in time.

The Mountain Pyre-maker's Best Friend

White pine (*Pinus strobus*), also called "mountain pine," is the tallest tree in Eastern North America. Of all the native pines in Southern Appalachia it is the only one that clusters its needles into groups of 5 and arranges its limbs almost exclusively in whorls. Easy to find, white pine's dead, low branches make superb kindling.

Gathering Kindling – Find a white pine with dead lower limbs still attached to the trunk. Ideal limbs are those that are complicated, spreading into many branches,

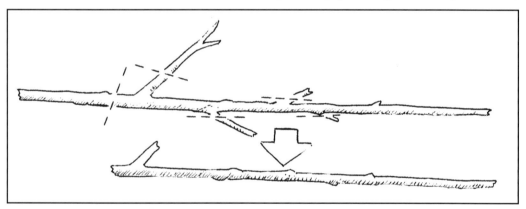

branchlets, and sub-branchlets that terminate in numerous slender twigs.

For limbs too high to reach, fashion a long-handled grappling-hook from any standing dead sapling as shown in the illustration. When snapping limbs from the trunk, guard your eyes from fast-flying splinters of wood. When harvesting at heights with the grappling hook, stand out of harm's way from the falling limb.

Carry harvested limbs to your fire site intact and do all further breaking there. It is easier to carry two large complex limbs rather than hundreds of broken parts.

Arranging Kindling and Fuse – Begin gathering your prime white pine kindling by snapping off the thin tip-ends

of the branches. These outer twigs are the thickness of pencil lead and highly flammable due to terpene content.

Collect a handful of tip-ends only – each narrow twig about 4"long and neither forked nor branched (to allow for compact grouping). These thinnest sticks will serve as your primary kindling. As you continue to break slightly thicker sticks for successive levels of the pyre, you'll be meeting the needs of the flame, which must encounter a gradual increase in size of fuel. (The thicker portions of your branches will be used as the first layer of poles for the "tipi" architecture that will eventually envelop the pyre shelf.)

Lay down parallel twigs (in a neat layer ½"high) perpendicular to the cross rafters so that twigs will not slip through the cracks in the shelf. Don't allow them to hang out over the doorway, where they might impede lighting the pyre. This is the time to insert the fuse.

Cut a long, dry sliver from a thick part of a dead white pine branch. If the sliver is not naturally curled, bend it gently into a C-shape. Carefully spear it through the top of this first stratum of kindling, working one end of the curled sliver downward through the twigs between 2 cross rafters until the bottom of the fuse can be seen well beneath the shelf. To prevent this fuse from falling through the kindling to the ground, anchor it on top with a second layer of white pine kindling (same sized twigs as the first layer), which should be oriented perpendicular to the first layer. (This crisscross of layers ensures that plenty of oxygen will be available as the flame travels up the pyre.)

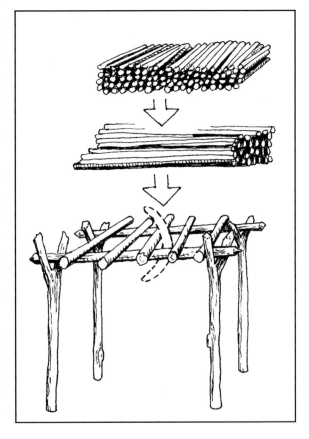

Add a third crisscrossed layer of white pine branchlets, these twigs only slightly thicker than the ones beneath it. And then a fourth – again, these pieces slightly thicker than the last. These layers comprise the first "rungs of the ladder" that the flame will climb.

At this point you should have amassed a fist-sized pile of kindling on your shelf. The next step will be a change in architecture: from the Indian *burial scaffold* to the Indian *tipi*.

A Pyre Without a Fuse – You can, of course, choose not to insert a fuse into your pyre and simply light the kindling between two rafters. (In doing this it is more difficult to hold the match at the optimum 45° angle and more difficult to see what your match flame is touching, but it can be done.) Still, plan ahead and identify the ideal lighting spot. Pinpoint one tiny stick above the cross rafters to serve as "the ignition point" and be loyal to it during the lighting.

The Tipi

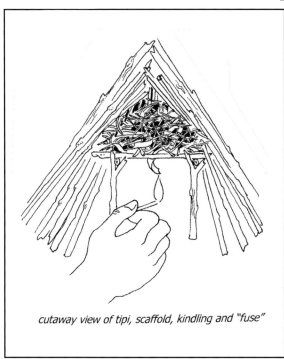

cutaway view of tipi, scaffold, kindling and "fuse"

The tipi will begin as a squat cone of pencil-thick sticks of white pine propped around the scaffold of kindling. The most common mistake in tipi construction is making the tipi poles too long, leaving an empty space between the kindling layers and the apex of the tipi. The first tipi poles should reach only to the center of the top of the kindling pile. This means angling the poles to make a low, wide tipi. Add enough sticks to hide the foundation of the pyre (the scaffold), except at the door. The tipi will become more upright as you add layers. With each layer, add slightly thicker, slightly longer tipi poles.

Arranging the Tipi – Still using the two original branches of white pine, break pencil-thick tipi poles that can lean against the scaffold and reach to the center apex of the mound of kindling. Using many sticks, extend the tipi all around the scaffold except at the door. As the tipi grows in size, hardwoods can be added. As taller poles are laid down, the tipi shape will become less squat and better resemble the abode for which it is named. At this stage, it is difficult to stack poles too tightly. Generally, novices tend to space them too loosely. On the rare occasion that poles are too tightly arranged, it is easy to open up a "chimney" to let smothering smoke escape. Just remove or adjust a pole or two.

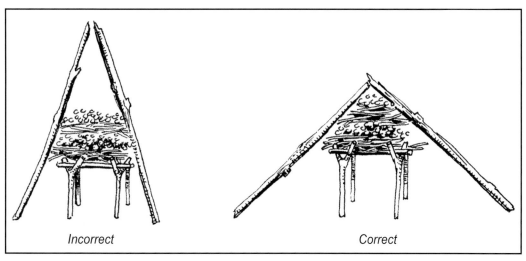

Incorrect   *Correct*

 ### **_Building a Tipi_** – Using the remainder of your white pine supply, break the thinnest parts to size and begin circling the scaffold with tipi poles, being sure

to leave the door uncovered. Tops of the first tipi poles should touch the top center of the kindling pile. Continue the process while using thicker and thicker poles until your pine is depleted. Subsequent layers of longer poles should lie against a previous layer and always reach to the center of the tipi's apex. Then start adding hardwood tipi poles, starting with 1"-thick sticks and increasing thickness as the circumference of the tipi widens.

Pyre Trouble-shooting

The most common mistakes at this stage of the tipi structure are:

1. Not enough primary kindling and/or kindling too loosely stacked.

2. Cross rafters too tightly laid down on the primary rafters, preventing access by match.

3. First tipi poles are too long and may not ignite because of the empty space between the apex of the kindling and the convergence of the tipi poles.

4. The tipi poles are too thick. The kindling flame cannot ignite them.

5. The shelf prematurely collapses due to poor construction or being made of highly flammable wood.

Ignition

Double-check that all extraneous flammable materials have been swept back 4'

from the fire pit or circle so that the flame cannot spread from the pyre. The lighter should crouch very low, kneel, or lie down before the pyre door in order to have a good view of the fuse. Strike, angle the match (hot-end lower than the cool-end), and touch the flame tip to the fuse. Watch the flame travel up the echelon of graduating stick-sizes to engulf the tipi. Once the flame appears active and dependable, fill in the door side of the tipi with hefty poles to balance out the cone with symmetry so that it won't collapse.

Lighting the Educated, One-Match Fire

Lighting the Educated, One-Match Fire – After the pyre lesson, give your students a second try at constructing a one-match pyre. Instruct each pyre-builder to collect dead, dry firewood from any species of hardwood trees to have on hand for closing off the door of the tipi. Encourage students to crouch low

or lie down to be sure that their match placement is accurate. Light the fuse. Once the pyre is burning reliably, add hefty tipi poles to the open section at the door to balance out the tipi. Always add sticks to a flame by holding them at the bottom, not the top. That way you can take your time, avoid being burned, and place the stick (rather than tossing it) exactly where you want it.

The best way to convince your students to lie down when lighting … is to do it with them!

A Fire to Call My Own – After the pyre lesson has been taught and successful fires have resulted for all, repeat this one-match fire challenge in a new, unfamiliar location. There your students will need to explore the land to find their needs, as opposed to having them pointed out (as in their original lesson.) By repeating this activity you are defining the importance of the skill. Never let them take one of these forest lessons as a "been-there, done-that" experience. You will likely find them eager to attack the challenge anew, to demonstrate their ability to harness fire – one of the great milestones of humankind.

A Lasting Fire

Once a fire is well established, stack tipi poles over the open side (doorway) so that the pyre will not collapse. Stack larger tipi poles all around to achieve the desired size of fire for the occasion. Finally, larger logs can be framed around the tipi as a retaining wall for the fire. Stack these log-cabin-style around the tipi in the shape of a rising square, pentagon, or hexagon … whatever best fits.

A tipi-fire is by far the easiest fire to keep going in rain. Even in a torrential storm, a wooden tipi can be laid so tightly as to shed water. The outer wood might

be soaked, but the fire inside is alive, intensified by the fact that it is contained like an oven. At this point wet hardwood can be constantly added to the tipi, allowing wet inner layers to dry and become part of the inner furnace. If the furnace appears to wane, thread fast-burning sticks like pine or tulip tree through cracks in the tipi all the way to the center of the furnace.

Wet-Day Fire – Build a fire when the forest is wet *after* a rain. Learn about that secret cache of dry wood inside all that seemingly wet wood. Before allowing young students to engage in knife-work, give a comprehensive lesson on knife safety.

Knife Safety

This lesson should include lots of visual demonstrations of carving, showing correct and incorrect methods of using a blade. It basically boils down to these rules:

1. Choose an isolated place to work … away from other people. Anytime someone approaches your workspace, you must stop work.

2. Never exert pressure on a blade that moves its edge toward any part of your body.

3. For any project other than shaving slivers of wood, use a log "workbench."

4. For every step of a project undertaken, visualize a slip of the knife that could occur, and then position yourself so that you will be out of harm's way.

5. A folding-blade knife should be used only for shaving wood or cutting notches. It should not be used like a drill or awl. Assume that even a lock-blade folding knife will unexpectedly close up with pressure.

Team Fire-Building – With a class of fire-building students, divide your group into teams of three or four. Assign a number to each of the team members (#1, #2, #3, etc.). Each team should clear a space for building a pyre then strike out to gather *all* the firewood needed to build a pyre – scaffold poles, rafters, kindling, and tipi poles. When a team has returned to its fire site, only then does the pyre-building begin. There can be no further wood gathered for fuel.

Team member #1 sets the first forked pole. Once set, the others must approve it. Is it the correct material? Will it burn up too fast? Is its fork the correct height off the ground? Is it thick enough? Will it fall over? If there is enough convincing disapproval of the pole, the pole must be replaced or improved by #1 until all approve.

Team member #2 sets the next Y-pole. Same critique. Same accountability. #3 sets the third pole. #4 sets the fourth. Then #1 lays down the first primary rafter. #2 lays the second. #3 lays down the first cross rafter. And so on. This alternating continues even through the meticulous laying down of tiny kindling pieces. This is one of the best learning experiences in

The pride of success

pyre-building, especially for those students who are not yet confident in their fire skills. The ones who are confident will enjoy teaching what they know.

Rain, Morale, and Fire

During one of my week-long wilderness summer camps, my twelve-year-old camp-ers were dismayed when the first day of solid rain stretched into two. By the third day of relentless rain, virtually the only words spoken were mumbles of complaint and oblique hints that maybe it was time to raise the white flag and head for home.

In our remote location (in those days we simply used the national forest), we had tents but no buildings to rescue us from the weather. By day-four there was still no let-up in the precipitation. No one had any more dry clothing as backup. We were wet and dirty from the work of keeping a fire going in the rain. Campers stood by our fire in the rain, holding out soaked articles of clothing in the hope of making them less wet. The concept of having something dry to wear seemed no longer a possibility for anyone.

All of the activities that I had planned for the week were scrapped. Nature had handed us a different agenda. We simply spent our waking time scouring the woods for fuel, hauling wood back to camp, breaking it or sawing it, feeding the fire and then going back out to repeat the ritual again. And again.

We cooked all our meals in the rain. We ate in the rain and cleaned up our dishes in the rain. In my mind we were the People of the Rain. Firewood was all we thought about. Finding a good piece of wood took on the import of finding a hidden treasure. But morale was low. By day-five those oblique hints about going home became more vocal.

Besides the rain, one other thing remained a constant during that week. Our fire stayed alive. We made that happen. We earned it. Yet the pride of achieve-ment could not yet surface in my campers. They were waterlogged to their souls. They moved about and spoke like prisoners of war.

When the week ended and we started for home, I wondered how many of those faces I might never see again at my camp. The prevailing mood seemed to be that we had just barely survived a wet war of attrition.

The next year, all but two of those campers returned … along with a few new ones who had been coaxed to join their friends. Every night around the campfire, someone stared into the flames and began to reminisce about the ordeal of the previous year. I watched them talk about it as they recounted the amount of work that had gone into the single task of keeping our fire alive. An unmistakable pride glowed in their faces, and confidence rang in their voices. They didn't brag about it, but they named it for what it was – "the summer of the fire."

One of the new campers remarked, "It rained every day? What a bummer!"

One of the veterans shook his head. "It was great." He looked around at his old comrades. They nodded and looked back into the dancing yellow and orange flames of our open fire. The solidarity of a job well done was now a part of them.

<u>Rainy Day Fire</u> – Build a fire *in the rain*. Don rain gear and, with young stu-dents, take along a small tarp under which to work and store wood shavings. For older students, give them a tarp-less challenge. They'll need to use their backs as

shelter from the rain as they hunker over their work. Often a student volunteers his back and flared raincoat as a permanent roof as others work beneath him. Modify the safety rules about knife use, because lots of bodies will necessarily be crowded where the knife-work will be done.

Building a Fire of Purpose

Building a Fire of Purpose – What better lesson of accountability than to build a fire for the purpose of cooking a meal on an outing? Let the building of a pyre be the primary project for a day outing in a forest. Once it is lighted, tend it to the desired size for cooking your group meal. To make it easy for a first-time outing, carry along a cooking grate and all the utensils you will need. Without a successful fire, there is no meal.

From here …   *… to there*

Notes for the teacher of a fire class

1. When a group of children is assigned the gathering of wood, there will be some who haul in inspiring bundles. Praise them within earshot of all. There will be others who wander back to the fire with just one or two sticks. Try presenting a quota of sticks that each person must bring in. They have their choice of twelve hefty sticks in one trip, three at a time in four trips, or one at a time in twelve trips. And keep in mind, it is easier to bring in a very long, multi-branched, dead tree balanced on the shoulder to break up closer to the fire than to break it up far out in the woods to haul in armloads.

2. Some "fire-hogs" like to stay by the fire and let sticks be brought to them. They are having all the fun of working directly with the fire. (We all have a little pyromania tucked away in our chromosomes, whereas hauling wood usually does not rank as one of the top-ten forms of entertainment for children.) Have each student do his fair share.

Gathering firewood: one tree, many hands, one trip

3. Keep a rake and containers of water on hand. If a fire unexpectedly spreads, especially in brisk winds, it can quickly grow out of control.

Wind Control

During the critical period, as the fire builds to engage the entire pyre, the wind might shift. If the wind reverses and pushes the flame back toward the doorway, remember that you can change the direction of the wind by creating an eddy with your body or with the collective bodies of friends. (See page 26.)

<u>Making a Wind Barrier</u> – Around a small campfire on a breezy day, practice manipulating the direction that a flame slants by forming a tight wall of bodies (or body). Get upwind of the fire and coax the flame to angle upwind toward the wall.

Safe Techniques for Children to Cut or Break Firewood

Two good tools for cutting firewood are a bow saw and a folding camp saw. Both are infinitely safer than a hatchet and more efficient if used properly.

A bow saw blade is thin and meant to glide <u>without bending</u>. If the sawyer's pressure does bend the blade, the cut becomes curved and the job of pushing a metal band through a serpentine slit in wood becomes quickly frustrating. The best technique for smooth sawing is to cut lightly and to position the body so that the gripping hand's forearm remains in a perfect line with the blade.

Using the bow saw can be a four-person project for children: one to anchor an end of the log (being cut) to the ground as it is propped over a small log (the workbench) … and one to push down on the higher free end of the log being cut. (This opens the pinch of the slit being cut.) Two other children work as a crosscut saw team – each holding an end of the saw.

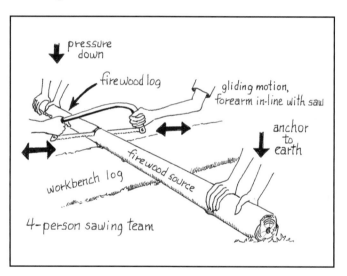

The blade should be working <u>near</u> the workbench, between the bench and the higher end of the log being cut. If the sawyers work the blade between the ground and the workbench, the inevitable pinch will stop the saw dead in its tracks.

The folding saw has a firmer blade and cuts more easily, but it is a one-person job, as far as the actual sawing goes. The downside of this tool is blade breakage. If the sawyer brings the blade back too far on the back-stroke and catches the tip end of the blade on the log at the beginning of the forward stroke, the blade will bend and possibly snap. A similar team can be set up for working with a folding saw, this time with only three members.

In a primitive camp where no saw is available, strength (as usual in woods-lore) becomes an asset for breaking the big pieces of dead wood. Herculean axe-like swings at a big rock can break some types of wood, but many hardwoods do not easily snap. Of course, you'll need hardwoods for long-lasting flames and coals.

Using two neighboring trees for a lever-and-fulcrum breaking technique is useful, but you must select your trees carefully as you can tear the bark off a tree or compress its inner bark tubes and do damage to the full height of the tree along that rank. Use mature trees with extremely thick, hard bark (hickory, chestnut oak, red oak) and do your levering gently. (Sourwood has thick outer bark, but it is more fragile than it appears.) Use padding of found slabs of bark or rotten wood to protect trees that you suspect are vulnerable to damage. At the first suspicion of bark injury, look for another pair of trees. Boulders, if available, or dead standing trees are a better choice. A good relationship with the Standing People living in your camping area is a big part of your experience.

padding

Beware the overhead hurling of a log at a rock. You may feel and look like Tarzan throwing a greedy fortune hunter over a cliff, but logs can bounce back and inspire a Tarzan yell … of pain. This technique should be performed only by the quick and agile adult. Logs that are too stubborn to break might be your very best fuel. Consider burning them into smaller segments by propping them over your fire.

For the smaller wood that needs breaking – say, sticks with a diameter of 1½"to 2"– don't assume that children know how to do it in a safe and efficient way. Again and again I see young students who feel so displaced in the alien world of the woods that their logic about simple tasks seems to get flustered. Countless times I have seen a child try to snap a very breakable three-foot-long stick by grasping it with their hands less than a foot apart and striking down on their thigh with the portion of the stick between their hands. If anything should break using this technique, it would seem to be the femur. Fortunately, that has never happened in my presence.

I discourage my young campers from using the time-honored practice of gripping a stick with both hands and pulling as they push the center of the stick with the fulcrum of a foot. Using a knee is less threatening … but still not ideal. Both techniques are potentially harmful to the spine. Show children how to prop one end of a stick on a log or rock and then stomp to break the stick.

"In the beginning there was no fire, and the world was cold, until the Thunders ... sent their lightning and put fire into the bottom of a hollow sycamore tree which grew on an island."

~ The First Fire, *old Cherokee myth, recorded by James Mooney in*
History, Myths and Sacred Formulas of the Cherokees

CHAPTER 3
The Trees That Swallowed Fire
~ finding the proper wood to create a fire by friction ~

The Cherokee once told a story about a lightning bolt that struck a dead, hollow sycamore on a river island. As the fire blazed into the night a menagerie of animals watched from the shore and decided to capture one of the bright flames to illuminate and warm their dens and burrows. Many creatures attempted the heroic ordeal – Owl, Raven, and Snake – but it was tiny Spider who finally achieved the task by shaping a silk (or mud ... there are variations to this story) bowl to carry a hot coal across the water.

The Lakotas' fire-acquisition story told of Coyote stealing fire from three witches. Forming a relay team, a host of animals passed the stolen burning stick from one runner to another – Coyote to Mountain Lion to Deer to Fox – each in his turn trying to outrun the witches. Each creature specialized in its familiar terrain and held its own against the pursuers, until Frog was cornered at the river. Just as it seemed that the old hags had triumphed, Frog spat the fire-stick into a dead stump, and the stump swallowed it!

As it turns out, many of the trees that can be used to make fire grow near a stream. If you know which species to look for ... and if you know how to ask for it ... that tree will give fire back to you.

Fire has been at the heart of our homes since early human history. It forever changed the way people would live. It became a magnet that attracted people into a new nocturnal social habit – gathering around the glow of flames. Even today, if you are near a campfire at night, those flames define the center of your world.

Lightning fires certainly introduced the power and worth of flames. But how did fire-creating begin? On each continent, at various times in the ancient days,

an industrious person labored long and hard to work out the method of coaxing fire from dry, dead wood. We don't know exactly who they were – man, woman or child. But I suspect that, at least in some cases, it might have been a child who pioneered friction heat with dead wood.

I have watched countless times as children have invented a way to amuse themselves in the wild. It often involves a stick or a rock or some other simple component of the forest. I witnessed one ten-year-old boy doing his best to drill through a slab of wood with a pointed rock. He spent over an hour on his self-appointed project. It is not difficult to imagine a paleo-child doing the same with a stick that he spun between his hands. When the friction produced smoke, I'll bet his father suddenly got keenly interested in his son's idle play.

This very image – twirling a thin straight stick between the palms, forcing the end of the stick to grind into a slab of wood – might depict the first technique of creating fire. A rising wisp of smoke was clear evidence of heat production. Around the bowl-like depression bored out by the rotating stick appeared a little dusting of dark ash that was hot to the touch. This ash cooled quickly. Still, it must have inspired more inventive thinking.

Exercising paleo-genius, someone cut a notch out of the wooden slab. This notch intruded into the bored-out bowl to allow the ash a place to accumulate compactly in a protected niche. Hot dust fell upon hot dust, reinforcing the heat of the ash trapped inside the notch.

I applaud that early inventor(s) for his/her brilliance and stamina, but I especially admire the concept of that notch.

On my first attempt to create fire, I came at the project by my favorite approach. I call it the "first-man" experiment. I pretended I was the first man of ancient times who would try to elicit fire from dead, dry wood. Without referring to any how-to books, I worked every night for two months with pieces of dead, dry pawpaw (the variety that always grows near water) and developed blood-red blisters that eventually hardened to calluses. Throughout the adventure I learned new definitions of exhaustion, but I had no success.

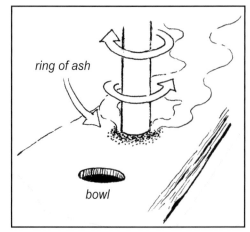

ring of ash

bowl

Rings of hot ash reliably built up at the lip of my bowl as the spinning wood produced lots of smoke. When the ring of ash piled up a quarter-inch high, I carefully deposited the charred powder into a kneaded nest of bark fibers from the tulip tree – the same material used by birds and squirrels as bedding and insulation in their homes. But always – even as I transferred the ash – I knew that it was already too cool to start a fire.

So I drilled harder … and longer … and amassed more and more ash. Yet I failed every time.

In truth, I had a lot going for me compared to the first fire-creators. For one thing, I knew that it could be done. At some time in my childhood I had probably seen glimpses of the skill performed in a National Geographic special or in a history book or on a museum painting. I had almost certainly picked up helpful hints, but apparently I hadn't paid close attention to the details.

My two months of failures were not without some benefits. I had gotten pretty good at spinning that stick. I was stronger. My hands were tougher. But two months without success was enough to transform me from "first-man" to "library-man."

In an outdated woods-lore book I found a hand-drawn illustration of a fire kit. My eye went immediately to a notch cut out of the wood slab. As I read the text I realized the brilliance of that V-shaped cut. When I got home I cut the notch into my kit and made fire on my first try.

The Good, the Bad, and the Improbable

As Frog from the Lakota story might say, not every tree swallowed fire; and so not every tree will give you fire – at least, within the limits of whatever strength

sycamore   *black willow*

a given fire-maker possesses. Generally, the trees that give the gift of fire are those oxymoronic "softer hardwoods" – like **basswood, buckeye, tulip magnolia, willow, sweetgum, birch, poplar, pawpaw** and a host of others. These are trees that grow fast on low, moist ground, suggesting that their high porosity (and resulting holey texture) is a factor in their success. But there are surprises on the list of fire-maker trees.

Hickory, redbud, sycamore, sassafras, and a few other trees with hard reputations can be used to create fire. Most pines (especially long-needled pines) prove too resinous. One exception is **white pine**, so plentiful in the Appalachians and the tallest of all the trees of the Eastern U.S. Another is **shortleaf pine**. Of the pines with very short needles, **hemlock** and **fir** are fire-makers.

I know better than to name a tree and say, "It cannot be used to make fire!" One day somebody might be successful with it. But I can say with confidence that certain trees loyally work for you (like white pine and basswood), while others are temperamental (like the tulip tree, sassafras, and sumac). Still, the majority of trees in the forest seem not to have swallowed fire.

white pine: of all the trees that swallowed fire, perhaps the easiest to find in the Appalachians

Even for those species that show the capacity for friction fire, success or failure depends upon the conditions of a particular tree's dead wood. For example, the degree of decomposition and the moisture content affect the outcome.

Listed below in alphabetical order are some fire-making candidates. Some are native, some aren't; but you'll find them in your local forests or wooded lots or in the yard of a neighbor who would probably welcome your taking a dead limb.

true poplar, an excellent choice

The Plants That Swallowed Fire

aspen*, basswood*, birch, box elder maple*, buckeye, catalpa, cedar*, chinaberry, cottonwood*, cracked-cap polyporous bracket fungus (growing on locust, pine, or oak), cucumber tree, cypress*, elderberry, white elm, fir, wild grapevine, hackberry, hazelnut, hemlock*, hickory, juniper*, red maple*, mimosa, pawpaw*, shortleaf pine, white pine*, poplar*, princess tree, redbud, redwood*, sagebrush, sassafras, sumac, sweetgum, sycamore*, tamarack, teasel, tree of heaven (ailanthus), trumpet creeper vine, tulip magnolia, virgin's bower, willow*, and yucca. That gives you over three dozen sources from which to choose. The items marked by an asterisk are especially good.

Making a Fire Kit
~ the bow-drill ~

We'll now start from scratch to create fire. We shall begin the challenge not by using the earliest known methods but by jumping ahead to an advanced technology that makes the process easier. Rather than using your hands to spin a stick, we'll employ a small bow (with rope) to do the rotating. This will spare your hands the abrasion that comes from vigorously spinning a stick between the palms, and it will apply a mechanical advantage to the spinning. Even using a bow, this project will be a worthy first-challenge. (The hand-drill will be covered in the following chapter.)

Few students succeed on their first attempts at creating fire. Your failures will ultimately teach you two things: 1.) the importance of careful knife-work as you carve the implements of your fire kit and 2.) the need for exemplary form.

Finding a Tree That Swallowed Fire

One theory suggests that the fire-making trees tend to be more porous than most. This porosity produces a less dense wood with rougher texture, while harder, heavier wood presents a denser grain. As an analogy, imagine rubbing together two wire window screens as compared to two smooth plates of sheet metal of the same material. Which would heat up faster? (There are notable exceptions to this arguable rule: hickory, sycamore, redbud, and sassafras, to name a few.)

Two pieces from the same dead porous tree can be ground against one another with more traction – more bite or grit, if you will – than trees with less texture.

Porous trees are the species that typically grow fast. Such trees need abundant water; therefore, they grow best in low areas, giving us a paradox in our tree selection: Some of the best fire-making species of trees are to be found in moist valleys, where virtually every night they are exposed to the cool humid air of the lowlands. This moisture, of course, is problematic to a fire-maker; but, with time, any wood can dry. Just remove any bark, split the wood into plank-like pieces about 1"thick,

and set these in the sun several feet off the ground. A living tree branch can serve as a drying rack, or you can construct your own at any place that receives direct rays of sunlight.

It is not necessary to hunt exclusively for a *dead* tree. All trees, as they get older, allow branches to die due to the fact that upper branches condemn the lowest to perpetual shade. Because these still-attached dead branches are well off the ground, they are considerably dryer than fallen wood. In this sense, every tree serves as a drying rack for its defunct branching.

The higher the branch, the better for your kit, because the nightly soup of airborne moisture mostly affects the lower stratum of air. Climbing a tree is usually not necessary. Instead, use the long-handled grappling-hook shown in Chapter 2.

You'll need one piece of wood for a cylindrical **drill** about 10"long and ¾"thick. For the slab or **hearth,** try for a 1"-thick plank-like piece that is at least 2"wide. Its length should be at least 6". In a best-case scenario, a big dead limb will splinter-snap so that the break resembles an alligator's partially open mouth. You can often pry open the gator's jaws to split the wood and have the **hearth** of your kit instantly. Elsewhere on the limb, you might find a perfectly straight **drill** section ready to be shaved to a point on each end.

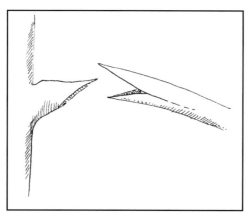

However, limbs generally contain decomposed wood in their outermost sap-wood, so choose a section thicker than desired to allow for carving away punky (rotting) wood. The most reliable drill and hearth come from the deeper woody tissue of a trunk.

Explore a flood plain for dead wood. Even if you are not sure what species of tree you find, test the firmness of a specimen with a thumbnail by attempting to press a dent into the wood. A dent does not guarantee that you have a viable fire-making tree, but it puts the odds in your favor.

If you find a dead tree with a broken trunk, work at the broken area to harvest the wood you need for your kit. To break open the tree use a heavy rock like a sledgehammer. If splitting is difficult, look for wedge-shaped rocks that can be hammered into a crack. It might take a dozen such wedges (getting progressively larger) to free up a slab. **Protect your eyes. Be careful of flying pieces of shattered rock.**

Splitting these two rough pieces into smaller blanks for drill and hearth can be accomplished with your knife and an improvised mallet. Set a to-be-split slab of wood vertically on the "workbench" of a sturdy log. (Don't use the ground as a workbench. You need firm resistance.) Use a divot in the log to hold the slab in place. Position your knife blade wedge-like on the upper end of the slab so that the portion of the blade closest to the handle will travel downward through the wood. Apply enough pressure with the knife to hold the slab vertical with only the knife-hand. With your free hand use a tough limb as a mallet to pound the back of the blade until it sinks into the wood.

With the blade buried in the wood, continue the pounding by striking the protruding tip end of the blade, all the while applying downward pressure on the

knife handle to counter the mallet blow and to keep the blade horizontal. Visualize what could go wrong if your mallet blow knocked the blade out of the wood or if the wood quickly split. Stand accordingly to keep yourself out of harm's way.

Once the mallet-work is complete, all other wood-shaping will be done by careful carving. Be demanding of yourself with this knife-work; it is all-important in having success with your kit. Imperfect carving ensures a number of problems and frustrations when you get to the spinning phase.

Searching for a Tree that Swallowed Fire – Using a field guide on

tree identification or with the help of a tree-savvy friend, locate a tree from the fire-making list on page 73 and, using a saw, harvest a dead portion of trunk 1'-long and 4"-5" thick. This will provide enough material to carve both the hearth and drill, both of which will soon be covered in detail.

basswood

pawpaw

juniper

buckeye

"Staring into the flames he began to make out the dark shapes of lithe figures dancing at the heart of the fire. As they came closer he thought he recognized the unbroken line of all his forgotten ancestors."

~ *Russell Storms,* Song of the Horseman

CHAPTER 4

First Friction Fire
~ *the bow-drill* ~

Though I have many large boxes filled with experimental fire kits, my trial-and-error learning continues. Run your own experiments and add to the list. Just make sure that the wood you are using is dead and dry but not rotten.

A few of the fire-making trees – namely, tulip magnolia, sweet gum, sassafras, and birch – tend to hold onto their outer-bark long after the limb or trunk is dead. This creates a sheath that keeps the enclosed wood moister than a limb whose bark has sloughed away. These damper woods named above may take considerable drying time.

Fashioning Your First Fire Kit
The Hearth

The drilling base or **hearth** of a kit is simply a slab of wood shaped like a plank. As it lies flat on the ground it needs to be at least two finger-widths wide (preferably three or four), one finger-width thick, and 6"or more in length (long enough for you to step firmly on one end and still have several inches showing beside your boot). A longer and wider hearth is even more stable, and it offers more space on its top surface for future fire-making sites. (Once you have used up the first drilling site by boring all the way through the hearth, you'll need to start another. One hearth might supply a dozen fire-making sites, each site providing several fires.)

If the ground is wet, insulate your board underneath with dry leaves, twigs, or whatever is available. Carve the bottom side of the hearth flat for perfect stability. As you will soon learn in the physical act of fire-making, keeping your hearth steady – without rocking or vibrating – is one of the many fine points that makes the quest for fire more easily attainable.

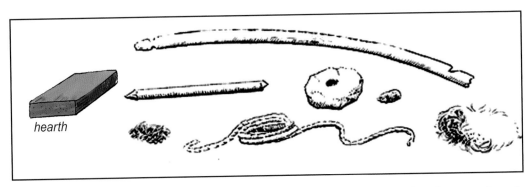

hearth

 <u>Making a Hearth</u> – From your harvested dead wood, split the wood with rock wedges (or knife) and a mallet. Then carve a level-bottom hearth with the appropriate dimensions: let's say 1' long, 3"wide, and 1"thick. Once completed, store it *off* the ground in a sunny place to dry.

The Drill

From a 10"X 1.5"X 1.5"block of wood carve a perfect, cylindrical **drill** that is slightly less than 1"thick. Take great care to carve your drill <u>straight with parallel sides</u>. Check it constantly as you carve, making sure that its sides (viewed from all angles) do not taper or bulge at any spots.

   The actual thickness of the drill varies with the strength of the fire-maker. For a first drill, carve one with a thickness that matches the widest knuckle of your long finger. As you become more experienced and stronger, you may prefer a thicker drill.

   A long drill – say 10"-12"– makes the work easier on your spine and opens up your view of the hearth. (With a short drill, your weak hand will block your view.) And, of course, a long drill lasts longer than a shorter one, because at the same time that the drill is boring through the hearth, the hearth is eating up the drill).

   Though the drill does need to be a perfect cylinder in silhouette, its sides do not have to be perfectly rounded. A flat knife blade is naturally going to carve flat facets into the sides, making its circumference a polygon. Make these facets narrow rather than wide. The many angles between facets will help the rope to gain traction on the drill for the spinning.

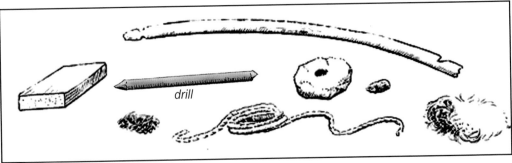

drill

   Once you are satisfied with the long, cylindrical shape of your drill, sharpen 1 ½" of one end to a long-tapering point. This will be the *cool end* of the drill that will be controlled by your weak hand. Carve ½" of the other end to a blunt point. This will be the *hot end*. The resulting drill should look like an oversized wooden pencil sharpened at both ends.

Finding a straight-grained section of wood is a blessing; but, of course, straight drills can be carved out of thick pieces with a crooked grain. As sculptors like to say: "Visualize the finished sculpture inside your raw wood and remove everything else."

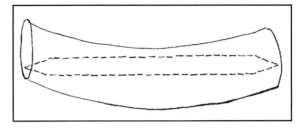

Never handle the **hot end**, as oil from your fingers can lubricate. Also, keep the hot end away from dirt and any other source of moisture. The **cool end** will benefit from any lubricants you might think of – nut oils, rotting mushroom, plant mucilage, facial oil, or ear wax.

<u>Making a Drill</u>

<u>Making a Drill</u> – Carve a 10"drill out of a larger piece of fire-making wood, matching its thickness to the knuckle of your long finger. Carve it straight and then test your work by studying its silhouette from every angle as you turn it. No part of the drill should be thicker or thinner than any other part. Taper 1 ½" of the cool end to a long point and ½" of the hot end to a blunt point. Set your finished drill in the sun with your hearth.

The Socket

Holding the spinning drill in a vertical axis is one of the most difficult and most important aspects of drilling. We will use a *socket* with a small divot to hold the top of the drill in place. (The bottom will be held by the depression or *bowl* bored into the hearth.) The socket can be made of oak, bone, stone, shell, glass, plastic, or any number of things you might find. It should be large enough to fill your hand when you grip it so that your fingers do not overlap and touch the spinning drill. If by chance you find an ideal socket material that is too small to grip, bulk up its top side with bark, bandana, or a sock so that it better fills your hand and provides more stability. Such padding will make the socket more comfortable to hold.

The socket probably used most often by primitive fire-makers is hardwood, simply because it is so available. But a wooden socket presents a problem. Though much harder than your drill's wood, oak is still a wood and there will be friction experienced at the top of the drill. This unwanted friction makes the drill more difficult to spin, reducing friction at the hot end. Ideally, we would like the cool end of the drill to be friction-less.

A wonderful socket awaits the fire-maker of red dirt country. The well-known red clay of the South is the result of abundant iron in the soil, which comes from the many rocks that contain iron. Because iron oxidizes (rusts), we can find rocks that have been weakened to varying degrees. Some reddish ferrous rocks are still too hard to be used. Others have rusted too much and become crumbly. But a good many can be crudely sculpted by a harder rock to create a divot large enough to accommodate the top of the drill. The size of rock-sockets varies from one hand to another, but in general they are about the shape of half a bagel (without the hole). We will add the divot to the flat side by grinding with shards of other stones.

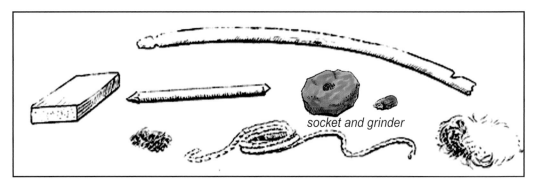

socket and grinder

Experiment with "grinder" stones by breaking larger non-ferrous rocks (careful of your eyes) to get random pieces, some of which will work nicely as tools for grinding into the ferrous rock. If both grinder and socket stones are ideal, you can make a completed socket in 15 seconds.

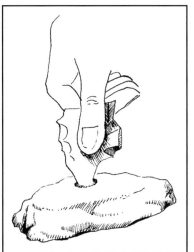

Georgia's reddish stone is self-lubricating with its own talc-like powder that is ground off the rock. But it is possible to find a rock overly oxidized, and its shower of powder will cover your hearth with rock debris. In this case, the drill will bore through this inferior socket too quickly, and you'll feel the cool end of the drill spinning against your palm!

 Making a Socket – If you live in red clay country, search for a light-weight, reddish rock shaped like a large biscuit to fill your hand. An uprooted tree is a good place to look. Root balls often pry up from the earth lots of underground rocks within their root system. Such rocks have had more exposure to water than surface rocks and are sure to be more oxidized.

Another promising site is a road cut. A road carved from a mountainside might have a six-foot bank of exposed dirt on the high side. Erosion exposes plenty of rocks. Also, scour east- and south-facing slopes that experience more temperature extremes. Rocks are more likely to surface there. If you live outside of red clay country, rock-grinding might prove too time-consuming. Search for a rock with a natural divot. Or keep an eye out for skeletons of dead wildlife. Large bones can be shaped by a crude rock tool. On the coast consider seashells and washed-up trash.

If nothing else can be found, you'll always have a back-up plan of hardwood. With your knife, carve a slab to fit your hand and cut a divot on one side at the center.

For the grinder use the hardest stone that you can break. The ideal shape for such a tool is a long spear point with the tip broken off square – like a crude flat-head screwdriver. No knapping skills are necessary for this. An accidental grinding tool will eventually present itself in one of the shards you have produced.

The Bow

The innovative high-tech component of the bow-drill kit is a small inflexible **bow**, which enhances the spinning of the drill by a mechanical advantage. It works much like a child's toy – the top, which is made to whirl by pulling a string that is wrapped around it a number of times. The string is pulled free of the top, and the top spins.

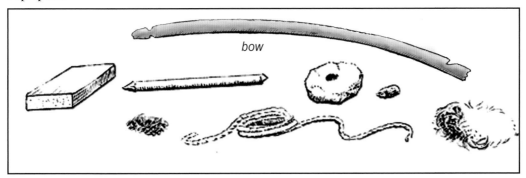
bow

The difference with the bow is that its rope wraps around the drill once and never lets go of the spinning drill. It works on the drill in alternating directions.

While a fire-maker works the bow, thrusting forward and then pulling back repeatedly to spin the drill, the rope is constantly exerting pressure on the drill, forward then back. What keeps the drill from flying off the hearth is the firm grip of the socket at the cool end of the drill and the bowl bored into the hearth at the hot end.

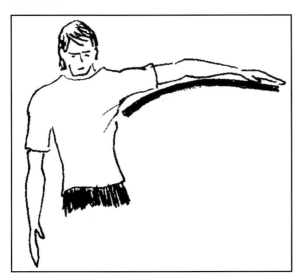

An ideal **bow** measures the length and follows the arc of your *slightly* curved arm from armpit to fingertips. The bow should be stiff (not green but dead) and strong (the hardest of hardwoods at least ¾"thick) and curved along *one plane only*, like an archer's bow. Hold the bow away from you like an archer shooting a bow, so that you see no curve in its silhouette. Rotate it 90° in your hand, and you should see the bow's only curve.

A shallow curve in the bow is best, because such a design transfers more of your work into the spinning of the drill. Furthermore, a shallow curve will not allow the bow to bend as easily as a

deep curve. Bow-bend results in a slack rope, which will slip rather than turn the drill. Such "flossing" results in no friction between drill and hearth.

Notch the bow on the convex side of each end. Using these you will tie a slightly slack **rope** from end to end. When done, it will resemble a miniature, thick

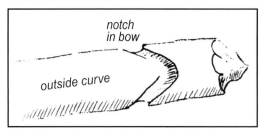

archer's bow with a thick, loose bow-string. How loose should the rope be? When you get to the act of loading the drill onto the bow, trial and error will teach you about looseness versus tautness. For all fire-makers, adjustments to rope tension are repetitive and part of the natural order of the bow-drill method. You'll adjust and readjust throughout the multiple attempts at making a fire.

Since the making of strong cordage (covered in *Secrets of The Forest, Volume 1*) and the replacement of broken cordage is the downside of the bow-drill, we'll use commercial rope for this first effort.

Making a Bow – Your best source for a fire-kit bow is a limb from a hardwood tree that has blown over from a storm and died. You'll have access to lots of curved limbs. Find a 1"-thick, inflexible section with a shallow curve in only one plane. Cut it to your arm's length and notch it for the rope. Use a non-slick, non-stretch rope 1/8"to 3/16"thick. Attach the rope so that it is barely slack. You will fine-tune that tautness when you first attempt to load the drill onto the bow.

Tinder

Tinder is any fluffy material that can burst into flame once the fire-kit has produced an ample amount of hot ash. For this we want a double-handful of fine, flammable fibers. There are many sources for tinder: fibers from dead dry weeds rubbed by hand to get rid of coarse chaff; dead dry inner tree bark frayed and softened by kneading; abandoned nests of mice and birds; bedding from squirrels' nests; downy seed fluff called "pappus" produced by certain plants; brown pine needles beat with a mallet until soft and cushiony; lint; dead grasses; etc. It has been claimed that grasses alone will not suffice (that grasses should merely bulk up your collection of better fibers), but this is not true. 100% dead grass tinder can be used successfully. Tinder must be dry, thinly fibrous, and compactly squeezed together to allow for continuous smoldering from one fiber to its neighboring fiber.

Damp fibers of potential tinder can dry while you complete your kit. Fray the fibers into hair-like filaments, then ball them up to crush between your palms in a rolling fashion, and then flatten these "hair balls" into wafer-thin disk shapes to dry on the branches of a tree in direct sunlight.

If a dry spell has been in place for a time, even on a rainy day in summer or autumn you might find fairly dry inner bark on dead limbs that still have intact outer bark. (Earlier I mentioned that outer bark holds in moisture, but it also keeps it out. The paradox is one about relative dampness. On a dry day, dead inner bark beneath a sleeve of outer bark can be damper than exposed inner bark. On a wet day, hidden inner bark can be much drier than exposed bark.)

notch in bow

outside curve

Plentiful Tinder in the Forest

Inner bark from dead tulip magnolia trees is the most easily found bulk of tinder in the forests of Southern Appalachia. (This is the tree incorrectly called "tulip poplar" or "yellow poplar" by many people, including the U.S. Forest Service.)

Even if you are not yet adept at identifying the tulip tree, you can often spot its "pennants" of frayed pale inner bark dangling from a dead limb, where a bird or squirrel has stripped the upper surface of the limb for nest material, leaving those harder-to-access fibers still attached beneath the limb. Let these streamers signal you to stop and harvest. These pennants are nicely air-dried. Bring down these limbs with a long-handled grappling-hook.

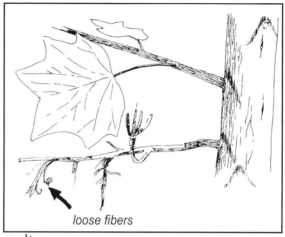

loose fibers

tulip tree

If rained upon recently, wet bark can be frayed and dried in direct sunlight in half an hour. Make identifying the tulip tree a priority in your fire-making education. Note that it is the only native tree whose leaves terminate not in points … but in notches.

Tinder Hunting – Locate a grove of young tulip trees growing on a bottomland or swale in the woods. Best results will come from a stand where the

majority of trees are no more than 3" in diameter. With all the competition among these trees, you should be able to find a few that are standing and dead. Break or saw them down and then gently break the trunk in various places to reveal any ribbons of persistent inner bark. In the right-hand photo on the previous page, note the long ribbon of inner bark draping down from the diagonal stick (near the left border of the picture.)

You'll find this inner bark in varying degrees of readiness to be used as tinder. Ideally, strip the tree and separate inner from outer bark. If the two barks are firmly attached, you'll need to soak this specimen in a creek for an indefinite time … until the layers separate. Soak 2 days; dry 2 days; repeat as needed.

 Tinder preparation – Once you have a collection of inner bark ribbons from the tulip tree, take a foot-long section and pull apart the parallel fibers from their midpoint without disengaging them; that is, allow the ends of the fibers to remain connected. Fray the ribbons into the thinnest strands that your fingers can manage.

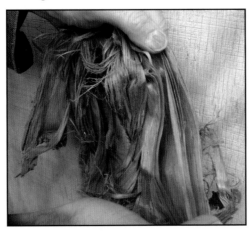 

Ball up the frayed sheet and crush it between your palms, rolling it, twisting it, and kneading the fibers in all directions. Beating it with a smooth stick (or dry river stone) against a dry, smooth, bark-less, log "workbench" is another softening technique.

An Urban Treasure

The most abundant, most accessible, and most flammable modern-day source for tinder can be found lying in the streets of urban neighborhoods where long-needled pines grow. Here fallen pine needles have been crushed, and softened by traffic until they collect in fluffy clusters that get run over again and again. The needles are kneaded and abraded down to their core fibers. When dry, the clusters might be wind-blown, rolling along the street like small, elongated, golden-brown tumbleweeds.

The combination of tire rubber … the weight of a car … a hard smooth street surface … and the highly flammable terpenes in the needles … all comprise a recipe for exceptional tinder. I can stop at a red light, lean out of my truck and in one scoop gather enough tinder for fifty fires. A three-minute stroll with a garbage bag has supplied me with a year's supply of tinder for fire-making classes and demonstrations.

This same tinder can be produced in the wild with a little time and patience. Needles picked up under pine trees do not work well unless they are processed, mainly because they slither apart too easily rather than forming a fibrous interwoven mass.

<u>Making Pine Needle Tinder the Primitive Way</u> – Set up at a

smooth, log workbench and beat lots of dead, brown pine needles with a mallet or smooth river stone. As the needles are worn down to their core fibers, their new wiry forms better mesh together to make a ball of fluff that is perfect for tinder.

Pappus, the Tinder Additive

Another helpful tinder material can be found on mature plants that produce soft, downy, fluffy pappus, which helps their seeds go airborne. Perhaps the most widely recognizable pappus is the gray ball of hair-like filaments seen on a gone-to-seed dandelion stalk. Other pappus-makers include: **thistle, cottonwood, asters, goldenrod, milkweed, wild lettuce, clematis, willow**, and the fire-maker's favorite – **cattail**. The seed down (pappus) from the female flower of the cattail can be laid on top of the tinder (just a thin layer of pappus will do), where the hot ash will fall into the notch. When heated by the ash, this botanical down molds to the hot ash, holding the "wedge of ash pie" together, so that it does not crumble and lose heat.

 ## Making Tinder on a Wet

Day – Excellent rainy day tinder can be scraped from dead cane, whether our native rivercane or introduced bamboos. With silica in the outer glaze of these canes, the woody material beneath remains quite dry during wet weather. By holding your knife blade perpendicular to a dead cane, scrape repeatedly in one direction to amass a clump of crepe-like ribbons of fibers. Use this same technique on prime hardwoods.

The Hearth Divot

If you try to spin a drill on a hearth without a depression to hold the drill in place, the drill will skitter chaotically across the surface of the slab. A **divot** is needed to prevent the hot end from roaming. This divot does not need to be perfectly carved to fit the point of the drill, for, in time, spinning the drill will sculpt the best fit possible between drill and hearth.

 ## Cutting the Divot – Lay your finished drill on its side on top of your hearth and flush with the edge of one long side of the hearth. Place your knife blade vertically and flat against the other side of the drill. This shows you how far from the edge of the hearth you will center the spin of the drill.

If your hearth is less than 8"long, position the divot toward one end of the plank. This will allow room for your foot to step on and stabilize the hearth at the other end. A hearth longer than 8"can be drilled anywhere.

Make a mark at the place you plan to drill. Then using the point of your knife, cut into the mark to make a crude, inverted-cone divot ¼"wide and 1/8"deep. To test your work, hold the drill vertically with its bluntly-tapered hot end in the divot and then determine the divot's lateral hold on the drill. You may need to sharpen the point of the drill more carefully so that it will better seat in the divot.

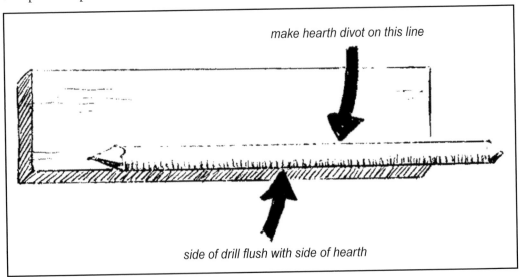

make hearth divot on this line

side of drill flush with side of hearth

This divot now needs to be enlarged by spinning the drill to create a bowl-shape. Therefore, we must now address loading the drill and working the bow.

Loading Drill to Bow

If you are right-handed, hold one end of the bow in your right hand (pointing the far end forward and away from you) with the rope on the left side of the bow. With your left hand bring the hot end of the drill perpendicularly toward the center of the bow (going under the rope) until the rope touches the drill's midpoint.

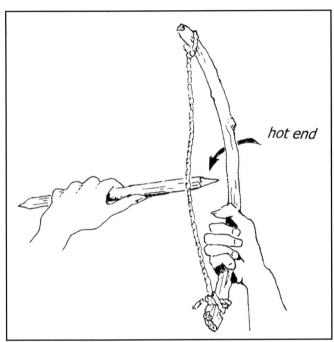

Now each end of the drill must be forced over the rope as the drill is turned counter-clockwise, as shown in the illustration.

To accomplish this you'll need both hands. Secure the near end of the bow in the hollow of your pelvis so you can use both hands to twist the rope around both ends of the drill. (At this point the bow hangs down beneath the rope.)

Propeller the drill counter-clockwise, forcing

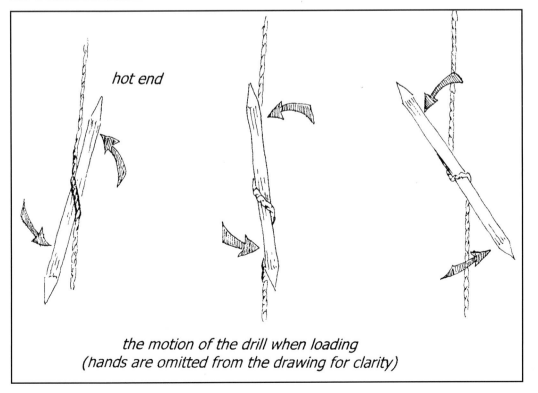

the motion of the drill when loading
(hands are omitted from the drawing for clarity)

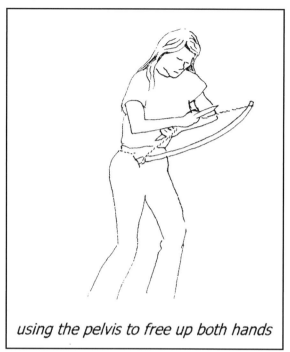

using the pelvis to free up both hands

the hot end of the drill up and over the half of the rope farthest from you … and the cool end of the drill up and over the half of the rope nearest you. Keep twisting, forcing the rope to take a tight turn around the midpoint of the drill. If the rope has the proper amount of tautness, the drill will "pop" into place. If there's no "pop," the rope is too loose and will need retying to make it shorter.

When the drill is loaded properly to the bow with the hot end pointed down, the drill will appear outside the letter "D" formed by bow and rope.

If the drill is loaded incorrectly *inside* the "D," its working space is more confined. In this position the drill may contact the inner curve of the bow during bowing and be knocked out of the divot, spoiling your efforts.

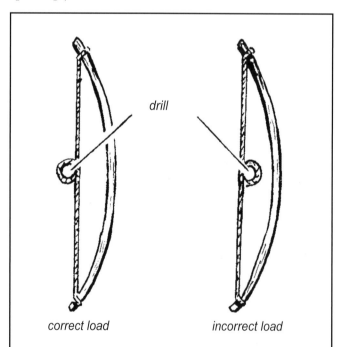

drill

correct load   *incorrect load*

bird's eye view

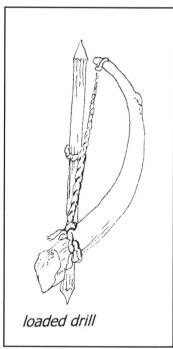

loaded drill

With the loaded drill locked in place by a firm grip of the right hand, kneel on your right knee with your left foot out in front holding down the hearth beneath the instep. Position the part of the hearth with the divot to the right of your left foot. Slide the *right* knee as far back from the hearth as possible while maintaining

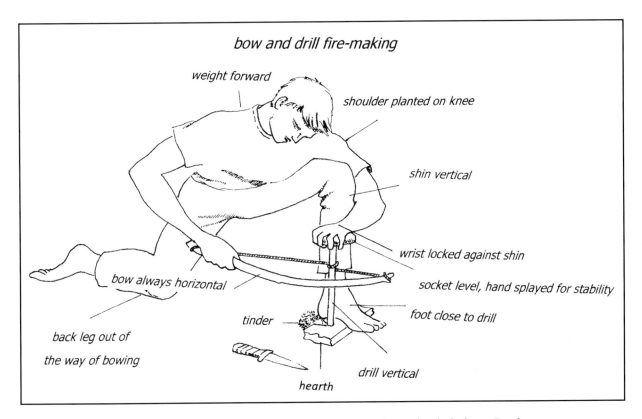

bow and drill fire-making

weight forward

shoulder planted on knee

shin vertical

wrist locked against shin

socket level, hand splayed for stability

foot close to drill

bow always horizontal

tinder

drill vertical

hearth

back leg out of
the way of bowing

a vertical *left* shin. Most of your weight should be *forward* on the left foot. In this pose you should feel ready to pounce forward. In other words, don't hunker back on the kneeling leg. This is the position you will assume whenever you use the bow. Of course, the left-right directions should be reversed for left-handed fire-makers.

Drilling a Bowl

Holding both the loaded drill and rope in your right hand to prevent the drill from flying out of its loaded tension, place the drill vertically on the hearth with the hot end in the hearth's divot. With your left hand lock the socket's divot over the cool end of the drill. Lower your left shoulder to your left knee and bend your left elbow out to your left so that your left forearm is horizontal as it *braces against your shin*.

With the drill trapped between socket and divot, you can let go of the drill and rope with your right hand and take a new grip on the close end of the bow. Pivot your left foot slightly (pigeon-toed) so you can press your left wrist firmly against the muscle just to the left of your shinbone. Now your left arm alone (braced against the shin) has the job of holding the drill vertically in place by your grip on the socket.

As it is in so many wilderness skills, strength is an undeniable asset, but form is the more important focus. Push and pull the bow in long, smooth, horizontal strokes and witness what may have been the world's first power-drill at work. *While bowing it is important to keep the <u>bow</u> and <u>rope</u> and <u>socket</u> all parallel to the earth at all times.* Don't let the bow follow the arc of a rocking chair's rocker, as most beginners tend to do. Keep the drill *vertical at all times*. Put only moderate pressure down on the socket. Increase pressure only as the wood heats up and releases smoke.

 ## Making the Bowl in the Hearth

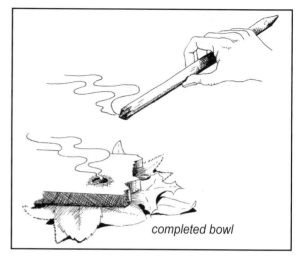

completed bowl

– Use a layer of dry leaves to separate your kit from the moist earth. Load the drill to the bow and kneel over your hearth in the posture described above. Firmly plant your left wrist against the left shin muscle. Now begin bowing. Keep the drill perfectly *vertical* and the socket and bow perfectly *horizontal*.

In the first few seconds of bowing the drilling is easy, for only a small portion of the drill's hot end is in contact with the hearth (the nascent bowl). As the hot end and bowl conform to one another, the friction increases and smoke begins to rise.

When the bowl has grown <u>to the full width of your drill</u>, stop bowing and set aside the bow and drill. You'll see a heat-blackened, recessed bowl in the hearth and a ring of dark, hot ash that rose from the bowl and encircled its lip on top of the hearth. As you can determine by touch, this ash cools quickly.

The Notch

Cutting the notch is like cutting the first slice from a just-baked pie, except that the knife point starts just shy of center. The blackened bowl in the hearth serves as the pie. Continue this wedge-shaped slice all the way out of the hearth as though you're getting extra "crust" with this slice of pie. The angle of the cut near the center of the bowl must be greater than 45°, less than 90°. Such a notch will allow an ample accumulation of hot ash but prevent the hot end of the drill

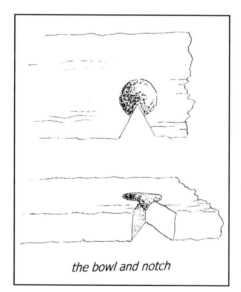

the bowl and notch

from slipping out of the bowl by way of the notch. This notch must be cut with smooth vertical walls that allow the ash particles to free-fall without impediment. Once you have cut the notch, you are ready to create fire.

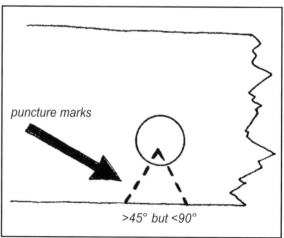

puncture marks

>45° but <90°

plannng the notch

starting the notch

Cutting the Notch – First, with your knife point, outline the notch you intend to cut out, taking care to position the point of the notch just short of the center of the bowl.

With the two straight lines scratched into the top of the hearth, use your knifepoint to turn these lines into "dotted lines" of perforations that you press straight down into the wood as deep as you can manage. (Don't attempt this with a folding knife.) Repeat this process, this time adding new dashes between the old ones. This knife-work establishes the notch angle deep into the hearth.

Now lay the hearth on its thin side and start cutting your notch from the "crust-side" of the "slice of pie." Set your knife blade on the hearth's edge in line with one of the perforated lines that you made. Apply pressure and rock the blade back and forth using the strength of your wrist to encourage the blade to sink ¼"deep into the edge of the hearth. Repeat this on the other perforated line. Then gently pry out the first quarter-inch of the notch from the edge of the hearth. Keep repeating to excavate the "pie-piece" by degrees. Cut true to the perforated lines so that the notch is completed with a sharp "V" point (not a "U"!) with its point *almost* extending to the center of the bowl. The precision of this "V" notch is crucial.

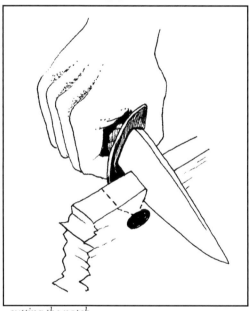

cutting the notch

Once the notch is established, carefully carve away any rough spots or splinters inside the V. These finishing touches make the inside planes absolutely smooth and straight, like a V-shaped box canyon with perfect vertical walls. You can cut the walls wider at the bottom of the hearth (like a canyon with overhung walls) but not the opposite (like a funnel) which would cause the falling ash to clog in the smaller space below.

The Serving Tray

A flat poker-chip-sized disk of tinder will be placed under the notch (and hearth) to catch the falling ash. This "**serving tray**" will be used to deliver the "wedge of ash pie" from the notch to the rest of the tinder, which lies waiting nearby.

Later you may decide that you prefer putting the full nest under the hearth so as to eliminate the need for transferring the hot coal to the nest by way of the tray. In that case you'll need to shim the hearth wherever necessary (using twigs, earth, pebbles, etc.) so that it cannot seesaw or wobble during the bowing. Ideally, only the bow moves and the drill spins. Nothing else.

Setting the Serving Tray

– Lay down a carpet of dry leaves to protect your kit from the moist earth. Use some of your prepared tinder supply to make a small flat disk that will fit under the hearth and notch without disturbing its stability. The tray should completely line the bottom of the notch and extend slightly from the edge of the hearth.

After placing your instep over the hearth, use your finger to push down any stray fibers of the serving tray that might be trying to rise up inside the notch. (If such a fiber were to be caught by the hot end of the drill, the fiber would be jerked upward, dashing away any ash that had accumulated in the notch.)

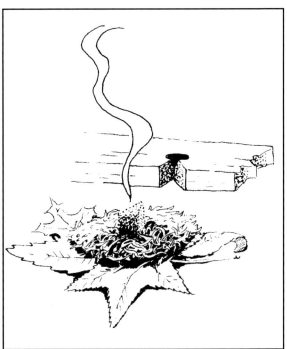

smoking ash on the serving tray ... what every fire-maker wants to see

First Fire

Shape the remainder of your tinder into a bird's nest and set it aside within reach. If you have cattail down, press a thin layer inside the notch on top of the serving tray. If there is a light to moderate wind, position yourself with the wind hitting the right side of your back. These currents will help breathe life into the hot ash that accumulates inside the notch. If wind is substantial, set up with the wind hitting your left side.

As you reload the drill onto the bow, you will probably find the need to tighten the rope. (Every series of bowing loosens the rope's tension.) Kneel and assume the bowing position: left foot on the hearth close to the drill, drill vertical in the bowl, left arm controlling the socket, left wrist locked against your shin, and right hand gripping the bow.

This is a good moment to pause, to acknowledge the gifts of wood and stone and plant fiber. (Be thankful for the store-bought rope, too.) Before you lies a set of primitive tools that has been used for eons by hands just like yours. Now dedicate yourself to the task: *Be strong, fire-maker … and of good form.*

Calling Up the Flame – Use long, smooth strokes, taking advantage of the full length of your bow. Soon you will feel and hear the drill "bite" into the wood with a serious grind.

Smoke production increases. Check the notch to assure that ash is falling down onto the serving tray. (If it's not, stop and use your knife to clean up the V-point of the notch where the ash first enters.) When the notch is half-full, speed up (still using long strokes, not short choppy ones) and apply more pressure down on the socket. When the notch has filled with hot, smoking ash, give the bow 10 more strong strokes to increase the heat. Now the bowing is done. Without disturbing the hearth, carefully remove the drill from the bowl and lay aside socket, bow, and drill.

This is a crucial moment. If the ash in the notch continues to smoke steadily, a fire is imminent. You may even see a bright red coal smoldering by the stir of the breeze. If smoke ceases to rise from the ash, then this is probably a failed attempt. But you never know for certain until you take the process through the final steps.

At this point many novice fire-makers get over-anxious and make the mistake of rushing their movements, only to see the ash collapse. (When this happens, heat dissipates quickly and the attempt usually fails.) Move with care. Holding the hearth in place with your freed-up hands, gently remove your foot from the hearth so as not to disturb the wedge of ash in the notch.

Holding the serving tray in place, lift the hearth up and away, leaving the wedge of ash on the tray. If the ash does not release from the hearth, carefully use a pine needle or twig to loosen it from the notch.

Once the smoking ash is sitting alone on the serving tray, lift the tray as if it is a grail filled to the brim with a precious liquid. If you break the brick of ash, it may cool off. Invert the reserve bird's nest of tinder over the serving tray, carefully enfolding the hot smoking ash with the larger nest. Now re-invert the joined tray and tinder, bird's nest below the serving tray, holding the mass with only your fingertips (so as not to smother the tinder with your palms) and blow into any tiny opening you find between the tray and the bird's nest. Compact the tinder with your fingertips to

ensure that fibers are contacting the hot ash. Blow quietly-but-firmly from the tight circle of your lips. (This minimizes moisture from your breath.) As needed, pinch the tinder tighter and blow until it glows and then ignites.

If the tinder is slow to ignite (moist), you may need to rotate the ball of fluff so as not to burn a smolder-hole out the back of the tinder and lose your glowing ash in the process. If you can see that the tinder has smoldered enough to form a cavity in the center of the tinder, gently press the surrounding tinder fibers closer together until they make contact with the hot ash or glowing fibers.

When the flame jumps to life, don't panic. Let the tinder burn enough to engage more fibers. Then place the burning tinder under your pyre. At this special moment you have joined a powerful alliance with the Standing People who swallowed fire.

A Solution for Bricks of Ash that Tend to Fall Apart and Lose Heat

Adverse conditions of some dead wood, when used in a fire kit, make it difficult for the granules of hot ash to cohere as a brick when the hearth is removed. When a brick breaks apart, the result is a sudden loss of heat. A tantalizing wisp of smoke may rise … but only for a second or two. Then the ash is dead. This situation coaxes a fire-maker to act more quickly (and carelessly), but seldom does such a kit show success.

By pressing a layer of downy plant pappus onto the top of the serving tray, you may be able to remedy the problem. Such material melts from the heat and serves as an envelope to hold the brick in its wedge-shape.

Pappus is the very light, filamentous, downy material that some plants use to carry their seeds airborne. A single cattail growing in a marshy area or river bank provides copious amounts of "tinder-enhancer." This pappus is packed so tightly that it stores well in the wild and remains relatively dry. Simply twist the seed head that resembles a hotdog on a stick and watch the pappus bulge out of the tear. Just a pinch between thumb and index will suffice. Layer it on top of the serving tray inside the notch of the hearth.

Other plant species with pappus include asters, cottonwood, thistle, wild lettuce, clematis, willow, goldenrod and milkweed.

Persistence

I've not yet met an ambitious fire-making student who did not eventually succeed in creating a flame. It may not happen on your first few tries but, by staying with it, you will earn it. What better way to acquire a skill? Respect the failures, for each brings its jewels of knowledge. The reference list below is designed to help you recognize some of the causes of failure.

Common bow-drill problems and > solutions

1. The rope slackens and won't spin the drill. > Pinch the rope to the bow using the fingers of the bow-hand. If the problem persists, stop and tighten the rope. You may have flossed or compressed the midsection of the drill with the rope.

It's still a usable drill but perhaps more challenging to load tightly onto the rope. If loading such a drill is too difficult, re-carve the drill into a cylinder to match the thinner midpoint.

2. *The rope travels up or down on the drill and slips off one end*. > Rather than keeping the bow horizontal while bowing, you are rocking it. Or perhaps your drill is not a true cylinder. If it tapers toward one end, carve it again with perfectly parallel sides. When the loop of the rope does begin to stray up or down during the bowing, you can guide the rope back into place with upward or downward pressure while bowing. Raise or lower the bow to the angle that will *push* the rope up or down.

3. *The rope is neither slack nor traveling up and down on the drill, but still it slips*. > (a.) The drill may be buffed to a slippery burnish by the rope. Rough the surface of the drill by scraping with your knife blade held at 90°. (b.) Otherwise, the problem might be that your bow is bending when you stroke. If so, replace this bow with a stiffer one. (c.) Your rope may be stretching. Select a new, non-stretch rope.

4. *The drill is too difficult to spin*. > (a.) The cool-end taper of the drill may be eroded and now the drill is too fat for the socket-divot, making unwanted friction. Re-taper the cool end. (b.) Just above the hot end the drill may now have some edges (angles formed by the facets made when carving the drill) that are now contacting the lip of the bowl (and probably sounding like a crazed seagull). Carefully carve away those edges, but *do not carve away any of the heat-blackened tip of the hot end*. (c.) The drill might be contacting the lip of the hearth-bowl because you are tilting the drill. Holding the drill vertical requires more strength than any other aspect of this fire-making method. (d.) The drill might be contacting the lip of the socket-divot because you are not maintaining a horizontal hold on the socket.

With each of the above problems, strength is your ally. Every fire attempt is worth something, if for nothing else, because it makes you stronger.

5. *The drill is flying off the hearth like a rocket*. > (a.) Your notch was cut too large, either with an angle too wide or by carving the notch to the center (or beyond) of the bowl. Start over. Create another bowl next to the first and cut a perfect notch. When you get more experienced, you can work around this problem by shimming up the notch-side of the hearth with rocks or wood wedges so that the hearth is tilted and the drill, though vertical, is angled on the hearth so that it can't escape. (This takes more strength.) b.) The socket divot is too shallow or has eroded an escape route. Improve the divot or replace the socket.

6. *The brick of accumulated ash seems too small to remain hot*. > (a.) The notch is too narrow. Carve it wider without intruding deeper into the bowl. (b.) Perhaps a few rough splinters at the top of the notch are causing a blockage for the ash. Carve them away.

7. *My wedge of ash keeps scattering*. > Before bowing be sure to press down all the tinder fibers inside the notch to make a good receiving pocket.

8. *When I remove the hearth after bowing, the ash falls apart right away. The grains of ash are like whiskers … or they are chunky like coarse sand in-*

stead of like powder. > The wood you are using is probably not going to work at this point in time … or possibly never. I believe that chunky grains or whiskers are symptoms of moisture or an unfavorable wood texture – perhaps due to rot. It is possible to encounter a more favorable stratum of wood as you drill deeper, but my best advice is to make a new kit out of some other, more promising tree specimen. (Predicting the success of what seems to be a good, dry fire-kit is always difficult until you make some ash and examine its texture.)

9. The drill is about to bore completely through the hearth into the ground. The bowl is almost used up. > To give that bowl more time for more tries, check to see if your hot end has become a long tapered point. If so, cut off its sharp point halfway up the blackened portion. At some point, of course, any bowl becomes a hole in the hearth. Before that happens, begin the process anew by creating a new bowl next to the old.

10. I give up! It's just not working! > Failures are inevitable. Even veteran fire-makers do not always succeed. Make a new fire-kit from another tree. Try and try again.

A Sly Mentor

Long ago, it is said, certain native teachers gave to their fire-making students pieces of oak from which to make a kit. The carving alone would have been challenging. After completing their kits, these students worked diligently at an impossible task. When the mentor finally approved of a student's form and temperament, he gave the acolyte a dry piece of cottonwood, sage, or some other prime fire-making material and watched (with a smile, no doubt) as the young one easily produced a flame.

The Fire-making Team

– I have known 12 year-olds who achieved a flame with the bow-drill; but, by and large, students under the age of 14 might find a solo effort beyond their capability. However, a team of three young students has a much better chance at success. One team member assumes the primary position as described previously. A second kneels across from him to grasp the far end of the bow, so that together they work the bow like a crosscut saw team. The third member kneels to the left of team member one and by using her hands as a vise she locks her friend's left wrist to his shin. Her clamping action is achieved by one hand on the wrist (pushing into the shin) and the other on the back of the calf. Have your students form balanced teams, carve fire kits, and then create fire.

A More Primitive Fire!

– To elevate a fire-making challenge to a more realistic emergency scenario, see what rope substitutes you can discover on your person or in your surroundings: bootlaces, twisted strips of fabric, a strip cut from a belt or backpack strap, litter, etc. Some materials may not find enough traction to spin the drill. Try twisting the strip to make it knottier and then moistening it with enough droplets of water to give the rope some "grip." (But not so moist as to drip water onto the hearth.)

A More-Primitive Fire-Kit Adventure

– Refer to the cordage section of *Secrets of the Forest, Volume 1*, and, after becoming proficient at making rope from plant fibers, substitute hand-made rope for the store-bought rope you have been using. Make three 4'-long ropes, each 1/8"-thick. Then tightly braid them into one stronger rope. Tulip tree bark, though prolific, is usually not strong enough for this challenge. Try yucca, green or dead basswood, green hickory, dried milkweed, or dogbane. Rawhide or buckskin rope is also recommended. (Making rope from animal skin is covered in *Secrets of the Forest, Volume 3*.)

The Purest Primitive Bow-Drill Fire

– Now achieve the making of every component of the fire-kit without using a metal tool – only stone. It's easier than you might think. You don't need to be skilled at knapping stone. Cruder methods of rock-work can suffice. This is a bonding experience for a group and a stellar solo challenge for the adventurous.

Four people work on a kit, one addressing the drill, one the bow, one the hearth, and one the socket. All will contribute to the making of rope for the many sections that ultimately will be needed to replace broken ropes.

For the drill consider a straight section of tree limb in the "prime of its death"; that is, possessing firm and crisp wood throughout. Break to length and then sharpen the two ends by scraping on a large, rough, flat surface of stone.

As you break larger limbs in search of a hearth, watch for a fortuitous split in the wood where you can continue the split to form a slab. (See the first illustration on page 48.) To make additional breaks, use leverage with neighboring boulders or trees padded for protection and push the free end with your body like a turnstile. (See the illustration on page 42.)

If a split just barely forms, continue it by using small rock wedges hammered into the crack by a mallet (stone or log). (See second illustration on page 48.)

Careful of your eyes whenever you strike stone! The hearth-divot, which is designed to hold the hot end of the drill in place, can be dug out by using a sharp pointed stone. The same is true for the rusty, ferrous socket.

making a primitive notch

The quest for the notch is what usually intimidates students until they are shown an efficient technique. With great care for your body parts, crash a big heavy rock down onto another rock until you achieve a long, straight, sharp ridgeline whose angle of facets is less than 90°. Two-handedly scrape the edge of the hearth against this edge of the rock. As you carefully scrape the side of the hearth on the stone's edge, make certain that you guide the notch so that it enters the bowl.

Fire-Making Woods for the Bow-Drill

ash	cottonwood	juniper	short-leaf pine
aspen	cracked-cap fungus	maple	sumac
bamboo	cucumber tree	mimosa	sweetgum
basswood	cypress	mullein (large specimen)	sycamore
birch	elm	pawpaw	tamarack
box elder	fir	poplar	tree of heaven
buckeye	hackberry	redbud	tulip magnolia
catalpa	hazelnut	redwood	willow
cedar	hemlock	sagebrush	white pine
chinaberry	hickory	sassafras	yucca (large specimen)

Tinder Sources

<u>Dead inner bark:</u> ash, basswood, cedar, cherry, cypress, juniper, black locust, oak (rarely), poplar, tulip magnolia, walnut, willow

<u>Dead scraped wood:</u> bamboo, rivercane, dry interior of hardwoods

<u>Dead leaf fibers:</u> cattail, mullein, pine needles, grass, and some deciduous leaves that have decomposed to their net of veins

<u>Pappus:</u> aster, cattail*, cottonwood, dandelion, goat's beard, goldenrod, grass plumes, wild lettuce, milkweed, sycamore, thistle, virgin's bower, willow (*Cattail offers the driest, most tightly packaged, and most available pappus through the winter.)

<u>Ready-made finds:</u> abandoned bird's nest or mouse nest; squirrel's fibrous bedding inside its leafy nest; dead pine needles crushed by automobile tires in streets

"... the fire-keeper ... made a new fire by rubbing an ihyâ'ga stalk against the under side of a hard dry fungus that grows upon locust trees."

~ James Mooney, History, Myths and Sacred Formulas of the Cherokees

CHAPTER 5
By These Two Hands
~ the hand-drill ~

There is some debate among anthropologists as to which method of fire-making came first in human history. The fact is, there have been many methods all over the world. We may never know with certainty the answer to the riddle, but the hand-drill is certainly one of the earliest – if not the original – of techniques. Though the bow-drill is considered an evolutionary leap forward with its mechanical advantage, the hand-drill appeals out of the simplicity of its parts.

Only three items make up the hand-drill kit: hearth, drill, and tinder. That's half the number of components of the bow-drill. Most importantly, one of the tools <u>not</u> needed is handmade rope, which is apt to break with multiple uses.

But if the materials are less complicated, the physical skill of using them are more demanding. Still, the skill can be mastered, and when you reach that level of reliable successes, the reward seems even greater. You'll never be quite the same human being after making fire with your bare hands.

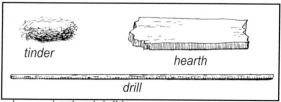

the complete hand-drill kit

Materials Needed for the Hand-drill Kit

The drill itself can be of almost any length from 10" up to several feet, but generally a hand-driller uses a drill longer and narrower than the previous one used in the bow-drill technique. Actually, any straight shaft will do, even if its wood-type is not conducive to creating fire; because a fore-shaft of fire-making wood can be spliced to the end of it.

With some materials this splice is a necessity because of the low probability of finding a straight section long enough to be an effective drill – like grapevine. Or perhaps you simply have trouble locating a straight stem of any species of plants on the hand-drill list. An arrow shaft could be sacrificed as a fire-making tool and tipped with a fore-shaft graft of ideal wood.

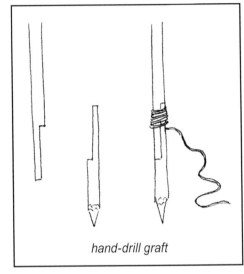

hand-drill graft

juniper

Eventually you will determine your own preferred length of drill. For starters try one 2'- to 2 ½'- long and ³/8"- to ½"- wide at the thick end. (By using the heftier end as the hot end of the drill, your hands will be working on the leaner end, taking advantage of a gear ratio in the spinning; that is, one smaller revolution at the top imparts a broader revolution at the bottom, creating more friction than a cylindrical drill.

Since creating friction by twirling the drill with the hands is physically more taxing than working a bow, you'll want to use the best materials you can find in order to have success. Many fire-makers say they prefer a dried yucca stalk for a drill. Since it is not always possible to use "like" substances for both drill and hearth (you might not find a yucca stalk thick enough to serve as the hearth), it becomes necessary to learn about mixing up different textures. (Though maximum friction is generally obtained from "like" materials, there are combinations that are very compatible for regular successes.)

juniper

yucca

For example, using a **mullein** stalk drill with a **juniper** hearth works well. So does **mullein** with **buckeye, basswood, pawpaw, white pine** and a number of other hearths. With juniper the sapwood (lighter color) is the premium friction material, but the purple heartwood can offer success, too.

Other drill materials for the hand-drill include **horseweed, evening primrose, cattail, lamb's quarters, shoots of box elder maple, elderberry, goldenrod,** and **dead dry <u>exposed</u> roots of hemlock** and other soft roots. Horseweed (*Erigernon canadensis*) is the stalk (*ihyâ'ga*) mentioned in the Mooney quote that opens this chapter.

stalks of dried mullein, horseweed, evening primrose

cross-section of tree

horseweed

cracked-cap polypore

primrose

The fungus from that same quote is cracked-cap polypore (*Phellinus rimosus*), which can be used as a hearth. This bracket fungus grows on black (yellow) locust and some oaks and pines.

Other hearth candidates for the hand-drill are: **cottonwood, box elder, princess tree, catalpa, tree of heaven, redwood, trumpet creeper,** and **white pine.** Besides mullein and juniper, three of the combinations that rise to the top of much experimentation are **horseweed on pawpaw, goldenrod on trumpet creeper,** and **evening primrose on white pine.** Virtually any woody winter remnant of a weed will work as a drill, as long as it is strong enough to hold up to the rigors of drilling on a wooden hearth. Once you have such a drill, you can try using it on various hearths to see which combination works best.

The basic principles for this technique are the same as for the bow-drill. Make a bowl. Cut a notch. Fluff tinder. Drill. When you accumulate a notch-full of hot ash on the serving tray, transfer the ash to the larger tinder and blow it into a flame. But the traction that runs this drill is supplied by your bare hands, and the engine is the muscles of your arms, chest, and shoulders. The drill is free-standing without anything like a socket to stabilize it, which makes the need for excellent

primrose

pawpaw

form take a quantum leap. It is more difficult to keep the drill vertical while spinning it back and forth between your hands, so you must think of the spinning in this way: You don't merely grind away to rotate the drill. Instead, you must make your hands work *around the constant verticality of the drill*. It will be necessary to learn how to apply aggressive energy to the spinning without compromising the vertical orientation of the drill.

Preparing the Drill

Mullein, an introduced biennial, prefers to grow on hard-packed soil in full sunlight. It can be found thriving on roadside right-of-ways, on slopes beside highways, as well as in grassy fields. It is easy to find mullein, especially where a guardrail has prevented road crews from cutting it.

In mullein's first year its milky-green, large, fuzzy leaves grow in a basal rosette. (So fuzzy are the leaves that the plant has earned the folk name "lamb's ears.")

When the flower stalk rises in the second year, leaves will sprout from this stalk – making it appear like a stem.

After the stalk dries and becomes woody in late fall, it will stand through the winter into spring and summer. In this woody stage it is, if straight, an ideal candidate for a hand-drill.

With mullein you will need to spend time smoothing the rough spots on the top-half of the drill. Your hands won't need to contact the bottom-half while drilling. There are swollen nodes and nubs of leaf stalks that need to be carefully carved away. To do this grasp the thicker end of the stalk in your left hand (narrower end pointing away from you) and position your knife blade almost flat on the stalk with the edge aimed at a bump to be removed. Push the back of the knife blade with the thumb of the holding hand as you apply shallow, scalloped cuts toward the top end of the plant. To achieve the scalloped cut, bend the knife-wrist upward at each stroke so that the blade will follow the dotted path shown in the illustration.

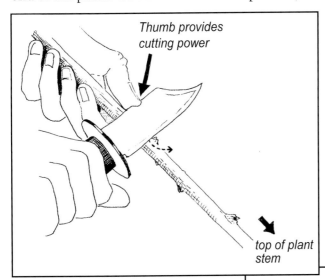

Thumb provides cutting power

top of plant stem

After all bumps and sharp nubs have been removed, smooth the stalk by gently scraping with your blade held at a perpendicular angle to the drill. Again, scrape toward the top of the plant.

Later, when drilling, if your hands find any rough spot that your knife might have missed, you might pay dearly for it with blisters or cuts. So take the time to make a smooth and comfortable drill. Injured hands will put a prompt halt to your fire-making efforts.

Mullein is generally good at producing a straight stalk, but choose the straightest section and

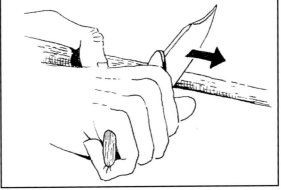

cut the hot end flat, like the end of a brand new, <u>unsharpened</u> pencil. On occasion I have used a mullein drill with a crooked midsection, but its two ends matched up as two disjointed segments of the same straight line.

One such drill was 6'-long. Its top straight portion was long enough for my hands to do the drilling. The crooked midsection whirled about wildly, acting like a flywheel to augment the spinning. I made fire with it as I stood back four feet with the drill stretching diagonally to a tilted hearth I had anchored to tree roots with heavy rocks. So, if a straight stalk is impossible to find, look for a stalk that has two distant segments that line up.

If a drill is crooked at the top end only, it will probably prevent you from making fire. Once your hands approach the midpoint of the stalk during the drilling, this bent end will wobble wildly and steal from your efforts.

The solution is to break off the angled end, assuming that leaves you a drill long enough to work. A shorter drill is better than a crooked one.

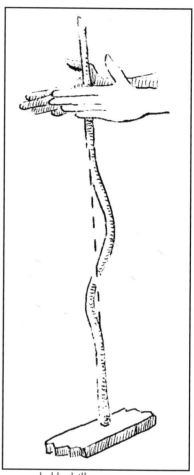

a workable drill

Mullein has a soft pith, so making a *centered* sharp point at its hot end would prove fruitless. As you drill with mullein, because the pith does not grind into the board with much abrasive effect, the bowl begins to show a nipple at its center. This raised bump is helpful in holding the drill in place. And though it is somewhat rare, this nipple can heat up the pith enough to create a hot coal *inside the pith*. This coal can be pried out with the tip of a knife to fall into the nest of tinder.

I have seen many a mullein stalk ruined by the student who is in a hurry to cut the drill's hot end. If he saws his knife against the stalk with a lot of downward pressure, due to the plant's soft center, the stalk cracks. As a result, problems usually crop up when the drilling begins, because cracks get worse. Pieces of the hot end break away.

You can achieve a perfect, flat, hot end by first circumcising a shallow ring around the stalk. (This ring serves merely as a marker.) Set your

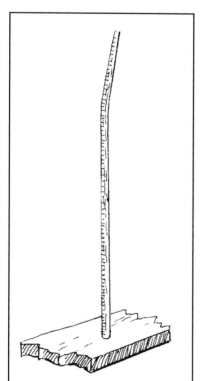

a problematic drill

knife blade in the groove of the ring and, holding the drill section in one hand, use the thumb-push technique on the back of your knife blade to shave away small scalloped pieces just as you did in removing rough spots on the stalk. Rotate the stalk and repeat again and again until you are shaving parts already scooped out – but now going a little deeper. The process is like a beaver felling a tree – patiently moving around the trunk, one little curved bite at a time. Let the discarded piece snap off on its own.

Hearth

The hand-drill's hearth is similar in design to the one used with the bow-drill, but the divot will be shaped differently. Cut into the top of the hearth a circular, flat-bottomed, 1/8"-deep depression that will accommodate the hot end of the drill.

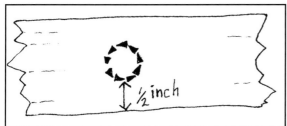

perforations

Cut it so that the drill fits perfectly and leaves ½"between divot edge and close edge of the hearth.

Begin this divot with perforations of your knifepoint pushed straight down to form a circle that precisely fits your drill's hot end. When you have connected all the perforations to a complete circle, insert the tip of your knife into the edge of the circle where the grain runs perpendicular to the flat of the knife blade. Gently pry out the wooden plug.

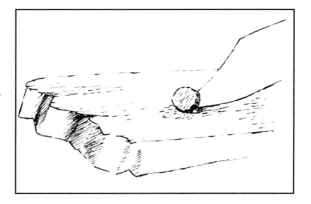

Once you have drilled enough to establish the bowl, cut a V-notch *to its center* with a 50°-60° angle. Just as with the bow-drill, cut this notch with great care, leaving clean, interior walls.

Making a Hand-drill Kit – Locate a source of prime dead wood from the

list of hand-drill hearths. If you don't have the plant I.D. capability to do that at this point, buy a board of kiln-dried redwood, cypress, or cedar. Locate a woody mullein stalk along a roadside and prepare it as instructed above, making your first drill 2 ½' long. With your knife, establish the flat, custom-made divot for the bowl at the halfway point of a 10"-long, ½" thick hearth.

After arranging a barrier of dry leaves, place the hearth on the ground and anchor it with one foot (or with two heavy rocks). Kneel (on one knee or both), center the drill in the flat bowl and lean over the vertical drill so that it points upward just in front of your preferred (strong) shoulder. To achieve the needed traction between palms and drill, spit on your hands and rub your palms together to distribute the spit. Too much or too little spit doesn't work. You'll learn by experience how to make your palms "barely sticky."

Take the drill on both sets of calluses of both hands and spin the drill by pumping both arms in opposing directions, alternating the direction each time you almost run out of palm on one hand and fingertips on the other. Be sure to keep the drill vertical. This start-up in creating a bowl can be a slow process. Be patient. Stay with the spinning until the bowl begins to smoke. At that point the needed friction is easier to achieve. Once the smoking drill and hearth have co-formed a perfect fit, lift the drill to see if the bowl has blackened and shows good definition. If not drill some more, putting a little more weight on the drill. After the bowl is established, cut a smooth, clean V-notch to its center.

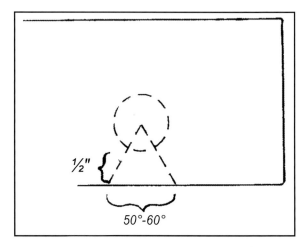

The Art of the Drilling

After applying the right amount of saliva to your hands, seat the hot end of the drill in the bowl. Center the very top section of the drill on the large calluses of your palms (just below the base of each finger). This placement will allow you to use the full surface of palms and fingers as you drill. Arch your palms slightly away from one another so that one hand will not contact the other. Now roll the drill back and forth mechanically, using all of each hand, being sure to keep the drill vertical. Remember, you must learn to work *both* moving hands (and arms) around the *constant verticality* of the drill. Move both elbows like pistons.

In this early stage, spin slowly. Learn the form before picking up speed. As you lean down to travel down the drill, apply weight to the drill for more friction, but don't push the drill *forward*, away from its vertical position. The axis of the drill remains beside your head.

When your hands come to the halfway point on the drill, you must now execute the hand-driller's "switch" by returning to the top of the drill smoothly, efficiently, and quickly – to avoid any cooling-off time. To do this, hold the midpoint of the drill in place with the left hand as you raise the right hand to the top of the drill to take over the duty of stability. (Try using a thumb to press down on the top of the drill.) Raise your body back up as you bring your left hand to the top of the drill to make a mirror image of the flattened right hand. Right away you are ready to take another downward pass on the drill with both hands whirring. Practice "the switch" until you can accomplish it in less than one second.

If your hands are too dry, on the way up you'll need to spit into your left hand and let the drilling distribute the spit to the other hand. Or you can apply the spit with an accurate shot after the hands have resumed the drilling process on the shaft. (Careful, don't spit into your bowl, ash, or tinder).

This split-second necessary for "the switch" is a cool-down instant for your drill and hearth. This is a weak-link in the hand-drill technique. If, time and again, you allow too much time to elapse in the transfer of hands, the switch might become your fire-making nemesis. If the ratio of cooling-off time to heating-up time is too great, fire will be elusive. But practice can make you fluid and efficient with hardly a break in the action.

In the early strokes of any attempt to create fire, keep your efforts smooth and relaxed as you heat up the kit. Depending upon the quality of your materials, this heating-up time might take more than a minute, maybe two, so this is not the time for giving it your all. Only after you are creating smoke and ash should you accelerate into more powerful strokes with more downward pressure.

At first, the drilling will feel slick and frictionless at the interface of drill and hearth. You'll probably hear a trebly rattle. If so, bear down with more weight. Soon you'll feel and hear the "bite" of the drill into the hearth. You'll sense a *grinding*. If you continue to hear more trebly, rattling sounds, it means that you are not putting enough weight down on the drill as you work.

Be patient, lest you find yourself collapsed into humble exhaustion. You must pace yourself. At this point of working by yourself, even to make smoke should be considered an accomplishment. But where there is smoke, there is not necessarily fire. Not yet. That will come. For now be satisfied to celebrate the rising wisps that mark this stage of your development as a fire-maker by the hand-drill.

Drilling for Form – You can learn and practice the proper hand-drill form

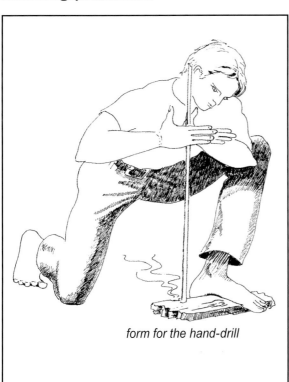

form for the hand-drill

with any straight, smoothed stick that's not too thick. An arrow shaft spun on a plank will work. Carve a blunt end on the shaft and cut a flat, round divot into the plank to practice. Try different body positions to see which you prefer: right knee up, left on the ground; vice versa; both knees down (hearth stabilized by rock or log weights); sitting with legs crossed and the outside of the feet anchoring the ends of the hearth; sitting with just one foot resting on the hearth; standing with the hearth raised on a makeshift platform.

Remember to use only the top half of the drill so that you will avoid wobbling the drill. After you feel you have gotten the hang of drilling, practice the switch after taking a pass down the drill so that you are ready to start on a new pass.

Ask a friend to watch your form to be sure you are keeping the drill vertical. When you feel that your form is right, increase the downward pressure and spinning speed for more heat.

Making Fire

As with the bow-drill, the serving tray should be positioned under the notch. Once again the goal is to fill the notch with hot ash. When it is full, give the drill four more aggressive passes as fast as you can spin and with as much weight on the drill as you can manage. Give it your all. Then carefully remove the hearth without disturbing the wedge of smoking ash, transfer the serving tray to the larger nest of tinder, and gently press the tinder with your fingertips to ensure that the hot coal contacts the fibers. Blow the coal into a flame by applying strong but quiet streams of air. If the ash or tinder stops smoking, it's time to start again … after a rest.

A Fire-making Team

A good way to break into this skill with success is to work with two or more friends as a team. Because teamwork gives each driller time to recover between passes on the drill, the feasibility of making fire is greatly enhanced.

 Team Drilling – Facing one another around a hearth stabilized by rocks, 3 or more people can alternate the drilling in a clockwise order. As one drills, the next driller spits on her hands and waits with hands hovering near the top of the drill. The one finishing his downward pass gives a vocal signal but continues to drill until he feels the new driller take control of the drill. Only then does he release the drill.

There is considerable rest time as the drilling goes around the circle, and that's what makes the team effort more likely to succeed. If any one member appears to be a weak-link in the process, you'll have to ask him to bow out and spectate until his drilling skills improve. Replace him with another driller.

 The Two-Person Team – A team of 2 is more demanding than a 3-man team and, therefore, the last training regimen before a solo attempt. Choose a partner who has proved her drilling skills. Set up facing one another over the stabile hearth and alternate with strong strokes and smooth exchanges.

 Making Smoke – For a young team of fire-makers, consider the worthy goal of simply making a kit and creating smoke for a first challenge. Gather the appropriate materials from forest and field to fashion the two "friction" parts of a kit – the drill and hearth. Smooth the drill, cut the divot, and go to work as a team.

If you try this activity inside a classroom, use a fireproof surface on which to set the hearth and temporarily deactivate smoke alarms if they are present.

The Boy With Magic Hands

I have seen many people of all ages and physiques make fire with the hand-drill, but by far the most impressive hand-driller I have ever witnessed was a fifth grader in a public school. This African-American boy was quiet and shy and with no fire-making experience before the day I had brought a program to his classroom. I did notice that he had very long hands – a good inch longer than mine. Before the day was over I would be referring to him as "the boy with magic hands."

The students worked as a team. Their goal was to make smoke – if they could. (A class so young often cannot produce a whiff of smoke, but the challenge takes them from the audience gallery and puts them into the arena of action.) Then after they had been immersed in the process, we planned to go outside on the school grounds, where I would take the skill to fruition to consummate their efforts.

Inside the classroom, each time the boy with magic hands took his turn, the drill came alive, roaring in the bowl like a mad dervish, with smoke rising in thick plumes. The drill remained vertical as he spun it at an impressive rpm. His class-mates looked on, spellbound. So did I.

Later, outside, he and I made fire together. Physically, he did most of the work, as I kept the skill on track. After our success, I could see that his presence in that classroom had expanded … as if the fire he had created had illuminated a part of him that his friends had never seen. They looked at him more closely, maybe wondering what other flames might be burning inside his quiet spirit.

Teamwork Etiquette, Do's and Don'ts

1.) As you finish your pass on the drill, don't get overly excited. Don't yell the exchange signal and "throw" the drill toward the one waiting to take it from you. Be strong and determined with a controlled demeanor. Give the signal calmly before you reach the halfway mark on the drill. <u>Don't stop spinning the drill until you feel new hands take it from you.</u>

2.) Never relax your downward pressure on the drill – not even for a split second. To lift the drill from its bowl during the exchange causes the next driller to gouge the drill into the dirt, where it will pick up moisture and/or splinter.

3.) Don't make a mere two or three-stroke pass on the drill and hand it off. Such an abbreviated turn takes your partner by surprise. Everyone is expected to put in his full time on the top half of the drill.

4.) No matter how many work in a team, be ready when it's your turn.

5.) After a reasonable try-out period, if some students can't find a way to drill efficiently, let them take on a new job, such as: anchoring the hearth by standing on its ends or holding it down with their hands.

6.) Don't apply so much saliva to the drill that you offend your teammates.

<u>Hand-drill Team Try-outs in a Classroom</u> – Go over the hand-drill
technique in detail and have each student practice with an arrow shaft and plank substitute-kit. After buying a single board of siding of cedar, cypress, or redwood, saw a 6"X 2"X 1"hearth for each fledgling fire-maker. Supply every student with a cedar arrow shaft. With a drill bit that matches the arrow thickness, drill a shallow divot in each hearth. Prepare to see your class enter into the epitome of industrious behavior. The gathering will take on the semblance of an army of beavers gnawing away at the same tree. Watch for lapses in form and coach each student toward perfect technique.

Lapses of Form with the Hand-drill – Problems [and Solutions]

1.) When I take a pass on the drill, the top of the drill continuously wobbles out of the vertical axis. [*You are moving one hand and its elbow only … or one more than the other. Pump equally with double pistons!*]

2.) I can't make the drill spin very much with each stroke of my hands. [*Start with the drill on the calluses in order to utilize the full surface area of palms and fingers.*]

3.) My hands contact one another during the drilling, and this slows down the drilling. [*Arch the hands slightly to eliminate contact.*]

4.) I hear a trebly, rattling sound as I drill and I'm making no smoke. [*Apply more downward pressure into the hearth with body weight, pectorals, and triceps.*]

5.) My hands slip wetly on the drill. [*Don't use so much saliva.*]

6.) My hands slip dryly on the drill. [*Use more saliva.*]

7.) When leaning down to take a pass on the drill, the drilling gets more difficult. [*As you lean you are levering the drill forward and away from verticality. This causes the drill to pinch inside the bowl. Rather than hinging your body forward from the waist like the closing of a trap door, lower yourself like an elevator.*]

8.) I can't seem to generate enough heat. [*You may be using only a fraction of the surface area of the palms and fingers. Use it all.*]

9.) After drilling down into the hearth a bit, the drill won't spin. It feels too tight. [*The drill is not vertical. Because it is now deeper in the hearth, a tilt causes the sides of the drill to pinch against the sides of the bowl. Keep the drill vertical.*]

10.) While drilling past the drill's halfway mark, the drill wobbles out of verticality. [*Use your hands only on the top half of the drill.*]

11.) I'm keeping the drill vertical, but it's harder to spin. [*Your drill may have abraded (gotten shorter) and now a rough spot on the side of the drill is bumping the rim of the bowl. Carefully carve off the projection.*]

12.) The drill locks up and won't spin. [*The hot end may have split, and the resulting crack catches on the edge of the notch. Cut a new hot end above the crack.*]

13.) The ash in my notch is scattering. [*The hot end of the drill has split and a fragment is projecting, rotating like a Weed-Eater. Cut a new hot end.*]

14.) Ash is not filling up my notch. It is collecting around the rim of the bowl. [*Cut a smoother opening in the narrow part of the notch. Make sure the V-notch reaches to the center of the bowl.*]

15.) The ash filling my notch is either chunky (like coarse sand) or narrow and whisker-like, and it won't sustain smoking. [*The hearth wood is problematic, either starting to go rotten or too moist. Select another hearth.*]

16.) The drill comes out of the bowl whenever I perform the switch. (This is the most serious infraction when working with a team, as the new driller is apt to grind the drill into the dirt and ruin the hot end.) [*Always keep pressure down on the drill.*]

 ### Arranging Large Numbers as a Hand-drill Team – When practice time is over, form two lines (east and west) on opposite sides of the hearth of

a viable kit. The first persons in both lines face one another. Driller E-1 (in the east line) begins by taking a pass on the drill. Before he reaches the halfway mark on the drill, E-1 signals driller W-1 (in the west line) to take over. When E-1 feels W-1 take over the drilling, E-1 moves to the back of the east line. W-1 spins the drill for one pass and then signals E-2 to take over. And so it continues. The exchange is a crucial moment. Keep that drill moving and keep its hot end in the bowl. Getting these teams to work smoothly might take a half-hour. During that time you will know which students are really contributing to the desired friction and which need to return to their individual kits for more coaching.

Eventually, to have success with a team, you'll have to cull out the weaker members. If you don't remove them, fire is highly improbable. Treat the culling process with honesty and respect and hopefully no feelings are hurt. I find that the less skilled ones actually realize that they are not helping the team as much as others, and they are anxious to see the fire that might follow if they bow out. If they show improvement in their individual practice, they can earn their way back into the team, especially as blisters and fatigue take their toll on the "varsity team."

Varsity Team Fire
– Simply to make smoke during try-outs is exciting, but you will also be able to assess which students most contribute to the challenge by the amount of smoke they produce. Keep a list of those who excel. They will make up the varsity team.

Choose a well-made fire-kit and set it on dry leaves in a clearing with a bucket of water on hand. Position the serving tray of tinder beneath the notch and hearth. Anchor the ends of the hearth with rocks or with the hands of volunteers from the "B-team." Have nearby the larger bundle of tinder ready to receive the smoking wedge of ash on the serving tray. It's time for your elite team to make fire.

When the notch is full of smoking ash or when a red glow is visible in the notch, show them the care needed in lifting away the hearth, picking up the serving tray, and combining the two tinder nests. Demonstrate holding the tinder by fingertips and blowing "strong but quiet" streams of air. Then let the team members take turns blowing until the bundle ignites.

A Team of Two Champions
– After success with an elite team, select two varsity students who demonstrated excellent form. Operating as a two-person team, they will face one another over the hearth and alternate drilling. The spectators often get so inspired that other two-person teams may demand their chance.

A Star Rises
– Of course, all this teamwork is heading toward the solo effort. This challenge will be out of reach for most youth, but someone will undoubtedly want to try it. Even if there is no success, this noble attempt makes for great classroom drama, accountability, and discussion of history.

Figure 8 Drilling or "Floating"

One of the weak links in the solo hand-drill process is the "switch." During that re-gripping of the top of the drill, the kit has a split-second to cool. This can be eliminated by an advanced drilling technique called "floating." It looks like a man lathering his palms with a bar of soap.

To introduce your hands to the motion, hold both hands, palms together, thumbs up, just in front of your belly, fingers pointing forward. Rather than pushing and pulling opposing hands as if the thick part of the hands are on a level tabletop, you'll follow a subtle serpentine path.

As you push the right hand forward, allow the fingertips to slightly rise. At the same time pull the left hand back toward you, letting those fingertips lower as the heel of the thumb rises. The resulting path of this dual movement of both hands is like the shallow arc of a rocking chair's rocker, each hand's path defining one-half of that arc.

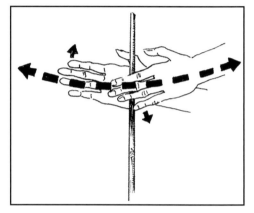

As the right hand reaches its forward-most position, fingertips should make a quick motion upward. This allows the palm calluses to purchase some rise on the drill. At this point you are ready to reverse directions for the next stroke.

This time, as you push the left hand forward (and pull the right back), the left follows the full "rocker" arc, allowing the fingertips to rise upward. At the forward-most position, flick the fingertips upward. The right hand follows the same full "rocker" arc in its backward motion, its fingertips eventually pointing slightly below the horizontal. Repeat in alternating fashion.

When you try this with a drill, the climbing motion may feel awkward at first, and you may find it more difficult to keep the drill vertical. But if you perfect this technique with adequate pressure exerted on the hearth, you may never have to switch again. Your hands can "float" in place or rise on the drill without traveling downward and necessitating a switch.

Most who can perform the "float" contribute only moderate pressure on the hearth. Their floating serves as a warm-up to the weightier drilling needed after the kit is primed. Those who achieve significant weight with the figure 8 have a crucial advantage as fire-makers.

Fine Points and Variations

In the beginning, before you catch on to the form, the hand drill is hard work. Like almost all who attempt the hand-drill solo, you will probably fail at first. Stick with it. Embrace the failures as necessary learning experiences, and you will earn your fire after you've paid your dues. Part of those dues includes toughening your hands. Another part of it is getting your muscles stronger for this specialized activity.

Once you've created fire, *knowing that you can do it* goes a long way toward your next success. This confidence inspires you to give that extra effort at the time when you feel too exhausted to go on.

If you abstain from practicing for long periods and come back to it, your hands will no longer be in shape. You will have to toughen them up again. If blisters develop, try using different parts of your hands. You may find that the thick edge of your hands (hands making a V shape on the drill) works for you. During this time of reconditioning – whenever your hands bruise or blister badly – you have no choice but to postpone your efforts and wait for healing.

There are other drilling positions to try for variety or to better suit your body – especially if you have knee or spinal problems. Try all the body positions previously mentioned or make up new ones.

Hand-drill Aids

As a way to anchor the top of the drill, I once carved a wooden socket to fit into my mouth. I clamped down on the mouthpiece with my teeth and held the drill in place within a divot centered in the outer part of the device. My hands simply spun the drill without making a downward pass, while my head and neck supplied the downward pressure. I never succeeded with this, nor did I find the technique comfortable. Each time that I made an attempt I felt as though I had taken a firm bite on the rear bumper of a truck that was roaring down a dirt road. Maybe you can figure out how to refine this technique.

Another attempt at improving the hand-drill calls for tying the midpoint of a leather strip to the top of your drill. Secure it tightly so that it cannot slip down the drill. Make loops on the free ends or cut a slit in each for your thumbs. As you spin the drill and apply downward pressure, the leather thumb-loops prevent your hands from lowering on a typical pass down the drill. Thumbs supply the downward pressure.

Many fires can be made from a single hearth.

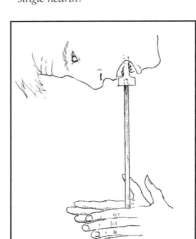

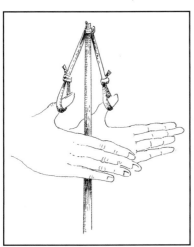

Thumb straps are a good idea but they do subtract from the speed of spinning the drill. I still prefer the free-held hand-drill. Employing that method I can apply a fast and aggressive pass on the drill when the last stage of the effort calls for it.

Advanced Hand-drillers

It is possible to create fire without a notch cut into the hearth, but this technique has been mastered by only a minority of fire-makers. The first time I performed this trick was by pure accident. Using a mullein stalk, I drilled long and hard into a juniper hearth and created a hot ember inside the mullein's soft pith. In this case, the hot coal that started my fire came from inside the drill. Very skilled fire-makers

box elder   *elderberry*

can perform this feat at will if they use carefully chosen materials. Some of these include elderberry on box elder and goldenrod on trumpet creeper vine. Sometimes the red coal materializes inside the bowl or in the ring of ash that encircles the bowl.

Drill Materials (dead) for the Hand-drill:

bamboo	horseweed
shoots of box elder maple	lamb's quarters
cattail	mullein
cottonwood	rivercane
elderberry	teasel
evening primrose	willow
goldenrod	roots, exposed and soft
grapevine	virtually any strong woody weed
hemlock roots	

goldenrod (left) and horseweed (right) are prime drill materials. Notice how both show branching clustered at the top of the stem, but golderod produces noticeable pappus.

Hearth Materials for Hand-drill:

all the trees that swallowed fire (see page 73)	trumpet creeper
	virgin's bower
cracked-cap polypore fungus	yucca
grapevine	

"I know how to make fire," the little boy says. "You rub two sticks together."

I admire the earnestness in his eyes. Then I pull two pieces of wood out of my supplies. "Show me," I say.

After a few minutes and a lot of overly dramatic scraping, he hands back the sticks. I feel for warmth. There is none. I press one of the sticks to his cheek so he can feel for himself.

He offers a vacuous smile. "Well, that's what I've always heard."

> *~ A conversation I've had countless times with a grade-schooler as I set up for a program in his classroom.*

CHAPTER 6
Rubbing Two Sticks Together
~ the fire-saw ~

I don't know that anyone has ever made fire rubbing two individual sticks together; that is, a stick in either hand, abrading one against the other with a fury. Maybe it is possible, but it's not likely. The closest thing to it might be the fire-saw.

This kit requires a single piece of 2'6"-long dead and dry bamboo with a 2" diameter. Such a piece will have a wall thickness about 3/16". Split the cane lengthwise down the middle, and you'll have the two pieces needed for friction – the **saw** and the notched **crosspiece** or **board**.

Scrapings from the outer curve of the cane supply tinder. A small branch of bamboo will be used to hold the tinder in place.

This saw kit is turned on its head when compared to traditional sawing. The

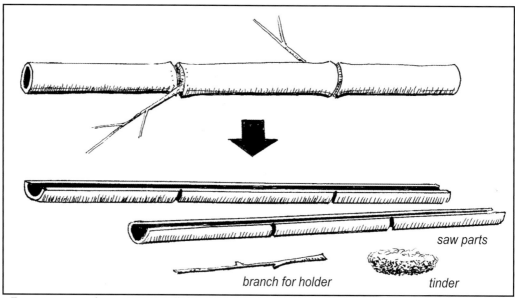

From one piece of cane … come all the components of the kit.

saw will be held in a stationary position, pinned between earth and chest. The board will be grasped by both hands and moved back and forth across the blade of the saw.

The Saw

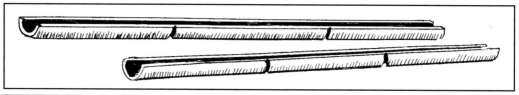

Because the bamboo was split down the center, the two newly exposed wall-thicknesses (the 3/16"-thick facets that attached to one another lengthwise before you made the split) will be in the same plane as the diameter of the former whole cane. Choose one of these split pieces for the saw's blade. At its mid-section carve one of these long facets to a sharp outer edge, like a knife blade honed from one side only. Do this sharpening of the 3/16"-thick facet, not from the rounded outside of the cane but from the inside.

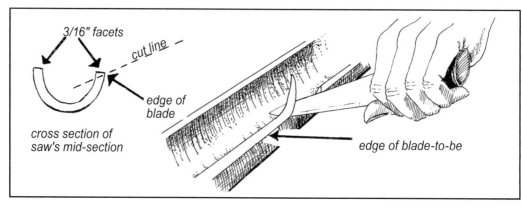

Narrow this long edge to about 45°. This honing need only be done to the middle 12" of the cane. This piece will be used to saw into the other half of the cane, the crosspiece.

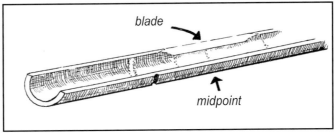

finished saw

The Crosspiece

The other piece of split cane needs a V-notch cut somewhere near the middle of its length, centered on the outer curve of the cane, and perpendicular to the grain. Using your knife, make two entry cuts to form the same angle you achieved on the edge of the saw (45°). To create friction you will scrape the crosspiece notch over the edge of the saw blade, the two pieces forming a cross. The notch should be 7/8"long and only open enough to show a crack of daylight. It is through this crack that hot ash will pass to get to the tinder.

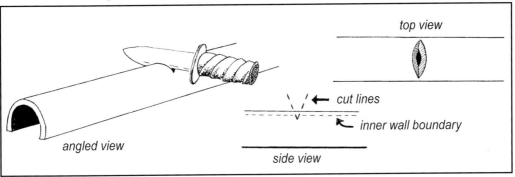

Making the notch in the crosspiece

Making a Fire-Saw Kit

Making a Fire-Saw Kit – Locate a bamboo stand and find a dead specimen with a 2" outer diameter. Saw a section 2'6" long. (This length, which varies according to your height, is determined by experience.) Prop the section vertically and position your knife blade on the top for a lengthwise split down the middle. Using a mallet, strike the back of the knife blade and split the cane. Sharpen the mid-section of one newly revealed, lengthwise facet (of the cane wall) to ~ 45° by carving not from the exterior of the cane but from the interior. This will serve as the stationary saw.

Into the other cane-half (crosspiece) cut a 45° notch just through the wall so that hot ash can pass through its slit. Then choose a slender, flexible, foot-long stick of any kind to hold the tinder in place. The nest of tinder should be placed inside the crosspiece just behind the notch.

Making Cane Tinder

One beauty of the bamboo kit is that every component of the kit can be derived from the original culm of dead bamboo – tinder included (as covered in Chapter 4). With your knife, scrape the outer curve of the cane to amass small crepe-like ribbons of tinder.

Working the Fire-Saw

Instead of the carpenter's habit of moving a handsaw across a board, you'll be scraping the board (notched crosspiece) against the saw. Kneel or sit and prop the saw on the ground before you with its sharpened edge facing away from you. Position chest padding (folded clothing) and lean on the saw so as to hold it firmly in place. Place a nest of tinder inside the concavity of the crosspiece behind the open slit of the notch. Lay a slender stick over the tinder (lengthwise inside the cane) by grasping the crosspiece and stick with both hands 4"- 8" apart, the tinder positioned between your two grips.

If any part of your saw's edge contains a septum (the inner-wall that divides sections of bamboo) that impedes any part of the sawing process, cut it away. Fit the now vertical notch onto the saw's edge and make repetitive downward strokes to produce friction.

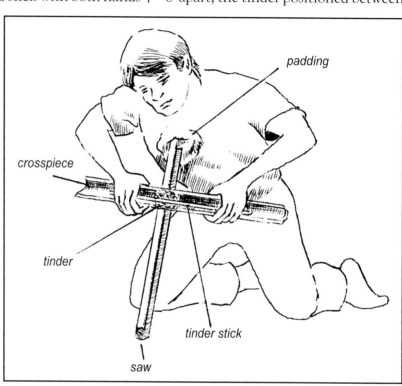

padding

crosspiece

tinder

tinder stick

saw

 <u>Making Fire With the Fire-Saw</u> – The down-strokes with this kit resemble the motions of a washer working laundry on a washboard. As with the hand-drill, warm up slowly before applying full-effort strokes. When smoking begins, pour on the power. When smoking becomes copious, give it 20 more strokes and then carefully check the tinder for a hot coal. If it's there, remove the tinder and blow it into a flame. If not, return to the sawing. You'll have one more try at it (another series of strokes) before the slit in the notch becomes too wide to accommodate the saw. If you fail again, cut another notch next to the old one, rest for a time, and try again.

 **<u>The Consequential All-Bamboo Fire</u>** – As a personal challenge to measure your skill and confidence, on your next camping trip take no matches or other fire starter. Instead, pack in a light piece of dead bamboo tied to your pack. Carry some food provisions that require cooking and some that don't. Having a warm meal and a companionable fire both depend upon your ability to create the bamboo fire.

" ... But the question was, How could she bring back the fire? 'I'll manage that,' said the Water Spider; so she spun a thread from her body and wove it into a tusti bowl, which she fastened on her back."

~ The First Fire, *old Cherokee myth, recorded by James Mooney* in History, Myths and Sacred Formulas of the Cherokees

CHAPTER 7
The Eternal Flame

~ Making a Lasting Fire ~

The effort of creating fire takes both time and energy, and so naturally you'll want to take care not to lose your flame to negligence or the inability to keep it alive in your temporary absence. Furthermore, you might need to relocate your camp-site. Taking your fire with you would be a handy skill. Throughout history the Native Americans perfected both techniques.

These days the rejuvenation of a fire is as easy as the flick of a thumb on the wheel of a lighter or the scrape of a match head across the scratch strip on a matchbox. But if those implements are not available, once again the tried and true methods of early fire-makers become a trustworthy store of knowledge.

The Keeper of the Fire

Among the migratory tribes of Native Americans, transporting fire from a former camp to a new one held spiritual significance. It might be thought of as a "ground-ing" factor – providing that sense of "home" that might seem elusive to a nomad.

A "Keeper of the Fire" – an honored position – was designated to carry fire on journeys that might stretch out over many weeks. When Plains Indians moved from a summer camp to a winter camp, such a journey might exceed a hundred miles. Oral tradition passed down through the centuries tells us that the Cherokees carried their "Appalachian fire" along the Trail of Tears – "the Long Walk" wrongfully imposed on them to trudge from Georgia to Oklahoma.

The Keeper of the Fire accomplished his job by making something akin to a giant cigar – one not smoked but carried and tended with care. A sheath of outer bark from a dead sapling or hefty limb could serve as an envelope for an assortment of tightly-packed, dead and dried materials: inner bark, mosses, lichens, scraped wood and vein networks from decomposed leaves. More fuel was added as needed along the journey, but the fire itself remained the "home fire" that lent a sense of continuity to a life on the move.

 ## Making a Fire-Carrier – Locate a source of dry inner bark fibers (a branch or trunk of dead tulip tree, basswood or locust, for example) and then strip away the combined inner/outer bark. Remove inner bark for tinder, and retain larger slabs of the outer bark (2"- to 4"-wide strips to use as a carrier for the tinder. The less damage done to the outer-bark, the more it is usable as a carrier.

Work the inner bark fibers into a fine fluff until you have a supply that, when tightly compressed, approximates the size of both your fists. If necessary, flatten this mass and set it aside in direct sunlight to dry.

Choose two strips of outer-bark that have the same width. Cut each strip 6"- 8" long and put them together like two half-pipes to form a cylinder. The fit does not have to be perfect, as irregularities in the seams will allow the entry of needed air. Take the halves apart and bore a hole in each end of each half (½" from the end) by cutting a small square with your knifepoint into the concave side. These

4 holes will allow you to secure a stout twig across the openings of the sleeve of outer-bark, thereby giving you a brace against which you can stuff bark fibers into the sleeve from either direction. For now, insert a twig in one end only.

A short-term sleeve could also be made by bending a long bark strip back on itself to form a small "quiver" – one end closed by the fold, the other end open.

Now use hand-made rope or a section of grapevine to hold the

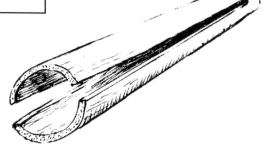

cylinder-halves together. With a simple spiral, wrap the sleeve with this string with a temporary knot. Pack the dry inner bark fibers firmly into the open end of the sleeve until all but 1½"of the container is filled. Use another half-pipe of outer bark as a scoop to pick up a marble-sized, red-hot, hardwood coal from your campfire and insert the coal into the sleeve. Stuff the rest of the sleeve with tinder and blow as needed to keep the coal active.

Smoke should steadily seep from one end of the sleeve. By simply angling it into the wind, you can achieve the desired smolder-rate … or more blowing might be needed. Any time smoke tapers off, loosen the wrapping string and open the sleeve to blow more directly on the coal to encourage the smolder. Once the smolder is well established, you'll probably not have to open it anymore. "Lock" the open end with a snug-fitting twig and walk with it, the swing of your arms sufficing to ensure airflow through the sleeve.

Keeping the Fire

– Plan a trek for your fire-makers from point A to B. At A they must build a fire of hardwoods to produce good coals. While the fire is building, instruct all to gather materials for a fire-carrier, while you safeguard the fire. Have each person prepare extra tinder to carry on the journey. When the carrier is complete, stuffed with tinder, and loaded with a coal, douse the home fire for an adventure of commitment. Let each of your wards take turns being the Keeper of the Fire at the head of the line as they journey to point B. For safety, haul the fire-carrier in a light metal bucket. Always have the second in line be responsible for fire safety. He must carry water and keep watch on the carrier to detect escaping embers, sparks, or hot fibers.

At the destination, build another pyre and use the smolder to start the new fire by opening up the sleeve to remove the smoldering tinder. Blow the tinder into a flame and insert it beneath your pyre to bring the fire home.

A Lasting Flame

On a Friday afternoon my young summer campers and I struck camp after a week-long wilderness outing in the mountains. As always, the heart of our base camp had been our campfire. On our first day we had worked as a team to draw our fire from the heart of a dead sumac trunk. These flames had cooked our food, warmed us at night, dried our wet clothing, and helped us bend the fibers inside the carved hickory staves we had fashioned into lacrosse sticks.

In the spirit of pioneer adventure, we had willingly entered into a no-match week. But our sumac fire kit had proved to be no easy task for twelve-year olds. After laboring long and hard over it, no one wanted to face the task of making fire

smooth sumac

again. To fend off the return of that ordeal, they had been very attentive to the flame, faithfully keeping it stoked and fueled. These children were proud that their original fire had lasted so long and served us in so many ways during the camping trip.

Before retiring each evening we had carefully *banked* the fire to ensure the presence of hot coals the next morning. Twice, rain had moved in during the night, but our coals remained protected by our banking structure. In the mornings the resurrection of our fire had served as a natural alarm clock, because everyone wanted to be first to uncover the treasure of glowing embers, lay down fresh kindling, and blow the coals into a flame.

The coals never failed to survive the night. And the magic of banking never lost its luster. We had reached into the heart of a tree for fire, stuffed it into the belly of the Earth to sleep each night, and then exhumed it at dawn. Seeing the flame resurrect was a morning ritual. Along with the rising of the sun, it marked the beginning of our day.

Because of the group's loyalty to this fire … and because a private adult group was scheduled to arrive at the campsite on the next Tuesday for a lesson in wild edibles, I proposed a challenge: that we save our fire for the incoming students. The campers were game. We cleared away all flammable materials from around the fire pit and banked the fire one last time. I was living in a tipi near this campsite and would be present over the weekend after I drove my campers back to the city. This satisfied my need for safety.

When I returned home late that Friday night, the fire pit faithfully emitted a steady stream of smoke. I built a cook-fire in my tipi and went about my chores, periodically checking the outside fire pit. Over the next few days smoke rose from that banked fire like the steady trickle of water from a mountain spring.

On Tuesday – late morning – my new students arrived ready for a class on wild foods. When our day's agenda called for the heating of water, I took these students to the banked fire, uncovered a bed of red coals, laid down fresh kindling, and blew up a flame. I told my guests that four days had passed since the fire had been buried by my summer campers. These adults stared at the fire as if it had emerged from the magma at the Earth's center. After talking among themselves, they asked if our plans could be suspended long enough for a lesson on how to put fire to sleep and then wake it up. And so we did.

How to Bank a Fire

The value of knowing how to bank a fire is immeasurable. If ever you found yourself in an unplanned and prolonged stay in wilderness, fire would be one of your most important assets. Having a usable fire includes these skills: efficient pyre building, creation of fire, and sustaining the fire.

In a survival situation one stays very busy with lots of chores, necessarily spending periods of time away from a base camp (such as in hunting, foraging, and checking traps). Coming back to a dead fire could be a morale-breaker. To a novice fire-maker, repeating the fire-creation process would take more time and energy than he might have to give.

Banking a fire is a process of slowing down the burn-rate to the extreme, without extinguishing the fire. This is accomplished by radically cutting down the availability of oxygen but at the same time making sure that plenty of fuel will be available to form an active bed of coals. There are different techniques to achieve this. The following method is straightforward and uncomplicated.

After establishing a fire in a safe fire pit, burn enough hardwood logs to accumulate a healthy bed of pulsing coals. Scrape the best coals into the center of the pit in the shape of a rectangle about 6" by 18". On top of this you are going to build a small room of logs that will become a self-sustaining oven.

For the two walls needed to support the roof of the oven, lay down two 2'-long logs of hardwood at least 6"in diameter, one on either of the long sides of the coals.

On top of these lay a cap of hardwood – a 2'-long log wide enough to span the gap between walls without touching the coals. If possible, use a cap that has

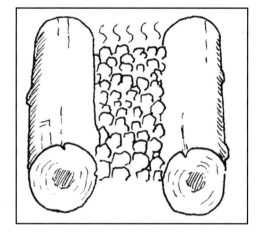

been split so that a flat surface can face the coals to better reflect heat. (A log can be split by driving a series of stone wedges into a preexisting crack. Hammer them deep into the wood by using a heavy log mallet.)

Using dirt and gray ashes, clog the open ends of the oven until it appears to be completely sealed. Now keep watch for ten minutes to see if smoke continues to escape. Usually a seal is not perfect

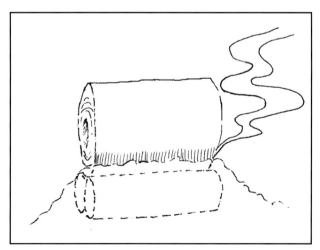

between a wall and the cap, and such a case is ideal. If after this time the construction is steadily smoking – and usually it is – the chore is done.

If the oven is sealed too well, open up a very small vent at the top of one clogged end. If smoke still does not emerge from the oven, open a second vent in the other end. If there are gaping cracks between walls and cap, you'll need to pack dirt there.

Finding (or cutting) a proper length log could be a problem in a survival situation. You might need to substitute lots of smaller logs put together as tightly as possible and then cover the outside portion of the walls with dirt. If multiple logs are used for a cap, mound and pack dirt over the whole affair then use a sharpened stick to create vents.

Banking a Fire – Before trying this on a camping trip, it would be prudent to attempt it at home with the help of a few tools and the safety of a cleared site and a nearby garden hose. Dig a fire pit the size of an inverted round garbage can top. Prepare your banking material with a saw and a maul or wood-splitter. Make it an event with your child by cooking outdoors and having your meal by the fire, giving the wood time to burn down to coals. When it is time to bank, rake the coals into a central rectangle, lay down walls, and set the cap firmly upon the walls. Use a shovel to heap on dirt and ash. When the buried coals show a small, steady stream of smoke, leave the banked fire to smolder for the night as you settle in for a backyard campout. Next morning it's time to uncover the coals, stoke the fire, and cook breakfast.

Primitive Banking – Without the help of cutting tools (like a saw and maul), construct your "log oven" with found pieces of wood. Look for thick chunks where hardwood trees have broken or dropped large limbs. You may need to burn through some of these to achieve manageable lengths for the oven, but large pieces can suffice with some modifications to your oven design. For example, consider using different lengths of logs for each of the three components and then covering the oven section with a mound of dirt. Before burying the structure, position two 3"-thick "vent-sticks" (round in cross-section, no branch nubs or knots), one running from each opening (end) of the oven, from coals to outside the fire pit. Pack dirt (no ash) tightly around these sticks to form a tight seal. When the mound is complete, gently work the vent-sticks free ("unscrewing" them) from the dirt to leave a tunnel for air on both sides.

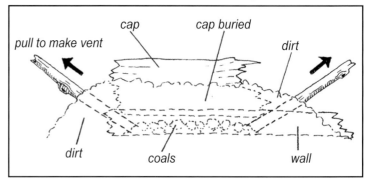

A Chain of Fires – Plan a backpacking trip with the main purpose being to carry your original fire to each subsequent campsite down the trail. For a true challenge of accountability, take only one match. Bank the fire each night and, as you strike camp the next morning, prepare a fire-carrier and insert a hardwood coal. Once the carrier has stabilized, douse and bury your original fire, return your campsite to its original natural appearance, and resume your journey with fire in hand.

PART 2

Storytelling and Ceremony

Author's Note

It is no wonder that fire – the ever-changing plasma, dancing and mesmerizing by its natural illuminating power – served as the canvas upon which ancient people painted the picture of a story being told to them. In the presence of a campfire and a storyteller, people today still fix their eyes on the flames. This is probably a replication of the way it has always been done.

Whether the details are manufactured by the skilled tongue of the raconteur or the inventive canvas of the listener's fertile mind, it is the listener who ultimately paints the picture. That's what sets it apart from modern media, where every visual and auditory detail is force-fed into the eyes and ears of its audience.

A beloved educator whom I know holds weekly visits at a school where he simply tells a story. Whenever he begins his story, he is always aware that a change comes over his audience – an indefinable but complete shift of loyalty to a spoken tale. He sees the students engage his words with an abstract tenacity. They change gears from their busy chattering to enter a mode of complete allegiance to his voice. He can't explain it, but each time the story begins to unfold he knows that he is reaching a place inside his audience that was, just seconds earlier, untapped.

A story is a powerful occasion. Few "non-experiential" events can top it as a permanent fixture of memory. What a paradox this is. Listening to a story appears to be a passive exercise. It would seem the antithesis of hands-on education, but there is a whirlwind of activity inside the listener's mind during the telling of a story. Unlike the experience of watching a story on a TV, movie, or computer screen, hearing a story told requires an interaction between words and listener. Every person within earshot of the narrative automatically begins constructing a mental image. In this way both teller and listener play an active role in the composition.

Though the storyteller does not ask the listener to produce a picture, still it happens. Inside the listener's mind a creative storm begins to stir up colors and voices, scents and facial expressions. A mental set of scenery is erected. A month of adventures can be lived in a matter of minutes. To the involved listener, the manufactured image is vivid … remarkably so for a thing unseen.

I am always impressed with the remembrances of my former young campers when they come back as adults to visit. They might not recall exactly how an activity or game worked, but their recall of details about a story is usually flawless.

Stories can be powerful tools, especially when they introduce a lesson scheduled for the next day. The students have no idea that they are being prepared for a project. On the following day they discover that they already have a mental picture for reference.

Ceremony brings the recognition of an important idea into a formal moment and a formal act. It might make use of tangible components, like bread and wine or a dusting of tobacco, even if these items are used only symbolically.

While a story can be light and of little consequence, a ceremony is about things that matter. For example, any act of creating fire-by-friction could be said to be symbolic of a do-or-die survival situation. Such an act of importance begs for ceremony, if only by including a prayer of thanks. And it could be argued that the reciprocal is true: that a ceremony begs for a fire, even if only by a lighted candle.

Each time I position myself over a fire kit for the work of drawing a flame from dead wood, I recall five Lakota words: "*Hanta yo! Wakanya hibu yelo.*" The recitation has, for me, become a ceremony that ties into the physical act of fire-making.

The first part (pronounced: *hahñ-TAH-yo*) means: "Clear the way!" I say the words quietly, privately; nevertheless, they serve as a declaration, announcing that I am fully present and dedicated to my goal with a "can-do" attitude.

The second part (pronounced: *wah-KAHÑ-yah hee-BOO yay-LO*) means: "In a sacred manner I come." With these closing words I express gratitude for the materials that go into the making of fire and for the fire-making technique passed down through the ages. The quiet recitation connects me to all people throughout history who labored over select pieces of dry wood to create a fire.

Like storytelling, a ceremony offers a stimulus to a student. Then it's up to the student to do something with that stimulus – something personal, like my commitment to spin a drill until I have made fire. Because of the personal nature of ceremony, we must tread carefully so as not to offend values and religiosities within the groups that we teach. Never lose sight of how the experience will be perceived by any individual student.

Because all of us entertain private concepts that are precious or reverent or emblematic of hope, it would seem that everyone could potentially make use of ceremony, yet, outside of a few ethnic exceptions, it seems that few Americans do. Even the simple saying of grace at the dining table has been lost in many households, largely because mealtimes are no longer opportunities for family gatherings. Busy schedules seem to interfere. This in itself is a loss of ceremony.

It has been my experience that most people (perhaps even secretly) crave ceremony … even those young ones who have never known it. Spiritual grounding might be one of the basic needs of humans, for it takes us beneath the surface of everyday events and connects us to the sacred aspects of simply being alive in this universe. Such grounding provides a kind of conversation with something grander than ourselves. Perhaps it is this conversation that makes us feel that, in this world, we count.

If a child regularly has an active part in the preparing of a meal, there is in that repeated practice the heart of ceremony. The mundane task of carrying platters to the table – observed by an anthropologist – might be labeled "a rite." This simple deed installs the child inside the equation of the working family. The child becomes integral, purposeful. Such a moment recognizes worth and, therefore, feeds self-esteem.

Throughout my career I have met many children who say they have no integrated involvement at home; that is, they have no pertinent or contributing chore within the family construct. Such a child has no experience in connecting a chore to the bounty of that chore (the washing of the potatoes to the enjoyment of eating the potatoes).

A camping situation might provide the best opportunity to grasp the logic of such a connection, because wilderness and accountability enjoy a close partnership. We can't eat until we cook. We can't cook until we make a fire. We can't have a fire until we gather wood. The chain of preparatory work in a camp setting takes on the feeling of ceremony, and if a child who is new to chores watches the others perform the work, there is a good chance he will feel the urge to join in the action, not only from peer pressure but from the good sense that the job will get us closer to eating.

But how do we pull off this idea of ceremony with a group of people from different backgrounds? That's what these pages will address.

"With some tribes the winter season and the night are the time for telling stories, but to the Cherokee all times are alike."

~ ~ *James Mooney*, History, Myths and Sacred Formulas of the Cherokees

CHAPTER 8
Tall Tale Teachers
~ the story that shares a lesson ~

Though this chapter does contain a few stories to read to your students, it is not intended as a treasury of tales to be shared from a book. Instead, it is a guide to help you recognize why and how to put a story together.

Most of the stories I have told around a campfire have been impromptu. I enjoy the unrehearsed exercise of creating imagery and storyline. But the important stories take planning, because they are designed to impart a lesson.

There are stories that champion values such as honesty and courage. These tales, hopefully, contribute to the larger picture of how to live one's life. Other stories can prepare a student for a specific project that is scheduled for the following day. What better way to introduce a lesson on wilderness skills than to dress it up in a story told around a campfire?

Long ago, when my students were scheduled for a beginning archery class on the day following, I created the story of "Flutterby." The purpose of the story was to prepare the students for the most difficult facet of archery – the string release. The secret to this skill is learning how to isolate the muscles of the string-hand and arm so that as the fingertips curl around the string, the rest of the hand, wrist, and forearm are relaxed, like a thick piece of rope. (This technique is covered in *Secrets of the Forest, Volume 4*.)

<u>A Story to Read to Archery Students</u> – Keep in mind that the purpose of this story is teaching the role of the string-hand and arm in the string-release when shooting with bow and arrow. The proper letting go of an arrow is

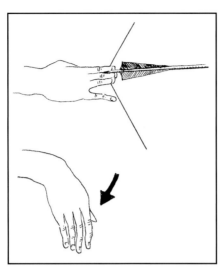

the single-most difficult part of archery and deserves much time in instruction. Though the act appears to be an easy motion when performed by one who understands it, it is not an instinctual maneuver. Everyone has to be taught how to do it. For this reason, it rates being the centerpiece of a story.

The story emphasizes the grace of the hand, wrist, and forearm and how that fluidity is applied to archery. The details of this story create a vocabulary for the conversation that follows in the next day's lesson.

~ Flutterby ~

There was an old Cherokee chieftain named Raven, whose great disappointment in life was that he had no son, only a daughter. Raven's reputation in warfare was widely admired, but as he aged he knew that his fighting skills were slipping away. He wished more than ever for a son to whom he could pass on his abilities as a warrior.

"My husband," his wife said, "my time for bearing babies is over. Perhaps you should adopt a young man from the village. There are several who have lost parents to the winter sickness."

Raven left his home, walking for the council lodge, where he would make the announcement of his intention to take a son. It was summer and many people were busy with their daily chores. As he passed a field of yellow flowers he happened to glimpse his daughter, Flutterby, standing among butterflies as they flitted about her in the sunlight. At the end of one outstretched arm, an orange butterfly perched on the back of her hand. Raven stopped, and as he watched, Flutterby remained motionless, as though she and the orange butterfly were speaking to one another without words. At the same moment that the butterfly lifted into the air, she let the hand drop so gently from the wrist that the orange wings and the slender hand seemed to contain the same grace.

"What are you doing?" Raven called out. "Should you not be helping your mother?"

The girl ran excitedly to Raven. "Father, I have learned how to help the butterflies fly a true path. The other girls flick them away with their fingers, and the little creatures go sailing off in dizzy spirals. But my way allows them to soar calmly to the place they want to go. I only have to wait until they are ready, and then we both part from one another with the same gentle movement."

Raven frowned. "But what good is this to know? Why does it matter what the butterfly does?"

Flutterby looked curiously at her father. "But, Father, you told me that Fox taught the People how to walk quietly in the forest? And Rabbit showed us how to hide. Even Worm taught us how to dig a small hole for our lodge posts."

Raven waved away her examples. "Yes … but butterflies?" He shook his head as he looked out at the busy little wings fluttering over the meadow. "Go home and help your mother. I am off to find a son, who will learn to be a warrior."

*

Three young men took up Raven's offer, and all came to live with him until it could be decided which one might make the greatest warrior. Raven would then train only that one and call him "son."

When the three arrived on that first day, Raven began their training with the war club. Each would take his turn hacking at an upright, rotting log to demonstrate his skill. The first, Wasp, had a narrow face and sharp nose. He struck the log only once and then stepped back.

"Why have you stopped?" Raven asked.

Wasp cracked half a smile. "Only one blow is needed if it is well-placed." He gestured toward the log. "I just cracked the skull of my enemy."

Crushing Bear, was bigger and stronger than the others and wielded the club with brutal force. By the time he had finished thrashing the log, it lay in shreds.

The third trainee, Whistler, took the club.

Pause in the story and ask your audience: "What would you do with the club if you were Whistler?"

Whistler stood before the pulverized log, and laughed. "Well, I have now seen the two extremes of war: the single blow and the endless barrage." He shrugged and smiled at Raven. "Which is best, Father?"

"Every situation presents its own problems," Raven counseled. "You must find a reason for whatever technique you choose."

Whistler studied the log for a moment and then handed the war club back to Raven. "I see no reason to fight where Crushing Bear has already been. Should I go look for another enemy?"

Raven looked at the shredded wood and laughed. "You are right. When we continue tomorrow, perhaps Crushing Bear should always take his turn last."

On the second day they gathered in the meadow for a footrace.

"I would never run from battle," Wasp declared. "Why practice running?"

"Speed on the battlefield," Raven explained, "will help you to get where you are most needed. You might save a friend's life this way."

When Raven gave the signal to start, Crushing Bear pushed both Wasp and Whistler down, and the Bear alone began lumbering across the field in a long, heavy stride.

Pause: "What do you think Wasp did now?"

Holding one elbow, Wasp stood and dusted himself off as he scowled at the distant figure of Crushing Bear.

Pause: "What do you think Whistler did?"

Whistler sprang up and sprinted to the finish, coming in several strides behind the winner.

"You must always expect the unexpected," Raven said to the three. "Learn to adapt your plans. I instructed Crushing Bear to surprise you." He looked at Wasp. "Why did you not run?"

Wasp raised his chin, and the tendons in his jaws rippled. "If an ally tricks me, he is my enemy." He nodded toward Crushing Bear. "I would not fight by his side."

Raven pointed at Whistler. "But he ran."

"And what good did it do?" Wasp replied. "He lost."

Flutterby had been watching from across the field. When the men started back for their midday meal, they walked within a few feet of her.

"I am Flutterby," she said, offering a shy smile. "Whichever among you my father chooses, I will be your sister and you will be my brother."

Crushing Bear looked over her attire. "I hope you can make sturdy moccasins. Mine are always falling apart."

Wasp showed his crooked smile. "That is because he is as heavy as a dead, bloated elk and half as intelligent."

Whistler stopped before the girl. "The butterflies seem to like you. What was that you were doing with them?"

"Teaching them to fly straight," Flutterby said.

Raven heard this and spoke over his shoulder. "She is just a girl who plays with the 'Painted Wings.' Come. It is time to eat."

On the third day Raven brought out bow and arrow to a fern bed in the forest. "We seldom make long shots with the arrow because our forests are so thick, but as a warrior you may need to silence a sentry from a distance. Only a shot to the head can drop him like a stone." He set a large dried gourd on top of a tree stump that stood the height of a man. Then he pointed across the creek. "You will shoot from there."

Wasp was first to shoot. When he drew back the arrow, his bow arm locked out straight, every vein and tendon bulging like taut vines buried beneath the skin. When he let go of the string, the shock of the bow jostled his stiff arm, causing the arrow to fly wide.

Taking the bow from him, Crushing Bear laughed, "You are not strong enough to hold the bow steady. I will show you." He loaded a new arrow and drew, aiming at the gourd. His bow arm seemed as thick and solid as the limb of a great oak.

"Well, you had better hit it at the center if you want to shatter it," Wasp challenged. "My arrow glanced off the side."

Bear snorted. "If that sentry even heard your arrow, he would have thought it was a mosquito buzzing through a distant valley."

"Enough bickering!" Raven scolded. "Whether Wasp hit it or not, he is right … hit it hard to put your enemy down!"

When Crushing Bear shot the arrow a grunt erupted from deep in his chest and his whole body suddenly thrust forward in his effort to empower the arrow. He looked like a man pushing a heavy boulder off a hill. The arrow sank deep into the stump and vibrated like a woodpecker.

Wasp laughed heartily. "Now there is a sentry screaming in pain at the arrow sticking in his belly. I wonder if his village can hear him?"

Crushing Bear started to swat Wasp like a fly but stopped when Raven took the bow from him and handed it to Whistler. "Now it is your turn," the old warrior said.

Whistler studied the bow and frowned. "An old bow-maker once told me," he began, "that the best archers – once they have drawn the arrow and aimed – let their bows do all the rest of the work. He said that the archer must get out of the way of the bow to let it do its work." He offered the bow back to Raven. "I have never learned how to do that. Can you teach me, Father?"

Raven pointed at Wasp. "He grasped the bow the way Hawk squeezes the life out of Mouse …" Then he nodded at Crushing Bear. "He seemed to throw all his weight at the gourd." Turning back to Whistler, he made a sly smile. "Neither of those worked."

"What does work?" Whistler asked.

Raven shrugged. "I am known for my close-fighting. I seldom use the bow." He slung the bow over his shoulder. "Perhaps I should give you all a day to learn the answer, and we shall repeat this contest tomorrow."

Crushing Bear and Wasp left right away for the village, where each planned to seek out guidance from anyone skilled in archery. Whistler walked to the stump and dug out the arrow imbedded there. Then he picked up the arrow that Wasp had shot. When he handed these to Raven, the old warrior seemed pleased.

"So," Raven said, "you see the wisdom of collecting your arrows."

Whistler nodded. "When I was a boy, I made arrows for the men who went to war. I know how much work goes into each shaft." Then he smiled. "Now I must learn how to make them fly."

As Whistler emerged from the forest he saw Flutterby standing in a swale of yellow-eyed daisies. A constellation of blue butterflies flitted around her, and he watched until one of the delicate creatures landed on her outstretched hand. Standing motionless she focused all her attention on the Painted Wings perched on her hand.

It was many heartbeats later that the butterfly took to flight. At the same instant, Flutterby's hand dropped limply from the wrist, a movement so gentle and dainty that her hand dangled like an alder catkin in a soft breeze. It was as if the Painted Wings and the girl's hand had worked as partners, each leaving the other by pre-arrangement, moving in opposite directions. The butterfly flew off in a path so straight that it looked like a distant hawk gliding on its open wings.

Fascinated, Whistler approached her and stopped at a respectful distance. "I've never seen the little Painted Wings fly so true," he said. "How do you do that?"

The girl was surprised that the young man had joined her. She looked around to see who else might be watching.

"My father would not want you learning such things. If you want to be the chosen son, you should not talk to me."

Whistler smiled, wagged his finger, and pointed it at her. "If you are going to be my sister, should we not know one another?"

At that moment one of the blue butterflies alit on Whistler's outstretched finger. Both the man's and the woman's eyes locked on it.

"So … what do I do?" Whistler said.

Flutterby stepped carefully toward him and stopped close enough that he could hear her whisper. "Watch it carefully until you see that it has chosen its destination."

Together they waited as the blue Painted Wings pivoted on his finger. Finally, it stopped and seemed to fix on some distant object.

"It is looking at that vine flowering at the edge of the woods," Whistler said quietly. "Should I move my hand now?"

"If you move your hand, you will use muscle. To use muscle, you will make the hand twitch, and this will alarm it, causing it to fly like a dog chasing its tail."

"Then what do I do?"

"You are going to stop holding your hand out."

Whistler kept his eyes fixed on the Painted Wings. "What does that mean?"

"To move your hand downward … and to stop holding your hand out … these are two different ideas entirely." Flutterby watched the butterfly crouch for take-off. "See how she bends her legs? She is ready. This is the moment. Now … stop holding!"

Just as Whistler's hand dropped downward and dangled, the butterfly lifted on steady wings and glided like a slow beam of blue light across the meadow to the flowers on the vine.

Whistler smiled, lifted his limp hand and let it flop again as if it were dead. "I can see why it took a woman to learn this skill. The graceful drop of the hand does not look very manly, does it?" He laughed and let the hand dangle again. Whistler squinted toward the butterfly on the vine. "Why does it work so well?"

"I think it is because the Painted Wings wants your partnership, and your role in that partnership is to get out of its way without disturbing it." Flutterby lowered her eyes. "But if I were you, I would not say anything about this to my father."

Whistler looked off toward the creek and smiled again. "We shall see about that."

On the following day when Raven and the three trainees returned to the forest, Bear carried a long leather sheath. Wasp walked to the stump and pointed to a bright scratch along one side of the gourd.

"You see?" he said, looking at the Bear. "I told you I hit it yesterday."

The Bear snorted. "I don't remember seeing that mark yesterday."

With his aging eyes Raven leaned to examine the gourd. As the trainees crossed the creek to get distance from the target, Raven touched the scrape, feeling a fine grit of crumbled stone clinging to the scar. He knew that the gourd had been scraped by a rock – but not the kind of clean-flaking rock that was used for arrowheads. At the base of the stump he picked up a speckled stone that lay atop a tuft of moss. Its surface was rough and grainy.

When the old man crossed the stream and they were all together, Raven handed the bow to Wasp and said, "Now we will see what you have learned since yesterday."

Wasp drew the arrow, and this time his entire body stiffened as though he were flexing every muscle. It was clear that he was making himself as rigid and unmoving as possible in order to keep the arrow on target. When he shot, he tried to maintain his wooden pose, but his body made a sudden jerking motion. In releasing the string his right hand flung open with fingers as crooked as an old woman's. And like before, his left arm bobbled from the shock of the bow. The arrow flew, wobbling like a wounded bird as it missed the gourd by two hand-spans.

"Did I hit it?" Wasp said, as though the matter were up for appraisal.

"No," Raven said, "but you might steal up on it tonight and cut off its other ear." He handed Wasp the speckled stone and watched the young man's face flush with embarrassment.

"My turn," said the Bear, pulling out a new bow from his leather sheath.

"And what have you learned in a day," Raven asked.

Bear smiled. "A man should use a bow that matches his strength. That bow of yours is for boys."

Now, when Bear drew back the arrow, he strained mightily to make the bow bend. He looked every bit as tense as Wasp had just moments before. As if this powerful bow were not enough to launch a lethal arrow, Bear – when he shot – lunged forward again, pushing the bow with a loud grunt, making it seem as though the arrow could drive through a solid tree. But it missed both stump and gourd and disappeared into the ferns.

Bear threw down the bow and started across the creek.

"Where are you going?" Raven called.

Bear stopped and turned. "To crush that sentry with my bare hands, as I should have done from the beginning. Like you, I have never relied on the bow."

Raven waved him back. "We are not done here," he explained and nodded toward Whistler. "Perhaps this one has learned something about the bow?"

Pause: "What do you think Whistler will do differently with the bow?"

"Yesterday," Whistler said, taking the lighter bow, "I told you about the secret I had been told as a boy. For many winters that advice has been only words to me. Now I have found a teacher who showed me how to let the bow do its work."

"A teacher in our village?" Raven said. "I know of no such archer."

"My teacher is not an archer," he replied. "Let me show you what I learned."

When he drew the arrow to his face, he thought of the partnership he had forged with the Painted Wings. Now he made such a pact with the arrow. When the shaft pointed perfectly at the gourd, he did not fling his fingers open … nor did he suddenly try to inject any strength into the arrow's flight. He let the bow do all the work by simply performing one simple feat: He stopped holding the string.

When he did this, his hand flopped and dangled daintily. The arrow sped through the air and cracked into the gourd, breaking it into many pieces. Once the shards of gourd had scattered and settled in the ferns, the forest was quiet and still. One by one the three spectators tore their eyes away from the shattered gourd to look at Whistler.

"Who was your teacher?" Raven asked solemnly. "I want all of our warriors to learn this lesson."

Whistler smiled. "We'll go to my teacher now," he offered. "I know that she will be happy to show all of you."

" 'She?' " Wasp and the Bear said, their voices sounding as one.

The four men walked to the meadow and stood for a time watching Flutterby patiently hold out her arms inside a swirl of butterflies of every color. Eventually an orange one landed on her hand, and she stood relaxed but motionless as she waited.

"Where is this teacher?" Raven demanded. He looked around the meadow in every direction.

Whistler pointed. "Watch your daughter. The lesson has already begun."

Raven frowned. "Where are you going?"

"To collect the arrows we shot into the ferns," Whistler said and pointed again at Flutterby. "Watch now … or you will miss the lesson, Father."

Raven could not help but chuckle. "Yes, my son," he said under his breath.

After the telling of such a story, on the next day you have a memorable reference for your archery students. You can touch someone's hand at full draw and say, "Let your hand and the arrow enter a partnership. When the arrow is ready, stop holding the string. Your hand will fall gracefully just like Flutterby's."

The students have already seen the act performed within the self-made imagery of the story. They themselves constructed the picture. A teacher could hardly ask for a better introduction to a lesson. How accurate that mental picture is depends upon the descriptive verbal skills of the storyteller.

Pacing the Story

A story needs to keep an audience curious about what will happen next. How will the protagonist solve a new problem? (What would I do in that situation?) Tension, as we all know from the best novels and movies, is a must. But resolving that tension too easily is a disservice to young students, who are already inundated with the convenient denouements of magicians, wizards, and sorcerers of movies and computer games.

Most crucial to a story, perhaps, is having your students involved. You can achieve this in different ways: creating empathy for the protagonist by giving him common ground with the listeners (age, gender, hobby, etc.); intensifying suspense so that the audience is anxious to hear what happens next (make some unexpected turns in the plot); and by giving the students a way to become part of the story. Help them slip into the skin of the protagonist by asking, "What would you do if you were this character in the story?" The answer you receive might help to shape your story.

Some girls who listen to the story of Flutterby might relate to her plight with her father. She's the real underdog in the story. Because she is so overlooked, the audience wants her to receive her due.

Most boys have to learn to play second-string to someone else who is better skilled in a given activity, because only one can be the best. The competition between the trainees in the story provides hope for those who are not natural athletes.

~ The Blind Medicine Woman ~

This story is designed for botany classes of all ages. It should be told after the students have learned plant anatomy in a comprehensive note-taking session. (This lesson, *The Botany Booklet*, is covered in full in *Secrets of the Forest, Volume 1*.) Around the campfire that night, let the story of The Blind Medicine Woman prepare students for the game of the same name, to be played the following day.

Before beginning the story, give the students a tantalizing bit of information: "The reason I am telling you this story is that two of the characters in this tale will actually visit us tomorrow. You'll probably have lots of questions for them."

Telling the Story of The Blind Medicine Woman – Blue Wolf
was an old healer, but her eyes were sharp and her thinking so clear that few people in her village ever thought ahead to a time when she would no longer be there for them. She served as the tribal storehouse for plant lore, versed in all the secrets hidden in roots and leaves, in flowers and seeds, and in the inner bark of trees. She knew how to make medicines and how to administer them. Her healing powers had saved the lives of many who had been sick or injured. She had been the medicine woman for as long as anyone could remember.

When one of the Elders of the Tribal Council developed a hacking cough, Blue Wolf brought him a cherry bark tea that calmed the tickle in his chest. As soon as the old man had drunk the brew, his coughing ended and he gained a much needed rest. From his bed, as he watched her pack up her herbs, he posed a question.

"What would happen to us, Blue Wolf, if you crossed over to the shadow world? What would become of the People?"

She shrugged and replied, "If I should become ill, I will heal myself."

"But, as you know, one day each of us must die," the Elder said.

Blue Wolf smiled and patted his shoulder. "I know my own health, old man. I have many winters yet to live."

He studied her wrinkled face, which he remembered had once been as smooth as a creek stone. He watched her shuffle to the door and noticed that her once straight spine was now bent like a pine sapling burdened with ice.

"Still," he said, "I will bring it up at the Council. We must think beyond ourselves … to the future of the People."

And so, this is how it was decided that Blue Wolf would take on an apprentice to ensure that her legacy of healing with plant medicines would continue through the generations. This new assistant must be old enough to absorb all the details of being a medicine woman but young enough to live many years as the tribal healer.

Insisting on her right to make the selection, Blue Wolf chose a quiet girl named Scratching Otter, who, even as a child, was known for her skills in drawing pictures in the dust and sand. The old woman knew that attention to detail was a most useful tool in the study of plants. Who would be more alert to those details than an artist? Scratching Otter was approved by the Elders, accepted the assignment, and began the apprenticeship right away.

On their first day together, student and mentor walked forest and field, talking only of the many shapes of leaves. There were round leaves, oval leaves, triangular leaves, leaves whose widest part was close to the base, others with the widest part near the tip of the leaf. There were leaves with lobes, and Blue Wolf had the girl look not just at the lobes but also at the shape of the empty space between each lobe.

(Make references to the vocabulary that the class learned in the botany lesson: "toothed," "entire," "pinnate veins," "clasping leaves," etc." With each mention of a familiar term, students in the audience are nodding and bonding to the story. They see, in their minds, exactly what Scratching Otter is seeing in the forest.)

On the second day of the apprenticeship, Blue Wolf introduced Scratching Otter to finer details, like minute hairs, complicated vein patterns, and surprising smells inside of leaves. She even learned to listen to the sounds of leaves when rubbed by fingertips.

On day three, the old woman showed the girl how some plants have more complicated leaves than others. She learned that some blades are not leaves but leaflets. Like sumac, from which Scratching Otter, herself, had made the tart drink, qualla, which her grandfather enjoyed.

sumac

Next they studied the formulas that plants followed in arranging their leaves. Some leaves grew opposite one another like the arms of a human, and those that did grew their limbs in a like manner. Other plants positioned their leaves in a staggered, alternating way. Still others grew leaves in multiple layers, making rings of foliage along the stem.

On the fifth day of the apprenticeship, as the two medicine women set out for another day of study, a young man appeared outside the medicine lodge, his face taut and anxious. He was the chief's son. Otter had seen him at the dances, where always there were many young girls eager to trill for him as he gyrated around the fire.

"What is wrong, Long Hand?" Blue Wolf said in a somber tone.

"My father," the young warrior said. "He was very ill through the night. He is hot and sweating. A redness is covering his back and chest."

"I will get my medicines," Blue Wolf said and turned quickly to the girl. "You must go with him and heat the water that I will need. Go quickly now!"

The two young ones made for the chief's lodge, Long Hand running ahead. "You are the new medicine woman?" he called over his shoulder.

"I am in training," Scratching Otter explained. Then, feeling that she had not spoken with the respect due a chief's son, she added, "I have seen you at the dances."

"You must heat the water quickly," he ordered. "Do not think of dances now."

When Blue Wolf arrived at the lodge, she found the chief too weak to talk. His eyes were tightly shut, and his breathing was labored. Rolling him over she found an angry boil about to erupt on his back.

"I have seen this sickness once before," she said. "A hunter had fallen down a steep slope and gashed his leg on an old stump. His blood became poisoned by rotting wood that had been lodged inside the cut." After inspecting the chief more thoroughly, she found a dirty, infected wound on the sole of his foot.

She made up two poultices, one to kill the crimson infection in the foot wound and another to draw the yellow sickness from the swollen boil. The girl lashed each poultice in place with a strip of skin she tore from the edge of her robe.

"Will these poultices heal him?" Long Hand asked.

"No, but they are needed," Blue Wolf explained. "I do not have the plant needed for this, for it cannot be stored. It must be harvested fresh to make the medicine."

"I will get it," Scratching Otter volunteered. "Tell me where to find it."

The medicine woman considered the offer, but finally she shook her head and lowered her voice so that the chief could not hear. "This plant grows on the

top of Sees Forever Mountain. If you bring the wrong plant, we will not have time for a second search before our chief dies. We must go to the mountain together … now!"

"It is a long climb for you, Grandmother. Please … I can find it alone."

The old woman shook her head. "You are not ready. We cannot afford a mistake."

Long Hand guided the two women to the door. "Go then. And waste no time."

Blue Wolf handed to him two more dry poultices. "When the sun stands at its highest, wet these in hot water and replace the old poultices. We should return before the sun dips below the ridge in the west."

At the base of Sees Forever Mountain they began the long ascent to the bald, where no trees grew. Along the way Blue Wolf watched the sky with interest, and by the time they reached the halfway point up the mountain, the sun was already hiding behind a dark wall of clouds.

"I must stop to catch my breath," she said. Even when she sat, her legs trembled.

"Grandmother, let me go on alone," Scratching Otter pleaded. "I will find the plant. I have taken your lessons to heart."

Blue Wolf shook her head and spoke between deep breaths. "Too easy … to mistake another plant … I must make sure … our chief gets the medicine … in time."

Just as they reached the crest, the forest gave way to a grassy glade with one lone tree standing at its center. Even in the dim light the bald provided an endless view of the mountains around them. Right away the vista dropped into darkness as the heavy clouds above turned the sky as black as the coat of Bear in his cave. Lightning bolts fired out of the sky and touched down on Screaming Cat Mountain one ridge over, creating sudden pulses of brightness and earth-shaking thunder. The wind began to roar in their ears.

"We will split up to cover more ground," Blue Wolf yelled over the wind. "Call me each time you find an herb with purple veins." She pointed across the clearing. "Walk to the other side and start there."

Blue Wolf began searching for the medicinal plant, when a lightning bolt cracked the sky closer to them. She turned to see the girl walking toward the tree isolated in the clearing, and Blue Wolf cupped her hand to her mouth and called out as loudly as she could.

"Stay away from the tree!"

locust

It was a yellow locust, which calls down lightning like a warrior taunts his enemy on the battlefield. When the girl continued toward it, Blue Wolf ran to stop her.

Before the old woman had hurried more than twenty steps, a great light flashed, outlining every blade of grass, every stone and stick with a white rime of fire. The air seemed to shatter with a terrible splintering sound, and Earth and sky sizzled for a sustained moment. The last sensation Blue Wolf experienced was her skin seeming to catch fire, as she fell through darkness and the scent of burned hair.

When Scratching Otter turned and looked behind her, she saw her mentor lying on her back in the grass. A wisp of smoke lifted from her gray hair.

"Grandmother!"

Scratching Otter ran to her teacher and was alarmed at the sight and smell of scorched hair. Rain began to fall, drenching them and everything around them. The girl could not lift the woman, so she knelt and raised Blue Wolf's head to rest in her lap. Leaning over her to protect her from the rain, Scratching Otter tried not to cry.

"Grandmother, please wake up! What shall I do?"

The old woman's eyes opened, but they were like two pools of dark water with neither light nor life in their depths. Her lips moved, but no sound issued forth.

"Grandmother, can you hear me?"

Blue Wolf's head made the barest movement, her chin slowly lowering then rising. The girl realized the woman had tried to nod. Scratching Otter lowered her face until she was eye to eye with Blue Wolf.

"Can you see me, Grandmother?"

The old woman's empty eyes showed nothing. Then her head strained to rock ever so slightly from side to side. Scratching Otter realized that the old medicine woman was both blind and mute.

"I will cover you and run for help, Grandmother. I will run as fast as–"

But Blue Wolf was shaking her head again. Her wrinkled hand tightened on Scratching Otter's wrist.

"But I cannot carry you," the girl said. "I need help to take you down the mountain."

The woman's grip loosened and her hand came up to point a finger at the girl … and then at the open field. Then she gestured with the finger toward her own eyes.

The girl's breathing stilled. "You want me to search for the plant for our chief?"

Blue Wolf nodded.

"But how will I do that? You cannot see. You cannot speak."

Again Blue Wolf nodded. Then she shook her head. And the girl understood.

"I will ask you questions, Grandmother. You can signal me if I am right or wrong."

Blue Wolf seemed to relax a little. Her head sank back on the grass, and her breathing settled.

"Does this plant cluster its leaves into a repeating number, Grandmother?"

Pause: "What is she asking?" Answer: "Is it a compound leaf divided into leaflets?"

Blue Wolf shook her head once. The girl looked off toward the grasses and herbs on the bald. Another lightning bolt struck somewhere down the ridge and for a moment the world shone with infinite detail.

"Is there a petiole?" the girl asked.

Pause: "What is she asking?" Answer: "Is the leaf stalked or sessile?"

When Blue Wolf nodded, the girl continued, "Is the leaf smaller than my hand?"

Blue Wolf nodded again.

"Are the leaves rough along the edges?"

Pause: "What is she asking?" Answer: "Are they serrate?"

Blue Wolf shook her head. The rain was steady now, and the lightning had moved to the mountains to the east. The old woman smiled, and this encouraged the girl.

"Are the leaves like two wings?" (*Do they show an opposite arrangement?*)

When the woman shook her head again, the girl said, "Do they stand alone?" (*Alternate?*) This time, Blue Wolf nodded.

Bolstered by this new information, Scratching Otter covered the woman with her robe and began crawling around the edge of the clearing, searching for the plant. In the next flash of light she found a low herb that seemed to fit the description. She bent low, stroked the leaves with her fingers, and quickly ran back to Blue Wolf.

"Are the purple veins covered with hairs … little stiff ones?"

Blue Wolf shook her head. Scratching Otter hurried back to the forest's edge and resumed her search, dismissing any plant that did not meet any of the known criteria. After three more questions to her mentor, Scratching Otter was sure she had found the proper plant, and so she used a digging stick to pry up the specimen with plenty of dirt to protect it. After nestling the herb in a curled slab of bark, she brought it to Blue Wolf. The old woman turned on her side, leaned into the leaves, sniffed, and smiled.

"Blue Wolf!" a voice yelled from the forest path. "Grandmother! Are you here?"

Scratching Otter turned to see two men step out on the grassy bald. "Over here!" she called. "Blue Wolf has been hurt! The Firebird streaked from the sky and found her."

One of the men was the chief's son, Long Hand, and he wasted no time in cutting saplings at the edge of the clearing to make a litter on which they could carry the old woman. Otter presented strips of her robe to be used in lashing the parts together.

"Did you find the medicine plant for my father?" Long Hand asked.

Scratching Otter picked up the plant in its bark carrier. "Here," she said.

Long Hand looked hard at the plant, and then his eyes showed a question when he turned back to the girl. "She found it before the Firebird struck her?"

"I found it," Otter said. "I asked her questions and she answered by nodding or shaking her head."

"You must have known the right questions to ask," he said. When the girl averted her eyes, he added, "I must look for you at the next dance."

Otter tore another tying-strip from her robe. "We cannot think of dances now," she said. "You and your friend must get Blue Wolf down the mountain so that we can make the medicine for your father."

As the men carried Blue Wolf down the slope, Scratching Otter was already asking the woman the questions that would help her make the healing concoction.

*

By the next morning the chief's color had much improved. Scratching Otter had mixed the medicine and administered it, using the same method of communication with Blue Wolf that they had employed on the mountain. Observing from the shadows, Long Hand waited as his father steadily improved.

Blue Wolf survived the lightning strike, though she forever lost her ability to see and to speak. During the day Scratching Otter continued to learn the plant secrets from Blue Wolf. At night the two healers prepared medicines and stored them for future use.

On the night of the next full moon, while Otter put away the bags of medicines they had prepared, Blue Wolf retired to her bed. Outside Hoot Owl serenaded the edge of the forest with his throaty call.

"We stopped our lesson early tonight, Grandmother. Are you feeling sick?"

Blue Wolf smiled and cupped her hand to her ear, as though listening to something in the distance. In this quiet they could hear the drums far down at the dancing grounds by the river. Blue Wolf pointed to the girl and then toward the drums.

Otter stared long and hard at Blue Wolf. "Are you telling me to go dance?"

The old woman pointed to herself and shook her head. Then she pressed her hand to the ground, making an outline of her palm and fingers in the dirt. Holding the hand hard against the earth she pushed the fingers forward to make the track much longer. When she lifted the hand, the girl stared down into the track.

"Long Hand? He told you to tell me?"

When Blue Wolf smiled, the girl walked over and kissed her forehead. Within the time it took Owl to ask his four-note question out in the night, Otter had put on her dancing robe and left the medicine lodge.

Here, at the end of the story, allow a silence to fall over those gathered at the campfire. Then remind your listeners:

"Remember … I told you that we would have two visitors tomorrow."

Someone might say, "You said these visitors were characters in the story. How's that gonna happen? Didn't the story take place a long time ago?"

"That's true. Nevertheless, Blue Wolf and Scratching Otter will be here most of the morning, and you will get a chance to talk to them. Just wait … you'll see tomorrow."

And that is a good way to close the evening.

 ### *Playing the Blind Medicine Woman game* – See *Secrets of the Forest, Volume 1.*

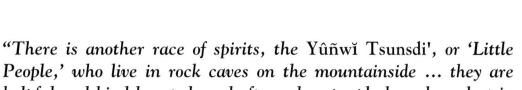

"There is another race of spirits, the Yûñwĭ Tsunsdi', or 'Little People,' who live in rock caves on the mountainside … they are helpful and kind-hearted, and often when people have been lost in the mountains, especially children who have strayed away from their parents … have found them and taken care of them and brought them back to their homes."

~ James Mooney, History, Myths and Sacred Formulas of the Cherokees

CHAPTER 9
Stories for Pure Entertainment
~ no audience member left behind ~

There are various methods I have seen employed to involve every listener in the making of a story around a campfire. For example, one participant might begin a storyline but must stop abruptly at a prearranged signal; such as, a teacher clapping her hands. At that point the next person picks up the narrative. Or perhaps each participant is allowed one minute (or five sentences) to add to the story. The tale is told as a chain of brief contributions as it travels around the circle, adding new characters and plot twists that make this exercise, if nothing else, unpredictable.

Usually these stories become difficult to follow, rambling with such aimlessness that they become disjointed and uninteresting. In an attempt to remedy the boredom factor, individual storytellers tend to concoct more and more outlandish events that render the story even more obtuse.

One storytelling technique that ensures audience involvement without surrendering control of the storyline is the "One-Two-Three Story." Every listener has some investment in the storyline, because each person – at a signal from the storyteller – provides a premeditated key ingredient of the story.

~ The One-Two-Three Story ~
(a meaningless, irrelevant, unforgettable, bonding experience)
As long as the subject matter remains inoffensive, a story creates its own worth,

especially when all the group takes a part in its creation. Such interaction is an impromptu team-building exercise. It doesn't matter what lesson or moral (if any) the story conveys, the group construction of a tale can't help but build camaraderie.

The One-Two-Three Story gives even the quietest student an equal voice in the gathering. Within the bounds of good taste, let the storyline go wherever it wants to go, but I recommend instant censuring for inappropriate entries.

 ### Developing the One-Two-Three Story – Think up three poignant questions to ask your students. (These questions should be gauged to elicit some memorable answers; such as, instead of: "Name a food." ... what about: "Name a food you would never want to find in your lunch box!") Each student must secretly write down his answer on a piece of paper. As an example, consider this trio of "loaded" questions:

1. What famous person would you least like to sit next to on a five-hour bus trip? (This can be any person from history or literature, no matter when he/she lived.)

2. What is the worst smelling thing you have ever discovered in your refrigerator?

3. What is the dumbest line you've ever heard in a children's song?

To avoid unwanted delays in the narrative, be sure that students jot down their answers. Once everyone has three ready answers on paper, begin the story (winging it, of course) and figure out how to integrate these answers into the tale.

A sample:

"Jacob Hammerhead is a twelve-year old, big-city, private eye who specializes in finding lost homework. Of course, he takes on other menial jobs – murders, extortion, kidnapping – but homework is his tour de force. He's expensive, but he's good.

One crisp autumn morning a knock rattles the pebble glass on his office door. In walks the most interesting woman he has ever seen. Her face is unforgettable ... in fact, she looks a little like ..."

(Pause at this point and call on one of the students by name and say the number of the question whose answer would best provide a description of a face.)

"Shelby, *one!*" you say.

Shelby looks surprised. She's already involved in the story and forgotten all about the instructions. Soon she rallies, opens her paper, and looks at her answer to question number one. "*Attila the Hun,*" she says ...

You continue without missing a beat. *"Even more interesting than her face was her breath. When she opened her mouth to speak the room filled with the aroma of ... "*

"Alex, *two!*"

"*Rotten liver paté with mold,*" Alex contributes proudly.

Wait for laughter to subside.

"Offensive as that was, it was what she said that made Jacob Hammerhead ease his hand toward his two-pint, Smith and Wesson water pistol that he kept hidden in his desk. The mysterious lady murmured in a low voice ..."

"Ben, *three!*"

Ben smiles broadly. "*Knick-knack, paddy-whack, give a dog a bone.*"

Again wait for laughter.

"Jacob digs through the waste paper basket in the hope of finding a bone from one of his lunches earlier this week, but all he can find is a small container of …"

"Nathan, *two!*"

And so on …

Creating a Fire Origin Story

In the Cherokees' story of a burning sycamore on an island (see page 43), there is a parallel theme woven into the narrative that adds color to the telling. A number of ambitious animals line up in a quest to be the story's hero by successfully bringing fire across the river to the animals. Utilizing comic relief, the tale shows how each creature's attempt backfired when it encountered an unexpected difficulty. The resulting foible forever changed its appearance (and magically branded all of its species to the same physical alteration). For example, Hoot Owl volunteers to approach the flames and capture fire for the benefit of all, but when he alights on the top of the burning tree and looks down into its hollow trunk, the fire surges from a gust of wind. Hot ashes spew upward from the cavity and almost blind him. The ash turns his face gray, giving him pale rings around his eyes, which hoot owls continue to demonstrate to this day.

Rat Snake tries too, but after scaling the tree he falls in and is scorched black before he can escape. The black rat snakes that exist today owe their color to that mishap.

These amusing twists to the story are similar to the Cherokees' animal-origin stories, which explain unique anatomical traits; such as, *Why the Possum's Tail is Bare* and *How the Deer Got Horns.* Expanding on this theme gives a storyteller's audience an opportunity to join in the story-creation process. Once a student has been a part of composing such a legend, he will feel more connected to the legends of old by relating to the storyteller's craft.

<u>Retelling the Story of Fire</u> – One night around a campfire, tell the Cherokee fire-acquisition story summarized in the first paragraph of chapter 3. Or better yet, read it in full from the quote source (Mooney's book) notated at the beginning of this chapter.

After that telling, assign to each student a wild animal that inhabits *your* area: gray squirrel, flying squirrel, rabbit, scorpion, blue jay, bobcat, praying mantis, deer, opossum, red-shouldered hawk, black widow spider (in some versions of the story, it was she who stole fire and retained that fire in her "bite" … in Mooney's version it was a water spider), rattlesnake, cricket, skink, skunk, ruby-throated humming-bird, earthworm, mosquito, bear, mountain lion, gray fox, etc.

Each student should research the assigned animal and choose one of its traits to use in a new story on fire creation. If, for example, one student takes on the study of Blue Jay, she will learn that this corvid's plumage includes a black "necklace" at its throat. She might then incorporate that necklace into the story, explaining how this Winged acquired it.

Perhaps Blue Jay flies to the island and hops around the burning tree for a time, looking for an opening to steal a hot coal. As he peers into the sycamore through a hole at the base, the loose necklace swings away from his body and catches fire. When he realizes his blunder he straightens up and the necklace singes the feathers at his neck. Panicked, he delivers an uncharacteristic, raspy cry and plunges into the river. When he surfaces on the shore where the other animals wait, he is a changed bird. Robin and Dove laugh at his charred and wet appearance.

"Was that you who cried out, Blue Jay? You sounded like more like Crow than you."

Blue Jay opens his beak to answer but only a croak issues from his syrinx. He can feel the damage done to his voice by the fire. The other Wingeds make the mistake of laughing again.

"You'll regret making fun of me," Blue Jay growled. "From this day on I will make my meals from the eggs in your nest!"

At this point the apprentice storyteller delivers the historic denouement: "Even today the blue jay still shows that burn-mark running around its throat, and one of its songs is a raspy whine. Whenever possible it steals other birds' eggs and eats them."

When you tell the story again over a new campfire, after setting up the scene of the burning sycamore lighting up the night from the island, call on each student (one at a time) to add her contribution of an animal blundering in its attempt to be the hero. Then that contributor ends her story by explaining how the experience forever changed that species' appearance, vocalization, scent, or behavior.

As a surprise to the group at large, secretly assign to one student the task of relating how his animal was the successful stealer of fire. During the telling of the story, of course, call on that student last.

Let's say, for example, that you assign flying squirrel to one student. In private, inform that student that it will be flying squirrel who successfully acquires fire from the sycamore. Here is a possibility for that student's end-of-the-story:

"Flying Squirrel, who in those days was known as 'Runt Squirrel' (because he was so small), swam to the island and assessed the situation. He knew that he could never hold a hot coal in his hands, so he chewed out the center of a hickory nut from one side to make a bowl. When he tried to enter the burning cavity of the tree through a hole at the base, it was too hot. The best he could do was to reach in with the hickory nut bowl and try to scoop up a coal. He pushed the bowl in with his right forepaw but failed to capture a coal. He didn't want to use the same paw again because the heat had almost burned it. He used the other forepaw but failed again. With a hind paw he tried a third time. Still, no coal. Finally, with his last foot he managed to snag a hot coal, but a sudden downdraft caused a roaring flame to surge out the hole. Runt Squirrel, holding the bowl by his teeth, instinctively scampered up the sycamore, but soon it was evident that he was trapped. The base of the tree was engulfed in flames. Runt Squirrel had no choice but to jump.

"When he leapt into the air he discovered that all that reaching with his legs and the intense heat from the tree had caused the skin at the base of each leg to stretch into a thin, wing-like membrane. He felt the wind lift him as he glided all the way across the river, with the bowl out in front clamped by his teeth. As he sailed, the wind breathed life into the hot coal, keeping it smoldering a bright orange. When he landed, the coal was intact and, using the tulip tree fibers that he always collected for the bedding in his nest, he blew it into a flame. All the animals praised him and took a piece of the fire back to their homes. To this day Runt Squirrel can still outstretch his legs to expose that thin layer of skin which allows him to soar through the air. Now they call him 'Flying Squirrel' in honor of his feat. And to make sure no one ever forgets his heroic act, Flying Squirrel always leaves behind a hickory shell shaped like a bowl to commemorate the night he stole fire from the sycamore."

Stories from Mysterious Sounds of the Forest – 1.) **The Medicine Crow:** Every now and then, an individual crow can be heard to "caw" with a strange, gargling effect. This call has the same pitch and down-slurred melody of typical crow-calls, but its texture is bubbly, like the purr of a cat … or the coo of a pigeon … or even the soft growl of a dog. Listen for it. Direct the attention of your students toward the unusual avian cry.

Secretly assign one student to develop a fictional story about that particular crow: How did it acquire this voice? Why does it use it? What is its message? The crow-protagonist of the story may have undergone some physical ordeal that damaged its syrinx (voice box.) Or perhaps the bird learned to affect this call for a specific reason. The crow might be displaying a penalty invoked on it each time it breaks its promise to a certain animal. The storylines are endless.

2.) **Ghost Timber:** When one tree leans against another (sometimes dead, sometimes alive), the wind can move one upon the other like a bow over violin strings. The sound can be eerie. Point it out to your students and ask for their ideas about the origin of the plaintive cry. Secretly assign to a student the composition of that tale. Why do the trees weep? There is, in this scenario, the potential for an epic love story between two trees. Or is it a struggle? It might be a call for help from tree to human … or from tree to tree. Or is it a warning?

3.) **Talking Creek**: Many young campers have commented on the alleged voices heard at night from a creek. In some cases, individual words have been heard (or so the child thought) from the lapping and gurgling and splashing of water. On a campout near such a creek, ask your students to listen for the nocturnal, aquatic conversation. Have each student make up the dialogue and relate it to the other campers in stories that explain the water's need to communicate at night.

4.) **Every sound from the forest** offers a centerpiece for a story. Listen for them as a group. Contrary to their typical chirrs and barks, gray squirrels sometimes make plaintive, mewing calls, as if they are lamenting or needing help. This sound is a perfect inspiration for a story. Every bird's call could be interpreted onomatopoetically, like the chuck-will's-widow, who says: "Just whittle the willow!" Or the black-throated green warbler, who says: "Come back, Robin Hood!"

By drawing your wards' attention to all the aforementioned sounds (and then providing their stories), you open up the ears of the young ones. They will always connect the stories to these sounds. And they will learn to listen for other mysteries.

 <u>A Thousand Words</u> – A story can be inspired by a single picture. Of course, you can choose any work of art to instigate a narrative, but I include several here to help you get started. 1.) a surreal face-to-face conversation between a red fox and a river otter … a perfect set-up for an Aesopic fable; 2.) a whitetail deer sniffing a beer can; 3.) a fox caught in a steel trap; and 4.) a fox receiving the gift of a feather from a bird.

Print out a copy of the picture you'd like to use and give one to each student to study. Based upon the picture, each writer composes a story. The artwork should serve as an illustration to some part of the story. Each day give a different student center stage to read his work. It will be fun for all to experience the variety of imaginative ideas spawned by a single drawing.

"... Almost every prominent rock and mountain, every deep bend in the river in the old Cherokee country has its accompanying legend."

~ James Mooney, History, Myths and Sacred Formulas of the Cherokees

CHAPTER 10
A Story of Place

~ the Legend of the Medicine Bow ~

I was in Belize working with a group of wealthy, privileged high school sophomores from a private academy in the States. We had rotated through a variety of daily activities ranging from reef snorkeling to floating through river caves to volunteering help in a local hospital. It was early spring.

On this day my group was taking a slow trip on a lazy river. The students were spread out over a painted, plywood deck of a homemade barge, pushed along by a purring outboard motor as our Belizean guide talked about the land, the water, and the wildlife. By midafternoon these American teenagers were strewn across the deck like corpses. No one even turned a head to look at the jungle as we traveled. Most dozed under the spell of the guide's droning voice.

I sat on the bow with my feet dangling over the smooth water, taking it all in. There were crocodiles here. And snakes I had never before seen. Birds with songs (and names) that carried intriguing sounds to my ear. The plant life along the shoreline was exotic to my eye, and I soaked up the history being narrated by our native companion.

Then came the news – an "aside" spoken as casually as if the narrator were explaining the life cycle of the botfly: "And over here on the left," the guide informed us, "that is where Harrison Ford filmed *Mosquito Coast*. What you see there is the scenery used for all the shots that involved ..."

He may as well have banged the end of a fifty-five gallon drum with a sledgehammer, because every student sat bolt upright at the familiar name of a celebrity. I was impressed. These kids, who had just been asleep or seemingly bored,

now looked like every teacher's dream of a classroom hungry for knowledge. With Harrison Ford in the mix, the students looked at everything: the tree canopy, the vines, the way the water lapped on the shore, the slope of the land. They looked hard into the shadows, trying to imprint the image of the place into memory. It looked like a thousand other places we'd seen that day, but it wasn't. Harrison Ford had been here. On some strange level, they were invested in this acre of earth.

It was a memorable lesson for me, seeing all those young minds light up with curiosity. Maybe one could argue that this sudden interest in the scenery was superficial and shallow. After all, the newly found importance of this place was based not upon the jungle ecology but upon our culture's fascination with "famous people." Yet it was undeniably Harrison Ford's connection to the place that got the students' attention. Here was a subject that – for whatever reason – mattered to them. Understanding this is what I mean when I tell teachers during an educator's workshop: *"Start where the students are!"*

If we could have gone ashore at that point for, say, a lesson on animal tracks, I wondered if I could have parlayed Mr. Ford's celebrity into the lesson.

I might say: *"See how this bird track in the sand shows that the bird leaned forward to sniff at or peck at something."* I might point to a small indentation in the sand just in front of the bird's footprint. *"Maybe Harrison Ford dropped a cigarette butt here, and the bird was curious about it."*

The point is this: The Harrison Ford-connection opened a door on *a place*, where five minutes ago there had been no door at all. Some of Mr. Ford's celebrity spilled over onto the land, making the land itself an icon to these youths.

This Belizean experience made me think about my own land back in the mountains of Southern Appalachia. How could I charge my little piece of geography with this same kind of energy? Would I need to convince Harrison Ford to visit my place?

"This morning we'll be learning about the insect repellents found in certain plants, like this bracken fern here next to me. It's simply a matter of bruising the frond and wearing it like a visor under your hat."

The students are standing three yards away from me, their hands in their pockets, their lackluster eyes moving to and then away from the fern.

"By the way, when Harrison Ford visited here, he took a frond from this very stand of bracken and wore it under his Indiana Jones fedora."

The students drop to the ground on hands and knees and begin sniffing the bracken. Thank you, Harrison.

Why not, I thought, inject my land with a similar energy from the original art form of make-believe from which cinema evolved … a story? So, that's what I did.

The Legend of the Medicine Bow is a long story – a "two-nighter" around the campfire – that centers around a Native American ceremonial bow, which was never used to kill but to guide the People. (Though the story is fiction, the *medicine bow* was a real part of history.) This tale includes landmarks that are nearby – streams, mountains, trails, and specific trees. It is about our valley and its surrounding peaks. And though it is a product of creative writing, it is a powerful asset for (a verisimilitude of) the reputation of the land.

Twenty yards away from our fire circle stands a totem of debarked juniper that I erected years ago. On it I painted a series of pictures that illustrates *The Legend of the Medicine Bow*, spiraling from bottom to top. At the top of this *legend pole* is the symbol of the medicine bow, itself – an arc of wood naturally sculpted by the constriction of a vine. The bow is bent by a bowstring and adorned with a blue feather.

Many of the students have walked past the pole and barely noticed it … not to mention the bow hovering fifteen feet above. But after the telling of the story at night, we visit the legend pole with our flashlights, and all eyes take in the fifty pictographs.

I include the legend here in full in the hope that you might see its worth and develop a story and legend pole for your land.

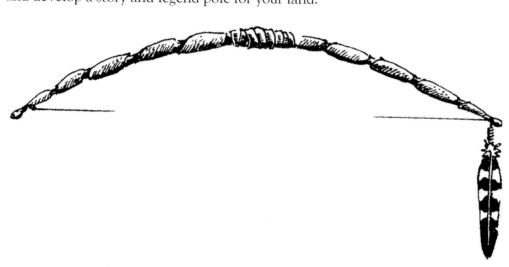

The Legend of the Medicine Bow

When the spring rains did not come for a fourth consecutive year, the People of Little Itawa (our valley) began to feel desperate. Once again the blistering summer sky flashed dry lightning over the parched mountains. The few ragged clouds that hung in the dead air refused to stack high into thunderheads that might quench the roots of the trees and fill the dwindling creeks so that the fish might run again.

Deer and Elk migrated north. And Turkey, too. Even Rabbit. Every creature sought greener places. Filling the void, new animals migrated into the valley of Little Itawa. They too were seeking relief. And like the animals before them, they could not know that the continental scope of the drought exceeded their ability to escape it.

One hunter summed it up when he said, "The whitetail I stalked today has a white patch of fur under one eye. I have never seen him before. He is new to our land, and so he is unsure, wary, and nervous. He is always looking, jerking his head this way and that. I was never closer than two throws of a stone, and so I did not shoot."

This was in the time before there were chiefs. There was no concept of that position of leadership, where one man told another how to live his life. It seemed natural that men and women follow their individualistic instincts for survival.

Before this drought had dried up the land, the People had always shared their surpluses with those who were in need. Now each family measured its wealth in morsels. Hunger has a way of pushing generosity into the shadows.

One man had little to worry about because of his unrivaled skill with bow and arrow. Crooked Bow, a master archer, had no need to stalk so close to the skittish creatures. He had been known to kill beaver when shooting across the full span of the River Itawa. But one man alone could not be expected to feed a village.

The deaths of three old ones on the same day heightened the alarm, so that the Elders took it upon themselves to meet in the Council Lodge. To a man and to a woman they decided that the village must assemble for the purpose of addressing the crisis of food shortage. The word spread quickly, and all the People met at the square-ground on that same day just as the sun touched the ridge to the west.

At that meeting someone came up with the idea that they take a lesson from the wolves, who live under the leadership of an alpha-male. The People should appoint such a chief. It was a startling idea for a village unaccustomed to a leader. But how would they choose this person? No one could say. The concept of voting was unknown.

"Let us go to our beds with this question," an Elder announced. "We ask that the Great Spirit give to one of us an answer in a dream. Tomorrow we meet again at midday and decide how we will choose our new chief."

That night, outside the lodge of one family, someone scratched at the elk skin door flap. (This was the manner by which visitors announced themselves in that time.) The father went to the door, where he was beckoned outside.

His family continued to boil an old rawhide war shield with the few roots they had gathered. This was to be their only meal for that day. The children of the family heard whispering outside the door and grew curious. When the father returned a short time later he carried a leg of Deer to the fire, and together they sliced chunks of meat from the thick muscle and dropped them into the stew.

By the expression the father carried on his face, the wife and children knew not to ask where he had gotten this treasure. They did not care. All they could think about was the hole in their bellies that would soon be filled with the unexpected venison.

At another lodge a woman answered a scratch at her door. She too stepped outside, and her family heard snatches of a whispered dialogue. When she returned she carried a dead Turkey by its legs. Without a word she began plucking the feathers, and the family prepared a cooking spit over the fire. At a third lodge the grandfather of the family stepped outside to converse with their visitor. Later, when the old man stooped through the door, he carried a dark fur folded upon itself. When he lay the package on the earth and opened it, his family's eyes widened at a heavy red slab of Bear meat.

This happened at four more lodges. Seven in all.

At noon the following day the People once again gathered in the square-ground. When the Elder asked the question that was on everyone's mind, to the surprise of all, an answer came right away.

"A contest of bow and arrow should decide who our leader will be!"

The crowd turned as one at this bewildering proposal, for no one could say what shooting an arrow had to do with governing the People. As they strained to see who had offered such a solution, another voice called from across the assembly.

"I agree, let the arrow decide!"

Then a third voice. "Yes, the bow will tell us the name of our chief."

Four more people spoke up supporting the archery contest. Seven in all.

By now everyone was thinking: *Well, this must be what all the People want. They who speak out are all saying the same thing.* And so the tournament was set for five days in the future.

As the crowd dispersed, one woman remained motionless, leaning on her walking staff in the square-ground. Singing Stone was old and blind and the villagers flowed respectfully around her, like a river parting around an island.

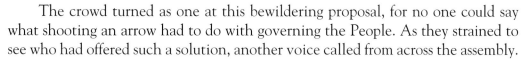

Like everyone else, she knew without a doubt who would win the archery contest and become chief. No one could match the skill of Crooked Bow with bow and arrow.

Because she was blind, Singing Stone could often sense what others could not. She could hear in a doubtful voice the subtle waver that marked a lie. She could smell fear on a man's body. She could feel a person's honor as if it were a radiant heat emanating from the heart. And likewise she could detect cowardice … or generosity.

"I must not let Crooked Bow become the leader of the People," she said to herself. And having said it, this became her mission.

To understand Crooked Bow, we must look back at his childhood. His mother, White Fawn, was one of those women whose physical beauty seemed to arise from within, from her love for every human, creature, and plant. When her marriage was arranged by her parents, she entered into the pact with obedience but not without a certain degree of doubt. Her husband, a warrior named "Scar," was known as a man of hot temper, even violence. White Fawn saw that the man's father had planted an anger in his heart when Scar was a boy. The red mark that he carried on his cheek and neck was a lasting symbol of that failed relationship.

White Fawn believed that by the mere application of gentle and patient love, she could heal that wound as well as the wounds hidden inside Scar's past. Unfortunately, she did not know that the legacy of hate can be every bit as powerful as the legacy of love.

After one winter of marriage, when White Fawn's efforts to change her husband had failed, she convinced herself that a child made by them would unlock the hidden joy that the Great Mystery had intended for every man. Within the year a boy was born and, because his first deliberate movement was to reach for the small jumping insect in the meadow grass, she called him "Cricket."

White Fawn's love for this baby was like a warm liquid dye soaking into every pore of a deer hide. On long walks through the forest she held the baby and sang songs to him. Then she would set him down on the forest floor and marvel at his little hands as they explored every texture of the Great Mystery's creation.

The more time she spent with Cricket, the more Scar smoldered with jealousy. When she asked her husband to take their baby in his arms to teach him the tracks of the wild animals, Scar picked up his lance and turned his back to her saying, "I am going hunting. I cannot take a noisy baby with me."

Even with such a loving mother, the boy's life was fragile and full of fear. Through thirteen winters Cricket tried to avoid being alone with his father, though by this time they should have been hunting together almost daily. Scar had not even made Cricket a bow – something the boy wanted more than anything … which was, of course, why the father had denied it.

From a distance, Cricket watched the other boys in the village play games with bow and arrow. He was embarrassed that he had no weapon of his own. Worse than that, he felt incomplete. If there was anything that Cricket knew in his unhappy world, it was that he was meant to shoot a bow.

And then he found one! On what was perhaps the greatest day of his life up to that point, he wandered behind the village looking for something to do. The bow lay atop a mound of discarded rotten skins and fractured stone tools where someone had piled trash. Cricket picked up the bow as if it had been handed to him by the Great Mystery. It did not matter that the bow was cracked. He boiled a strip of rawhide and wrapped the flaw tightly with the flaccid skin. As the bandage dried and tightened, he fashioned an arrow from a straight rivercane growing near the creek. This he fletched with duck feathers and tipped with a crude stone point he had scraped on a boulder.

He shot the bow all day, learning how to compensate for its imperfection, until he surprised himself by hitting several targets. He was so excited when he returned home that, in the absence of his mother, he spilled out the news to his father, who was building a fire for the evening meal.

Snatching up the bow, Scar examined it with a sneer and then looked at his son. "This is why I have come home to a cold lodge without a fire? This is why I will have to wait for my meal? Because you were out playing with a worthless bow?"

Cricket pointed to the bow. "But look how I have wrapped it with–"

Scar slapped the boy so hard that Cricket fell sprawling into the dusty fire pit. In that moment White Fawn stooped through the doorway and stared at the two, who were as frozen in time as a pictograph scratched into stone. Cricket's left cheek was as bright as the prickly pear fruit, and Scar's face was hard.

She dropped the firewood she was carrying and pointed at the door, her arm stretched out stiff as a spear. "Get out," she said quietly, glaring at her husband.

The father sneered. "Make me something to eat, woman."

White Fawn took a step toward him. "Leave!" she commanded. In a quieter voice she added, "I cut the knot forever."

Scar laughed and slapped open the door. "Cook my meal before I return or you will wear one of these!" He jabbed a thumb at the bright scar on his face, and then he left.

When he returned to the lodge later that evening, Scar found every possession that was rightfully his thrown into a heap outside the door. This was the way that a woman divorced a man in those days. By tribal custom, he could never again enter that abode, which belonged wholly to the woman.

Even without having a man to provide for the family, Cricket's life was much improved. In fact, necessity had placed him in the role of hunter, and now with his imperfect bow he stepped into the life that had waited for him. He became a hunter.

When the bow finally broke – as any flawed bow must – Cricket visited his uncle and asked that he make a bow for him. The tradition of the tribe called for this. But the uncle was busy burning out a dugout canoe and said he must finish before the net-makers completed their fishing seine. When Cricket approached his grandfather, the old man

complained of the pain in his hands that would not allow him to make a good bow. Every man that Cricket asked had an excuse waiting on the tip of his tongue – just as each man tried to hide the nervous darting of his eye as he looked away from Cricket's request. The boy knew that his father had spoken to each of these men. Though he tried to learn, Cricket discovered that the making of a bow was a mystery. And so he resorted to visiting the middens of trash every day until finally good fortune struck again. He found a second bow. It was twisted and could not be repaired, yet he learned to shoot it fairly well by flicking his wrist as he released the arrow.

When Cricket was fifteen winters old, a runner came into the village, and all the People became excited and gathered in the square-ground. Long-distance communication like this was a big event, and this message proved to be especially so for Cricket.

"I have carried this news to all the villages," the messenger announced, "traveling in a great spiral throughout Katuah (Southern Appalachia) and your village is last to receive it."

The runner raised a long feather, and the crowd looked on in stunned silence. No one in the village had ever seen such a plume – slate blue and mottled with black. He turned it in the sunlight, and the onlookers tried to imagine the Hawk to which it had been attached. The blue color seemed to blink off the feather like sunlight reflecting off the river.

"It has been decided," he continued, "that a contest will be held to determine the greatest archer of all Katuah. The champion will receive this feather from the Sacred Hawk to wear in his hair. It has been decided that the tournament will be held here in your village. Prepare lodging for your guests, People of Little Itawa, and make ready your bows and arrows. The contest comes in one moon."

Cricket could hardly believe his ears. He would be granted the gift of seeing the greatest archers of his time. He would learn from them simply by watching their techniques. This thrill lived inside his heart for only one day before it was replaced by yet a greater sensation. *Why not!* he thought. *I will stand beside these archers and shoot in the contest. I will be one of them!*

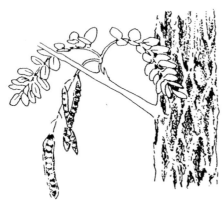

More than ever now he needed a good bow. Still, no one was willing to make one for him. Perhaps he should go to the grove of sacred trees – the garden of yellow locust trees carefully cultivated by the People – cut his own stave and do the best he could with his limited knowledge of bow-making. The prospect excited him, so he ran to the grove with a stone axe. When he reached the place, he felt a great sadness. Someone had mutilated the grove. Every tree was ruined – slashed, chopped, and scarred beyond utility.

A few days before the contest, strangers began drifting into the village. Their arrival was, for Cricket, an education about the size of the world that lay beyond Little Itawa. A woman arrived from the North wearing white furs that he had never before seen. Everyone who walked from the East wore shells around their necks – shells like those of River Clam but full of varied colors and twisted shapes. One man who had traveled from the South drew so much attention that Cricket had to ask him what manner of creature owned so many teeth like the jawbone the man wore like a necklace.

"It is the giant Lizard who lives in the swamp," he said. "I killed this one with my bow and ate his tail. This is his skin." The man pointed to his scaly quiver of arrows, and Cricket swallowed at the prospect of facing such an animal.

From the West came a man whose arrows were tipped in shiny, black stone.

Over the next three days new archers arrived, and Cricket's education stretched to new boundaries. The anticipation of the contest set the People chattering like birds on their morning perches.

Finally, the tournament day arrived. Holding his twisted bow, Cricket felt very small among the other archers as they gathered together. Soon a man began beating a drum, drawing everyone's attention. Then he stopped and explained the rules of the contest.

"Five archers will stand at this line." He pointed to a scrape in the dirt. "Each archer will hold a bow with one hand. The other hand must be empty. Arrows remain in the quiver until I begin beating the drum. I will strike the skin seven times – as fast as a sleeping heart beats. At the first drumbeat, you may snatch an arrow and load. Then shoot whenever you are ready, but you must get off your shot before the seventh beat has sounded."

He pointed to a furry object suspended from a tree limb by an arm's-length of rope. "There is the target, the skin of Woodchuck stuffed with dried grasses. If you are fast and the first to shoot, you have the good fortune of aiming at a target that is not moving. But if someone hits it before you shoot, your target will be more difficult. All who hit the target within the seven drumbeats will shoot in the next round from a farther distance. Then we will repeat this until a winner emerges."

(At this moment in the story I pause the narration and point at an old oak with a stout limb eight feet off the ground. "That tree," I say.)

Cricket was nervous. He had never shot at a moving target. He knew he must load quickly and be first to shoot. The first five archers were called to the line; and,

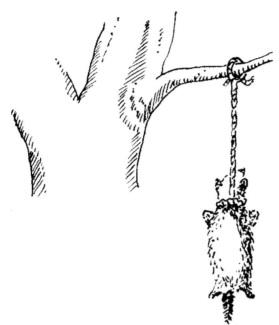

when all were ready, the drumming began. Arrows rattled in quivers and swished the air as the archers hurried to load. A tall man from the North was first to shoot, but he missed. A woman, who had been just as swift with her loading but had taken an extra blink of the eye to aim, struck the skin squarely, and it began swinging wildly. Of the three other archers, only one was able to score a hit. Two out of five had qualified.

Cricket's name was called in the next group. He felt proud to step to the line. He might make a fool of himself as an archer, but he had done more than any other youth in his village by entering the contest. Alone between two muscular men, he felt like he was standing at the bottom of a gorge where the sun seldom shone.

The drum sounded, and he whipped out his arrow and notched it to the string unerringly. He believed that he was the first to draw a string, so it surprised him when he heard the twang of a bowstring. But he forced his mind and his eye to focus and took that tiniest fraction of a breath to align his shaft on the perfect track. He released the string with a soft downy lightness that made his fingers drop like feathers dangling in the wind. At the same time he curled his wrist as the twisted bow had taught that he must. When his arrow hit the mark, the crowd roared. Two others hit the moving target after Cricket.

Cricket had not just shown up for this contest. He was in it!

The drummer stepped off seven paces to move the shooting line farther from the target. In the first group of five called to the line, Cricket took his place and determined to be the first to shoot at the more distant target. When the signal was given, he loaded, drew, and shot before any of the others. His aim was true again, and the impact of his arrow spoiled the plans of his competitors, who adjusted for a moving target with their arrows waving in the air like the antennae of probing insects. But their efforts were anticlimactic beneath the cheering from the villagers for one of their own. Only one other from his group – a woman – joined Cricket in qualifying for the third round. When the remaining contestants had completed their second turn, eleven archers remained in the contest.

The distance was now formidable. For Cricket, to hit a moving target at this range was unthinkable. The drum thudded its steady cadence, and Cricket rushed through the loading process with all the speed with which his muscles were capable. He sensed that the archer at his back had matched him move for move, and so he drew the bow quickly.

The snap of the twisted bow was like the sound of ice cracking open a tree during a hard freeze. Cricket felt the violent liberation of the bow's tension fly around him like crazed birds on a tether. The bow had broken apart in two places. The two pieces still connected by the string slapped his back and thigh. At

the sixth drumbeat the drummer unexpectedly stopped, and Cricket turned to see that the other four archers had lowered their bows.

Before the confused drummer could ask his question, a stocky archer with a broad chest spoke up. "If we are to surpass this boy's shooting, it should not be because of a broken bow. Let him replace it and we will start again."

The newcomers to Little Itawa waited for a villager to step forward to loan Cricket a bow, but no one moved. The Peoples' eyes strayed with caution toward a man whose cheek and neck shone with a garish red scar. If a visitor made a move to offer a bow, a hand stayed that person and a mouth leaned close to whisper in that one's ear.

A woman whose shoulders were adorned with tiny shells sewn around her shirt began a chant: "Give the boy a bow … give the boy a bow …"

Soon the demand gained momentum with a chorus of ten women. Then the men joined in, giving ballast to the song. All eyes gravitated toward Scar, whose face turned so dark that his old facial wound appeared to glow.

"All right!" he yelled. "Enough!"

He strode off in a stiff gait, his footsteps the only sound among the crowd. As they waited, Cricket avoided all the eyes looking at him. When Scar returned he carried a singular bow, which he held out to his son. The bow was made of knotty wood, asymmetrical and wrought with odd angles that jutted from the intended arc of the bow like a terribly injured bone that had not healed properly. The father had finally given his son a gift – and a bow, at that – but the gift was so obviously invested with malicious intent that those who witnessed the presentation felt nothing but pity for the boy.

But remember: Cricket was accustomed to inferior bows. He tested the pull of the string, and by the wood's convoluted bend, he knew that the arrow would shoot high and to the left. There was no time to practice. He would aim low and to the right.

The drumming began, and Cricket loaded and shot, his arrow smacking into the center of the target. No one else in his group was able to pin the swinging skin. When the villagers roared their approval, a chill of pride washed up Cricket's spine, but he hid his smile by clenching his teeth.

Two more groups shot, only three more archers qualifying.

Seven more paces were stepped off, and the few archers remaining were visibly more focused. More than ever, Cricket dedicated himself to the most rapid load humanly possible. Then he must force himself into a calm that would deliver the graceful release of the arrow. For the first time since hearing of this tournament, now he allowed himself to imagine the glory of winning the blue feather.

When the drumming began, Cricket's nervous fingers fumbled with the arrow. It took him two tries to successfully set it to string. Even before he had drawn

his bow, two arrows flew, one arrow clipping the edge of the target, sending it reeling in a wobbly circle. He made an instant decision to shoot at it as it swung toward him at the outside edge of its orbit, but he sensed that he must send the arrow before the target filled that space. That way the arrow and woodchuck would meet at the same place at the same moment.

At the sixth beat of the drum the shaft leaped from his bow, arced high, and fell back to the appropriate height. But the target had come and gone. His arrow soared into noth-ingness and skittered across the dirt.

The audience groaned, but Cricket did not sag … nor did he show anger or disapproval. No excuse sprang prepared from his lips. He held his head high and met the eyes of his competitors. He nodded and walked from the line to the place where the disquali-fied archers had banded together. The People watched him stand without a word to his peers, as he rested the tip of the crooked bow upon his moccasin and became a spectator to the final rounds of the tournament.

That night White Fawn knelt by Cricket's bed and stroked the hair from his fore-head. Though his eyes were closed, she knew that he was not asleep. She watched the firelight flicker on his face as she put together a mother's words for a son who had made her proud. Before she could speak, two scratches on the door-flap broke the silence inside their lodge. White Fawn rose and went to the door.

Just outside, one of the Elders stood bent in the dark. "We wish to speak to your son at the Council Lodge." And with that, the old man left as quietly as he had arrived. White Fawn turned to Cricket, but the boy was already up and dressed. Without a word he left, jogged across the square-ground, and made his way to the Council Lodge.

Inside the lodge, nine Elders sat in an incomplete circle around a blazing fire. "Sit here," a woman said and gestured to the empty slot in the circle. He sat. The flame in the fire-pit was steady and strangely without sound. For a long time the Elders were motionless.

"Today you made us very proud," said the woman finally. "We wish to do for you that which is right and timely … something that ought to be done by one who will not." The others mumbled agreement and nodded, but Cricket had no clue what she meant. "No longer do you walk this Earth as a boy with a boy's name. From this day forward, you take the long steps of a man, and you shall be called 'Crooked Bow.' "

With this announcement, she handed him a bow. It looked very old but strong. The wood was yellow and the handle wrapping was tight and smooth from use.

When he returned home and slipped back into his bedding, White Fawn saw the bow, came to him, knelt, and placed her hand on his chest. "Cricket, what–"

"No, mother," he corrected her. "I am a man now. I am Crooked Bow."

She looked at his dark silhouette for a long time. Her heart was like the river swollen with rain. His heart was like an arrow shot from a powerful bow – an arrow that might never land. Then without another word, she leaned, kissed his cheek, and went to her bed.

The next morning, with his new bow in hand, Crooked Bow walked every byway of the village. Indeed, his steps did feel longer. He felt taller. Everywhere he lingered, he overheard someone talking about him.

"Look, there is the boy who shot with the archers."

"They say he is no longer a boy."

"See … he carries a man's bow."

"Cricket was touched by magic to shoot so well with a bow so poorly made."

"No, not 'Cricket' … 'Crooked Bow' is his name."

To Crooked Bow these words were like water to a thirsty man.

When his rambling took him to the river, he saw many children playing in the water. Their games seemed distant and irrelevant to him – like a place where he would never have need to return. *It is good to be a man*, he thought. *To rise above the weaknesses of childhood and carry this new weapon.*

A young man sat on the river bank and watched over the children like a mother bird. He was the same age as Crooked Bow but taller and his muscles etched with a history of labor. But, as Crooked Bow knew, this one did not yet possess a man-name. This one was still a boy.

Across the river, Crooked Bow spotted a large black Snake curled on top of a log. Filled with the newness of manhood, he called out to the children, "Ho! Watch me, little ones! See what it is to be a man!" He loaded an arrow and took aim at the far bank. The children stood transfixed at this spectacle, and Crooked Bow felt their attention like a beam of light shining on him. He drew the bow and looked down the arrow shaft.

"Wait!" someone said, and Crooked Bow heard the rhythmic *slash-slash-slash* of a long stride moving toward him in the water. He pretended not to hear as he aimed. Then the wading sound stopped only a few feet away.

"Do not kill Snake," said the same voice. The calm and quietness in these words were somehow startling. Crooked Bow knew it was the tall boy who had approached. Holding the string at full draw, he sneered.

"I will kill whatever I want," he boasted without looking at the boy.

The young man moved a step closer. "No, it is wrong. Snake eats Mouse, who eats our winter storage. Snake is our brother."

Crooked Bow felt his stomach churn like the foam below a waterfall. What was it about this boy that affected him so? Something about his manner … his confidence.

"Go play with your children. I have a shot to make." He aimed again and heard the boy step closer.

"No, you will not." The boy's voice was quieter but somehow more commanding.

"Yes!" Crooked Bow hissed, the sound of his voice surprising him. Fuming with nervous energy, he pulled the string back even farther and glared at Snake.

Several things happened at once. The tall boy's hand flew out to snatch the shaft and stop its flight. The string twanged with an unusual sound. The arrow flew a wobbling arc. Trembling with anger, Crooked Bow flushed with color and turned to the boy.

"I could kill you for that!" This time his words reminded him of his father, and his reaction was to become even more angry.

"No," the boy stated evenly. "You will not kill me."

With every child's eye bearing down on him, Crooked Bow kicked at the water as he strode away, his steps choppy now … making him feel like one of those children, who earlier had been splashing mindlessly in the river.

The tall boy looked at his hand. The arrow had opened a gash across his palm, and blood ran freely. Pressing his wound with his other hand, he peered across the river but could not see Snake. The children watched as he forded the river and began searching in the ferns. When he found the arrow impaled into the ground, he was relieved to see that it had not pierced the serpent. He had an idea. He would break the arrow and leave it as a sign to Snake that the alliance between Black Snake and the People was still intact.

When he reached for the shaft, a thing happened that let him know that the Great Mystery was present. Black Snake appeared from the fronds and slid across his wounded hand. It emerged glistening red, its body covered in the boy's blood.

The Snake slithered away just a few feet, stopped, turned its head and looked squarely into the eyes of the boy. Not knowing what else to do, the boy snapped the arrow and dropped the pieces on the ground. When Snake finally crawled out of sight, the boy found himself wondering if all this had really happened. As if to answer his question, he looked at his palm and saw that the blood had ceased its flow from the cut. In fact, but for a fresh scar, it was healed.

So now you know something of the man Crooked Bow. And perhaps you understand why Singing Stone worried over the method that the People had agreed upon for choosing their chief. It may forever be a mystery how the legacy of cruelty can survive from generation to generation. People often think that a victim of cruelty will repair such injustice when he comes of age. But, so often, it is not so.

Singing Stone knew that she must somehow find another candidate for chief. She had no idea how she would convince the People to accept another person to lead them, but she knew she must try.

In her search Singing Stone made her way to the Lodge of the Basket-Makers. There she listened to women complain about their husbands or belittle the skills of the hunters. Carping and criticizing seemed to be the only sounds there. Not hearing the voice she needed to hear, she moved on.

At the Lodge of the Arrow-Makers, two craftsmen argued about the better oil to use on their cane shafts. Bear or Beaver … Opossum or Mink. Though grown men, they bickered like children. Singing Stone moved on.

At the Lodge of the Hide-Scrapers, three women forecasted the demise of the People. They were sure that the drought was a punishment from the Great Spirit. Hearing no hope in their voices, Singing Stone did not linger here.

She made the rounds to the village garden, to the Dugout-Makers, and finally, dejected, found herself at the river, where she sat and soaked her tired feet. The laughter of the children playing in the water was the sweetest sound she had heard all day. But then – as if everything in this day must sour – a fight broke out among two children and a chorus of cheering filled the air.

Singing Stone heard a long stride cut through the water, and soon the excited voices softened to a murmur. A man spoke and the fighting stopped. When the man's voice spoke again, there was laughter. Soon the children were playing again, and all was normal.

A little girl happened to walk from the water near Singing Stone. "Child," the blind woman said, "who was the one who spoke to the fighting children?"

"Oh, that was Fish. He watches us at the river when our mothers cannot."

"Tell Fish that Singing Stone wishes to speak to him."

In a short time, Singing Stone heard the long legs slice through the water and slow in front of her. "You wish to speak to me, Grandmother?"

"Yes," she said patting the ground next to her. "Sit with me."

They talked until the stars came out overhead. The children had long ago returned to their lodges. The sound of the river current was peaceful to their ears in the long stretches of silence that fell between the many topics that they discussed.

"Tomorrow morning," Singing Stone said, "before the sun climbs over the ridge, I want you to come to my lodge. I need you to guide me."

"I will be there, Grandmother," Fish promised.

*

Just as the eastern sky bloomed with light, Singing Stone stepped from her home and stood very still. She wore a yucca robe adorned with Turkey's feathers, and she carried her walking staff. She knew that Fish was there waiting. She could sense him.

"Where are we going, Grandmother?" Fish said.

She slowly pointed northeast. "Take me to Hogback Mountain."

(Just as Singing Stone did in the story, I pause in the telling long enough to point northeast toward the mountain that, in daytime, is just visible to us through a gap in the trees. I ask, "Does anyone remember the name of that mountain?" "Hogback," one of the students recalls. Then I continue with the tale.)

Fish stared into the dead eyes of the aged woman, who seemed much too frail to climb the mountain, much less undertake a Vision Quest, which was the reason anyone ever visited Hogback. But it was not his place to question an Elder. Without another word, she gripped his arm for guidance, and they trekked off toward the mountain.

Part way up the slope, Singing Stone felt Fish's body tilt back, as though stretching his spine. This happened repeatedly as they climbed.

"What is wrong?" she asked.

"Nothing is wrong, Grandmother. I am watching a Winged. It has been circling us."

"What Winged?"

"Well, I'm not sure. Certainly in Hawk's family, but ... I don't recognize it."

The trail finally stopped climbing ever upward and began snaking through a boulder field to a flat shelf of stone that overlooked the great valley of Itawa. Singing Stone seemed to know where she was, for she leaned her staff against the natural wall of rock and stepped to the perfect center of the stone.

"I will stay here for three nights. On the fourth morning, come back for me and bring me some broth. I will be hungry."

Now he knew that she did, indeed, plan on a Vision Quest. "But, Grandmother, four days?" He wanted to ask her if someone her age could endure such an ordeal. She had no food, no water. He looked around the rock shelf. There was no wood for a fire.

"If I am to learn how you are to become our chief, then I must empty myself so that the proper dream can enter the darkness in my mind."

Fish's eyes widened. "Chief?" he said. "But I am not very skilled at shooting a–"

"It is not the bow and arrow we should be concerned with," Singing Stone interrupted. "We must think beyond that."

He looked up into the sky, wondering what alliance already had been formed between Singing Stone and the Great Mystery.

"Go now," she said. "And remember to bring the broth."

Throughout that first day she sat on the rock and sang a song, her sightless eyes pointing toward the mountain ranges that stacked one behind the other like swollen waves spanning a broad, green river. That was how her father had described it when he had brought her here a lifetime ago. When the dusk-whistler Winged (Whip-poor-will) finished its repetitive calls and the cool of night washed over her, she lay down to enter the dream world, but sleep would not come. She was nervous about this rendezvous with the Great Mystery.

So, she thought, *I am not so different from the child I once was.* Recalling the time she had fasted on this mountain in her search for womanhood, she remembered it had taken three days to empty her mind of childish prattle.

In the morning she decided to be quiet throughout the new day. Again she sat, simply biding time with prayer and feeling the path of the sun by the warmth touching her face. When she lay down that evening, her back ached from sitting so long, and – once again – sleep did not come.

On the third day she determined to stand throughout the day, her feet firmly planted on the stone, her back against the rock wall. When she snapped awake at dusk, she was disoriented. Had she been asleep? She was still standing. Had there been a dream? No. She sighed and shook her head, worried now that she might not sleep during the night. She feared that she had spoiled her chances. From below in the trees, Owl seemed to reprimand her, and then there was no sound at all. It was the longest night of her life. When the first morning songs of the Wingeds rose from the valley below, Singing Stone was exhausted. As the new day dawned, she felt herself fading. Then … like a fog creeping into a valley … sleep filled her head. And with it came the dream.

Three poles stood in a row on an island of green. The pole at the center began to move – slowly at first, then swaying as if in a dance. A bright red bead of liquid – like a drop of blood – oozed down the pole, spiraling like a vine in reverse. Then a piercing scream split the air above her.

(At this point I capitalize on the opportunity to surprise my audience by rendering the high-pitched cry of a hawk.)

Something fluttered from the sky. Was it snow? Blue-tinted snow? The red-streaked pole now lay on its side on the green island. And that was all.

Awake now, Singing Stone lay very still, letting the details of the dream settle in her memory. Having been blind most of her life, she clung to the remarkable mental scenes that had formed in her mind. Though the dream had come, just as she had prayed it would, she had no idea what it meant. A light tread of moccasins

on stone told her that Fish had stepped onto the shelf. She sat up and drank the bladder of broth that was placed in her hands. Without the trespass of words on this fragile reunion, they descended on the mountain trail. Once again Singing Stone felt Fish slow from time to time and lean backward. He was looking up into the sky again, she knew. Once again, Blue Hawk was with them.

Where the trail leveled off, they stopped. Fish studied Singing Stone's face, wondering what message from the Great Mystery she might now share. Singing Stone felt his eyes on her. She knew he awaited her instructions, but what was she to do or say? Tell him about a dancing pole that bled and then fell?

"This is the day of the archery tournament," she said.

"Yes, Grandmother. The people are gathered at the sharp bend in the river."

"Then we must go there," she said.

Fish looked around at the unfamiliar forest and then at the sun. "I believe we can cut through the woods here," he said and led her off the trail.

They had walked only a short distance when Fish stepped into a clearing and made a simple sound in his throat, one that this entire story hinges upon. "Hmm," he hummed to himself. It was a barely audible utterance, a mere sign of mild curiosity.

"What is it?" she asked.

"Oh, nothing really, Grandmother," he replied. "This is a place I did not know existed. I have not been here before."

"What do you see?" she asked.

Fish looked around the clearing "It is an opening, shaped in a circle. The grasses here are thick and soft like the under-fur of Beaver. Three trees grow here in a line."

Singing Stone's grip tightened on Fish's arm. "Tell me about the trees," she said.

"The one on the left is the Crooked Arrow Tree *(sourwood)*. On the right is the Shadowtree *(hemlock)*. In the middle is the Sacred Bow Tree *(yellow locust)*." Fish stopped breathing. "Grandmother! The Bow Tree is trembling!"

Singing Stone felt Fish lean back again to look at the sky. "Watch the tree, Fish. Watch for the blood."

Looking back at the locust tree, he exclaimed, "Something is coming down the trunk, Grandmother. It is a Snake … Red Snake! I have seen him once before!"

Snake spiraled down the tree, stopped, and lifted its head so that it was looking squarely into the eyes of Fish. Then Snake swelled its muscles and constricted, compressing the wood into a dense spiral. Fish described to Singing Stone every detail of the strange event unfolding before him: Snake gliding to the ground, leaving the tree trunk distorted and misshapen, Snake stopping, looking back at Fish and then disappearing into the forest.

(Here I pause and look around at rapt faces. The audience is silent and expectant. Quickly, unexpectedly, I make the hawk cry again!)

Above them a scream filled the sky. Blue Hawk was so close that both witnesses felt the air from its powerful wing-flaps.

"Grandmother!" Fish breathed. "It is the Sacred Hawk! The one that no man of Katuah has ever seen."

Hawk hovered in place. From a sudden flurry of wing-flaps, three blue feathers fluttered to the ground. Then Hawk began to rise in a spiral.

"Hawk has left us three feathers, Grandmother."

The stillness of the forest gathered around them. Singing Stone took in a deep breath of thanks.

"Collect the feathers and lead me to the Crooked Arrow Tree," she said. "I will make an arrow. You must cut down Snake's tree and make a bow."

Fish fashioned a crude hand-axe and chopped at the tough trunk. Singing Stone slid her hands along the Crooked Arrow Tree until she found a straight branch. She broke it from the tree and tied the blue feathers to the shaft using a strand of yucca fiber torn from her robe. Stripping more fibers from her robe, she twisted a bowstring. When Fish had a bow completed from the distorted wood, together they bent it and fastened the string.

"Break a small bough from the Shadowtree," she instructed. He did. Taking the evergreen needles, she rubbed down the bow and then the arrow and said a prayer.

"Now," she said, "we must hurry to the river."

The tournament was almost over. Standing on the far side of the River Itawa from the villagers, Fish described to Singing Stone the scene of the contest. Three archers remained. There was Runner, Gray Otter Woman and, of course, Crooked Bow. They were backing up to the river, preparing to shoot at a distant target suspended from a tree limb. A drumbeat began a steady cadence, and the three archers sprang into action.

Only those who were close to the contestants heard the trick employed by Crooked Bow. It was a twanging sound he made with his tongue, making the others believe he had shot. Runner fell for the trick and rushed his shot, missing by a good arm's length, but Gray Otter maintained her composure and gracefully released the string. Her arrow struck the edge of the target and spun it in a shallow

circle. The People cheered. At the sixth drumbeat Crooked Bow loosed his arrow, which smacked the target at its center. The roar of the crowd doubled at such a shot.

For the final round, these two contestants now stood at the edge of the bank with their backs to the river. When the drum started, Crooked Bow said something to Gray Otter – something that made her hesitate. When she saw that he was already loaded, she hurried. He made the sound with his tongue once again and followed this with an airy whistle through his teeth. The woman seemed to abandon the grace that had carried her so far in the tournament. Her arrow flew wide, missing the target by a hand-span.

The drum beat a fourth time, then a fifth. Crooked Bow casually drew his string and aimed. The People did what all spectators do when an arrow is about to be launched. They turned their eyes to the target to see the moment of impact. When the arrow flew, it fairly screamed. (*I make the hawk cry again!*) It seemed to sail in on a blue wind. The shaft struck with a decisive slap, pierced deeply into the target, and sent the stuffed woodchuck spinning so wildly that no one at first noticed the blue feathers. The seventh drumbeat struck and the crowd roared. It was the grandest shot they had ever witnessed.

The People looked to Crooked Bow to see what his face might register after such a magnificent performance, but they saw only the back of his head as he searched across the river to see who had sent this arrow fletched with the feathers of the Sacred Hawk. Crooked Bow's arrow was still resting across his bow.

Across the river a man stood alone on the sand. In his hand was an oddly shaped bow. No one noticed Blue Hawk perched in the tree high above the target, just as they had missed its arrival with the arrow clutched in its talons.

Into the river ran the People, splashing and laughing as they surrounded Fish. Lifting him onto their shoulders, they carried him to the contest side. Crooked Bow, knowing he could never make such a shot as the one Fish had performed, slunk away into the forest where he would not have to witness the rejoicing.

*

That night around a large fire in the square-ground, Fish laid out a plan for group hunting strategies, for dispensing food among the people, and for overseeing the old ones who had no family to care for them. These were the first of many ideas that would win him a place in the hearts of the People as a great chief.

Two moons after Fish had assumed his role as chief of Little Itawa, on a night so dark that torches of pine knots were lit in the square-ground, someone scratched at the door-flap of the chief's lodge. As he always did, Fish called out for his visitor to enter. When Singing Stone stooped through the doorway, Fish dropped the fishing net he was repairing and crossed the floor to meet her.

"Grandmother, where have you been all this time? I have not seen you since the day of the tournament."

"I have come to ask a favor," she said.

"Anything, Grandmother. What favor can I do for you?"

"Give me the Medicine Bow. I have found the place for it."

Fish looked at the twisted bow hanging on his wall. "It is yours, Grandmother. I had never intended to shoot it again."

He lifted down the bow and handed it to her. Then she opened her arms and he stepped into her embrace, the bow nestled into his back.

"Stay strong for the People," she said.

Those were the last words anyone heard spoken from the old blind woman named Singing Stone. When she shuffled across the square-ground carrying the bow, the torches cast flickering shadows across her stooped back. This was the last time anyone saw her.

But not so the Medicine Bow.

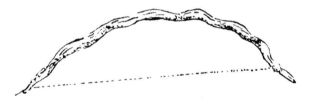

Three decades ago near the Etowah River, a bow was found in a cave, the location of which is known to only one person. The finder's name has never been made public. On the ceiling of the cave are fifty faint pictographs painted upon the stone. These pictures depict the story that has just been told to you – beginning with the drought that lasted for four years and climaxing at the tournament that decided who would lead the People.

The series of illustrations was interpreted by anthropologists from various universities across the Southeast. Most curious was the closing part of the story:

"And the Medicine Bow was laid to rest, having never been used to pierce the flesh of man or any living creature … but for the good of the People. The Medicine Bow shall rise again, and all who pass under it shall become as an arrow, taking its good medicine with them wherever they go."

I pause at this point and do not reveal that this is the end of the story ... for there is no end. Even though someone always asks, I do not label the story as real or fiction. Its importance, I explain, lies in what happens next ... after these listeners leave this place called Medicine Bow. I look at the confused faces around me and inform the listeners. "Did you know that you have passed under the Medicine Bow?"

Blank stares encircle the fire. I stand up.

"Would you like to see it?"

When we leave the glow of the fire circle and enter the darkness, the act of moving into the forest on its terms is like a symbol of our recognition that the real world waits for us to step outside the boundaries that have been imposed on us by custom. Atop a fifteen-foot juniper totem that I have planted upright in the earth rests the arc of twisted wood that symbolizes the Medicine Bow. It is an eye-catching shape – a five-foot section of arced sapling that had been strangled by a vine, leaving a corkscrew sculpture, its ends stretching the bowstring tightly.

I click on my flashlight and spotlight the bow as all gaze upon it in silence. It is a memorable moment. Running up the totem are fifty scenes that I have painted on the wood, each rendering a prominent scene from the story. I highlight the chapters of the story with my beam and listen to the children's excitement as they discover familiar images and fill in the text for each illustration. When I turn off my light, I repeat the last lines of the story.

"The Medicine Bow shall rise again, and all who pass under it shall become as an arrow, taking its good medicine with them wherever they go."

Erecting a Legend Pole – After your "story of place" has firmed up over time, make sketches of the story's salient moments. These will be used as "starter" templates for the totem's pictographs. Choose a dead juniper or locust tree (or buy a treated 4"X 4"X 14' post) that will resist rotting when buried in the ground. Use post-hole diggers to excavate a 3'-deep vertical cylinder into which the base of the pole will be sunk. Erect the pole and tamp dirt firmly as you fill around the base. Paint the pictographs in order from bottom to top, allowing the sequence to spiral up the pole. Apply varnish after drying.

A Group-made Story Totem or Legend Pole – As an alternative to creating this monument yourself, ask students to contribute a few of the paintings after each telling of the story. This provides a long-term project completed by multiple artists over the years.

A Story of Place Epilog – I have learned that students (of all ages) love to be tested on the details of an epic story. The day after I complete the 2-night telling of the *Legend of the Medicine Bow*, I hold a "Wilderness Quiz Show!" This contest monopolizes our time around the campfire for that night. It never fails to be a favorite evening program.

To set up this fun event, let each student know that his/her name serves as a quiz-show buzzer. When a contestant (anyone around the fire) knows the answer to one of your questions, she tries to be first to say her name. (The first name you hear is the person to call on to answer.) Think up a question about your storyline and phrase it in such a way so that the most important word(s) come last. (This prevents too many buzzers from going off before you have completed your question.) Here's an example of a wrong way and a right way to compose a quiz question:

Wrong: "*Singing Stone's robe was made of the fibers from a certain plant – what was it?*" (By the time you have said "made of," several buzzers are, no doubt, going off.)

Right: "*What plant was used to make … Singing Stone's robe?*" (Answer: *yucca*)

If an incorrect answer is given, go on to another question and return to this one at a later time. This quiz can be performed with or without keeping score. If the former, have one who answers correctly pick up a dead stick. At the game's end the participants add their sticks to the fire in ascending order as the teacher counts out loud. The winner has the honor of being last to feed the flames with the most fuel.

Other question samples: "*Of all the places visited by Singing Stone in her search for a chief, name two groups of specialists where she listened.*" (*Lodge of the Basket-Makers, Arrow-Makers, Stone-Knappers, Hide-Scrapers, Dugout-Makers, or gardeners.*) "*What materials were used to make the tournament target?*" (*Woodchuck or groundhog skin, dried grass*) "*Where did Fish give the gift of broth?*" (*Hogback Mountain*) "*How far did Crooked Bow shoot when he shot at the black rat snake?*" (*The width of the River Itawa*) "*What physical possession distinguished the visiting archer competitor from the west?*" (*Arrowheads of shiny black rock [obsidian]*)

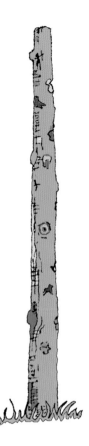

"Though scientists may never verify an answer as to what fundamental, defining trait differentiates man from the creatures of the wild, I will set forth this theory: Could it be that we alone can imagine what it is to be someone or something other than ourselves? And if so, then by practicing that God-given skill, are we not only more human ... but also more humane?"

~ Shadowfox

CHAPTER 11
Slipping into Someone Else's Skin
~ teaching empathy through storytelling ~

Early in my career as an environmental educator, I had the good fortune to meet a timber wolf in Georgia. He was fully-grown with long sinewy legs, huge feet, a scruffy coat, and eyes that penetrated deep into my soul. This animal had been illegally raised from a pup by a man who faced criminal charges for his transgression. The wolf had been confiscated by Fish and Wildlife and secretly penned in a temporary holding cage on National Park land one mile from my home. A park ranger friend passed along this "classified" information to me, and naturally I visited the wolf. What naturalist wouldn't? The outcome of this fortuitous meeting provided a wonderful educational opportunity for fifteen fourth-graders on the following day.

I had been consigned to lead a small field trip for a nearby school with the expressed purpose of using Nature as the venue for a creative writing exercise. According to plan – and with the permission of the Park Service – I met the school vans at a pre-arranged spot on a backroad at the edge of the forest. The students and their teacher had no idea what was in store for them.

With notebooks and pens in hand, we walked a half-mile through the woods, stopping sometimes to investigate and explore whatever caught our fancy.

Only when we were one-hundred yards from the wolf did I gather the students together to let them know that they were about to experience something out of the ordinary. Everyone promised not to utter a word. And they all promised to walk quietly and move slowly.

By the time we reached the clearing with the cage, the students behind me were faithfully following my stalking example and as quiet as mice (though that might seem a risky creature to emulate for the situation). Like a class of dedicated Tai Chi devotees, we inched into the clearing and approached the pen. The wolf was waiting with his fiery glare, having heard and smelled us long before we emerged from the foliage.

No one needed to be told this was a wolf. There can be no mistaking an adult timber wolf. Moving in respectful quiet, we slowly sat in the grass in a semi-circle and simply observed. The wolf remained a statue, looking back at us. He gave no indication that he was familiar with humans. His eyes were intense.

For five minutes no one moved or spoke, including the wolf. Then I slowly, gracefully stood and gestured to the others that they rise. They followed my lead as we backtracked into the forest. The mode of stealth they had adopted earlier stayed with them as we traveled well out of earshot of the wolf. There we stopped, and I gave them their instructions.

"I'm sure you know that you have just visited an honest-to-goodness wolf. You will be the only people privileged to do so. Later I will explain to you the circumstances of this wolf's captivity, but first you have an assignment.

"By walking through these woods and stepping out into that clearing, you had quite a unique experience. I'm sure you'll relate the story to many people tonight. But your experience was mild compared to the wolf's. What was it like for him? What was it like to hear our approach from the woods? To smell our varied scents? What did he feel as we revealed ourselves in such a careful way? When we sat and settled in, what went through his mind? Throughout those silent minutes as we watched him, what did he presume was going on? Did he have expectations, fears, hopes, or confusion? What were his thoughts as we so unobtrusively exited and left him to his solitude?

"I want each of you to find a private place, get comfortable, and settle in for your assignment. Write the wolf's story. Crawl into his skin, wear his fur, and think like him to relate the story of his visitation by us. Cover every moment of those five minutes."

And so they did. And the results were wonderful. For the thirty minutes that these children sat in the silence of the forest and imagined the feelings of a wolf, they had transcended to a place outside themselves to experience a new perspective. I'm willing to bet that they never again saw a wolf in a film or magazine without revisiting some relic of the empathy they had practiced that day in their fourth-grade class in the woods. That kind of shift from the daily mechanizations of the ego has got to be of value.

An Essay of Empathy

– It is not at all necessary to have such a unique animal as the wolf for an exercise in creative writing. Looking through the eyes of any creature is a worthwhile project. The central subject of an essay could be a squirrel, a cricket, a wren, or a spider. As a teacher you simply need to provide an opportunity for your students to observe any wild animal. The ideal venue for this study is in the animal's natural habitat, so that the students are able to witness a part of its daily agenda in the wild.

Build a blind (hiding place) or gather your students in a room near a window where all can watch a chapter in the life of a squirrel. Take notes on each physical action the squirrel performs. Fifteen minutes into the study, tap on the window just enough to get the squirrel's attention. Observe its reaction. Finally send one student outside to walk past the squirrel's arena of activity until it reacts to human presence.

The students now have enough data to construct a story that reveals the squirrel's point of view. Here are some writing points to help them get started.

1. Based upon this animal's actions or personality, make up its name.

2. Why was the animal at this particular place?

3. Make an assumption about exactly where it lives.

4. What, precisely, was the animal doing?

5. What sensory experiences did the animal encounter?

6. What did it have to worry about during the entire scenario?

7. What precautions did it take regarding these potential dangers?

8. What did it think when the glass was tapped?

9. What went through its mind when the human approached?

For a first experience this exercise can be performed as a group, as written here. On subsequent occasions ask each student to make the project a solo effort done completely outside. Such an experience is infinitely more meaningful. It involves constructing a blind and then employing secrecy, stealth, and patience. Each essay can be told as a story. One story per day will afford each writer the respect his work is due. With so many different animal species to write about, this could be the never-ending exercise.

Plant Stories

– For an advanced empathy exercise, consider using a tree as the main subject. First, read to your class some of the fascinating research

about what plants sense and how they react to stimuli. Preparatory reading for the teacher might include: *What a Plant Knows* by David Chamovitz, Scientific American/Farrar, Straus and Giroux and *The New Yorker* article *The Intelligent Plant* by Michael Pollan, Dec. 23 &30, 2013.

"She opened her palms to the sky and waited until the sun floated above the river. Through the din of the falls, she sent a prayer, using words that had been spoken for centuries in the land south of her from the Alleghenies to the Appalachian foothills in Georgia."

~ Natalie Tudachi, *Blue Panther Woman of the Anigilogi clan,*
Let Their Tears Drown Them

CHAPTER 12
Giving Birth to Transition
~ *the voice of ceremony* ~

When a worthy idea – such as a promise to oneself or a vote of gratitude – becomes important enough to us that we have need to pull it from the abstract world into the physical world of speaking and showing, we begin that transformation through ceremony. By performing ceremony we create a tangible, historical, quantitative act that can take its place in memory alongside all the other physical chapters of our lives. Ceremony passes a mystical light over the unseen so that it may be seen. It is a conversation that begins in the deepest chamber of the spirit and connects with the highest Power to which we acknowledge our existence.

As an example, if a person begins a quest to acquire courage, it is one thing to carry around a notion defined by weightless, untouchable words; but it is quite another to go through the steps of a ceremony. The ceremony is a physical act performed on a specific date at a specific time at a specific place. In this case, the one seeking courage might carve a stick down to clean wood and dab on it nine red dots of paint along its length. Each time he consciously performs an act of bravery, he carves away one red mark. Such a physical experience (the carving) becomes a moment indelibly marked in memory. Such an event will produce a memento – the stick freed of all paint – that will remind, insist, and inspire. Courage has taken its first step.

Religions use ceremony. That fact alone suggests that ceremony is a special practice. Some religions set aside exclusive times for certain rites – a day of the week, a time of the day, certain weeks of the year. Native American spirituality might be said to be more inclusive, for – by tribal custom – life and religion are integrated equally during every moment of every day. This does not mean that, for native people, every second is somber and reverential … or even peaceful. It simply means that the religious ethic suffuses all aspects of life.

It does not matter what healthy religion a person embraces, ceremony can enrich any life, if for no other reason, because the experience asks one to stop and pay attention. One need not belong to a special sect, tribe, nation, team, or affiliation. Anyone has the right to create and implement ceremony.

I encourage teachers to create ceremony for a class. Perhaps the way students walk with minimal footfall through the forest is a ceremony. Or maybe sitting in silence among the trees to *listen* for the varied calls of birds is a ceremony. Especially if these activities are given a repeated place on the class agenda. For acts like these to be considered ceremony, one has only to name it so; and, by naming it, we give it a loftier position of importance. Both of these simple examples serve to strengthen the bond between the human and the real world. Is that not reason enough to employ them?

Here I will share with you six ceremonies whose roots lie in the philosophies of Native American tradition, but these events cannot be called Native American ceremonies. I have not sought to replicate exactly what has been done before, but to absorb the points that resonate with me, assimilate them, and redirect them for my own needs both as an individual and as a teacher. I have found inspirations in other ancient cultures, too, (some European, some Asian) and I have just as readily adopted ideas from these philosophies. If there is something here in these pages on ceremony to enrich the manner in which you and your students live your lives, I am gratified. If not, I hope that the prospect of creating ceremony will at least stir up your own ideas.

A Way with Plants

Whenever I ask a group of people – adult or youth – to sit on the ground, I watch them to see what they do with their hands. Most cannot remain idle. Fingers get busy dismantling, digging, tearing, or breaking something within reach, all this in a distracted, unconscious way. If the group is sitting on grass, that patch of grass invariably gets hand-pruned.

This simple observation might be a telling statement about modern humans. Busy hands are unconsciously disassembling leaves, peeling bark off dead sticks, breaking twigs, or digging a hole. Sitting in the forest with hands at rest … at peace … is a very different experience. One is *controlling*; the other is *open to something larger than self*.

A person moving through a forest generally exhibits a similar mentality in the manner by which he handles the plants he passes along the way. Does he weave through shrubs and saplings by sliding through the foliage or leave a trail of minor wounds – breaking, ripping and crushing. Such damage is probably subconscious, nevertheless it brands the wayfarer's experience, as intrusive rather than integrating with Nature.

It is an arguable point, but I am suggesting that such "automatic" destruction of plant life – even on this small scale – is symbolic of a mindset which is, at the least, foreign and removed, if not adversarial and fearful. It could be said that this rough handling of the forest is simply a failure to recognize plants as fellow living beings. (An average person walking through a crowd of strangers on a sidewalk certainly does not pinch or pluck or tear at a passerby's clothing.) However, for one holding a deep-seated fear about the unknowns of the forest, that reaching-out-to-do-harm could very well be an involuntary and preemptive effort to show Nature who's in charge!

Raising a person's awareness about plants is sure to cure this habit of unpremeditated harm. In fact, the way one handles plants can be ceremonious. Invariably, as students learn more about plants, they begin to handle a leaf as if it were a brittle page from an historical document. This way of interacting with plants (or anything else in Nature) goes a long way in creating the elevated relationship for which so many strive with the natural world. It is the human who must recognize Nature's long-standing invitation to intimacy and initiate the interaction by *choice*. (Long ago, there was no choice. Every human enjoyed this bond with the Earth as a matter of course.)

The concept of ceremony with a plant is certainly germane when you consider taking a part of or all of a plant for food, medicine, or craft. It was not so long ago that most Americans probably "said grace" before a meal. Replicating this rite in the forest would seem to make sense to one who capitalizes on the edibility and nutritional contributions of a wild plant. Unfortunately, most urban American children of today do not recognize grocery greens as actual plants that once rooted in the soil, just as they do not see a red slab of meat wrapped in plastic on a Styrofoam tray as part of a once-living animal. They may know the source of these commodities in an academic sense, but they do not connect source to commodity without some prompting.

Some native teachers have suggested that, if you approach a plant in a careless or selfish manner, that plant might change its chemistry and deny you the very quality for which you harvest it. Whether or not this is true, the respectful approach allows the harvest to transcend to a more meaningful experience, where awareness and intent is crystal clear … where the harvester is fully in the present tense and acknowledging the worth of a plant. Recognizing the worth of anything is, in itself, a worthy practice.

An ancient Cherokee harvest ritual once included circling a plant specimen a certain number of times and then approaching it from a certain direction before taking a part of it. Often a gift was offered and buried in the soil. Words were spoken.

Whether a ceremony is Cherokee or Jewish, Episcopalian or Druid, most of its details are probably more symbolic than utilitarian. Formulas are often very arbitrary. This leaves the realm of ceremony wide open to any and all who would

enter it. A practitioner of ritual is free to design any approach he or she deems suitable for the occasion. Inventing and carrying out ceremony transforms man's use of plants to a sacred act.

The Harvest Ceremony

 – It begins with you, the teacher. Create a personalized way of saying grace to the plants at harvest time. Even if you are merely utilizing one blade of broad-leaved plantain for a wasp sting, the ceremony that you employ has the effect of lifting the experience from a *taking* scenario to one of *gratitude*. Whether the words are spoken aloud or internally, researchers suggest that chemicals (pheromones) waft through the air and carry a message. Is this conversation a monologue or a dialogue? There are differing opinions on this point, but by initiating the conversation you at least open yourself to the perspective of the forest. In such an empathetic state, are you not better equipped to absorb the world around you? I maintain that you will better feel, hear, see, and smell the forest, as if your senses have been heightened. Furthermore, gratitude is a positive practice that works for the good of the harvester.

Introducing Ceremony

– Many students feel awkward about the idea of engaging in ceremony. To introduce the concept, have each pupil research one ceremony of any culture around the world and then demonstrate it. Class discussions can probe into the origins of these rites: Why did people invent them? What purpose do they serve? Why do some topics of people's day-to-day lives include the practice of ceremony while others do not? What ceremonies still exist within your students' family lives?

Now that the subject of ritual is out on the table, reveal to your students an overview of the Cherokees' plant harvest: circling four times, approaching from the south, bestowing a gift. Ask for ideas about what these acts symbolized.

Next, share with them the harvest ceremony that you created for yourself. Tell them matter-of-factly why the practice feels appropriate for you. Then give each of your wards this project: Imagine that you are a member of a tribe, and it is your job to devise a <u>silent</u> harvest ceremony for your people to follow. (Without having to speak, these young students will be more apt to follow through on the project without embarrassment.) Have each inventor pantomime her formula for the class, and then ask the others to attempt to interpret it, to see who can accurately analyze it. Finally, allow each "author" to explain the details and symbols of the performance.

After this academic interaction of invented rites, students may feel less inhibited about personally entering into a ceremony, which is where we are heading. You can begin an introduction to ceremony participation by declaring a special day in your class, in which everyone honors the resources used that day.

"Origins Day" in the Classroom

 – On a prominent shelf in the classroom establish a row of jars to serve as receptacles for a simple ongoing ceremony. Label each jar with a symbol to represent one resource in Nature: tree, river, rock, soil, four-legged animal, bird, fish, insect, plant, and wind. On the other side of the room hang a large bag of marbles. These marbles will be dispensed like an offering to the natural sources of the items the class uses on a regular basis.

At arbitrary moments throughout the day, ring a bell – the signal for all to pause to consider whatever item(s) they might be touching at that moment. Choose a student as a starting place and help initiate the recognition process.

"Robert, I see you are holding your science book. Where do books come from?"

Robert ponders his textbook. "A bookstore?"

"Before that," you say. "What do we use from nature to create books?"

Robert taps a page. "Paper is made from trees!"

Now Robert has earned the right to walk to the bag, remove a marble, and walk it to the shelf of jars, where – as all watch – he drops it into the "tree" receptacle. It is important to suspend the discussion of resources until Robert has returned to his desk. It is this pause that elevates the event to ceremony.

Going down the row, you call on the next student. "Marion, you are writing on a piece of paper. Besides paper, anything to recognize as a source?"

She holds up her pencil. "This is made of wood."

Marion drops another marble into the tree jar. The next student is chewing after taking a bite of sandwich.

"What kind of sandwich, Will?"

Will studies his food. "Wheat, mayo, turkey, lettuce, tomato, salt, pepper …"

"What if we concentrate only upon the second and third items?" you suggest.

Will frowns. "Well, I know a turkey is a bird … but what about mayonnaise?"

"Can anybody help Will?" you ask.

Anne raises her hand. "My mom and I made mayo once … with eggs."

"Hens lay eggs!" Will announces. "Another bird!" He places two marbles in the "bird" jar.

As you can see, there are lots of opportunities for discussions (and revelations) about sources. In Will's sandwich description alone, he brought up three categories: plant, bird, bird, plant, plant, rock, plant. Take nothing for granted about your students' knowledge about sources. Chances are good that someone will learn something new about every subject.

If, down the line, a student near the end of the seating cannot think of any new item to cover, remind him of an article of clothing he is wearing: a cotton shirt (plant), leather belt (four-legged), metal necklace (rock), etc. Or consider the electric lighting in the room. In your geographical area, is it powered by coal (rock) or hydroelectric (river)? Don't forget to include air (wind) as a topic. If, when you ring the bell, someone is on her way to the water fountain or bathroom, suggest she give her attention to the water she is soon to drink, wash with, or flush.

Each time you ring the bell, start the discussion at a new beginning point among the rows of desks, so that the same students are not always burdened with thinking up those last, less obvious ideas.

At the close of the day, have the students count marbles to determine which resources were most frequently tapped.

The Pragmatic Side of Ceremony

One winter I returned to the hickory tree that I had only days before chosen for a bow that I planned to make. I knelt before the tree and laid my hatchet on the ground. Taking the trunk in my hands I said the words that had become my chosen ceremony – assuring the tree, the forest, and the Creator of the respect I would afford the tree, its wood, the future bow, explaining my need for the bow, and asking for forgiveness in the cutting. I looked up at the story of the tree, at its history as it was recorded in the shape of trunk and branches.

In this moment of quiet, a tiny shower of fine particles wafted down through the air and sprinkled over my hands. Looking back up at the trunk I saw a tiny hole where more of these fine particles seemed to puff out of the tree. It was very fine sawdust. A beetle was inside the tree gnawing at dead wood to establish tunnels for laying eggs. Sawdust and dead wood means "dry-rot."

Though that tree is still alive today, it was not a good candidate for a bow. My harvesting it would have been a waste. I have often wondered if the time spent in a plant-harvest ritual also serves as an intentional and last opportunity for inspection. Those few quiet seconds that I spent watching sawdust drift down from a hole in the bark spared the needless killing of the tree.

In these times of instant gratification and electronic immediacy, anything that causes a person to pause and consider his surroundings, by my estimation, has value.

Medicine Bundle

Everyone who spends time in the wild eventually develops special ties to certain trees or animals or rock outcrops or rivers or other landmarks. This attraction might be purely aesthetic. Or perhaps the bond is the result of an experience or a moment of enlightenment that occurred at that locale.

Your relationship with natural objects can be as important as the bonds you enjoy with intimate friends and life-changing teachers. Perhaps all things that exercise positive influences on us should be considered sacred. One need never search for the explanation or appropriateness for such a bond. It is beyond scrutiny. Such a tie is a matter of the heart – intimate, and fulfilling … and, possibly, atavistic.

There are even places that I consider parental, based upon what they did for me in my coming-of-age time, things my human parents could not or did not know how to do. When I revisit these places, I feel the need to acknowledge what was given to me. Such places are worthy recipients for a gift from the spirit. Such is the medicine bundle.

The medicine bundle, a Native American concept, is a simple collection of gathered materials (usually natural, but not always), bound together by some kind of wrapping. There are no rules or requirements about the materials. The significance of the contents and the wrapping is known only to the bundle-maker.

Decades ago, when I was exploring the forests along the St. Croix River in Wisconsin, I found a three-foot tall maple sapling with a dozen tea-bag-sized packets wrapped in bright-red felt and tied to the branches. This little tree possessed all the festive appearance of a Christmas tree. Less than a quarter-mile from Ojibwa land, I knew I had stumbled upon a place of special import to someone living on the reservation.

Moving on, I was left to wonder about what momentous event had inspired the gift of so many medicine bundles. Perhaps someone had repeatedly begun his hunt for meat in this place … or spent time on a Vision Quest … or conceived a child there. The reason was not mine to know, but I understood that this place had been celebrated by some individual, and the power invested into that celebration changed my experience in those woods. The feeling was like visiting the site of some famous historical event, only the event would forever remain a mystery.

The red felt covering of these bundles stood out like fire, making the array of gifts a bright contrast to the surrounding trees, ferns, and mosses. This was, no doubt, the intention of the bundle-maker. Today those red bags would be gone, returned to the earth by natural means, placing this ceremonial practice in the realm of evanescent art … like sand painting.

For reasons that I could never adequately explain to another person, I have a close tie to our native gray fox. I can say the same for the hemlock tree. From time to time, I find a fox that has been recently killed by a vehicle on the road. It is difficult for me to move on and ignore the corpse. If decomposition is not advanced and if skin damage is not prohibitive, I honor the fox by respectfully skinning, tanning, and preserving its pelt. Finally, in a quiet ceremony I bury the remains deep in the forest. (Skinning and tanning is covered in *Secrets of the Forest, Volume 3*.) I store this pelt for wrapping medicine bundles. The other part of my bundle, an evergreen sprig of hemlock needles, is available at any time of the year in the forest.

Making a Medicine Bundle — After making a one-foot length of bark cordage (see *Secrets of the Forest, Volume 1*), gather select materials from Nature (or from your personal belongings) that are in some way integral to you. This might include a chip of bark from a favorite tree, a pebble from a meaningful place, a lock of your hair, words written on a piece of paper, etc. Fold these items inside a small scrap of material (consider cutting this from clothing that you once wore) and secure the wrapping with the rope. Choose a location that holds significance for you and then tie the bundle there to honor that place. **Alert: Using or possessing any "non-game" or "non-vermin" bird's feather is a federal offense that carries a steep fine. This law is designed to protect birds from people who would kill these animals and then lie about how they obtained the feathers. (Examples of legal feathers: turkey, grouse, duck, goose, crow. Examples of illegal feathers: eagle, hawk, robin, wren, bluebird, vireo, jay.)**

Leaving a medicine bundle tied to a tree changes your relationship with that place. At any moment in your life, you can pause to visualize your gift in the quiet of the forest. It is like a memento forever reminding you of the importance of place … and, if you will, reminding the place of you. Whenever you return to that site, you will feel a heightened sense of belonging to that piece of the land.

Medicine bundles are used in any number of ways to honor a place or event. They have been left on riverbanks at the outset of a canoeing trip. Some mark a spot whence a prayer was sent or where a marriage proposal was accepted. Others denote the site of a personal victory (whether emotional, occupational, physical, or mental) or where a special animal sighting occurred. It might be said that medicine bundles are bookmarks that highlight the important pages in one's life. They are both anonymous and personal, never to be deciphered by another, which, to my mind, makes the presentation all the more powerful. Both the making of the bundle and tying it in place embody ceremony. It is a simple act but a profound declaration of one's regard for how he leads his life.

The Hunter's Prayer

The Cherokees whispered a prayer to the animal they were about to slay. Or if time did not allow for a preparatory prayer, hunters spoke their words of gratitude over the slain body. This prayer acknowledged the Cherokees' dependence on the animal's skin, meat, bones, brain, sinew, feathers, antlers, and the many other usable parts. They understood that they became part-deer or -turkey or -squirrel after ingesting that animal's meat. The truth of that interconnectedness is as valid for a person eating in a fast food restaurant today as it was for a hunter stalking with bow and arrow eight-hundred years ago.

Consider this prayer whispered by a hunter as he slowly raises his arrow and draws his bowstring:

"Deer, my brother, forgive me. I take your life and give it to my family. Your muscle becomes our own, so that we may run like you – swift and quiet. Your skin will cover us, as we borrow your beauty and blend with the colors of the Earth. Your stomach will cook our meals. The oils in your hooves will keep our clothing dry. Your antler will sharpen the stone tips of my arrows. I honor your life through my own."

Since most of us do not kill the animal-food that we eat, we are left with the option of saying a belated prayer at mealtime.

Composing a Hunter's Prayer

– Help your students to learn about the sources of their foods. In order for them to connect to *the real world*, they need to know the facts about what they put into their stomachs. Trace the history that explains the transition from hunting in the wild to domestication on the farm or ranch.

Give each student a topic to research regarding one of the foods they eat. Then, armed with that knowledge, have each one compose a prayer of thanks for that food. Each prayer should reveal something about the life of the plant or animal as it was raised for food, where and under what conditions it was grown, and how the nutrients, vitamins, and minerals of that particular food are utilized by the human body. Give each student a chance, over time, to say the prayer aloud over a meal that includes that dish.

The Spirit Stick

Discussing a spirit stick should be a one-on-one conversation – just as talking to an individual about any personal topic ought to be. This preparatory conversation does not ask the student to talk about anything too private. The details of how he might utilize the ceremony of a spirit stick need not be disclosed.

A person interested in bettering himself in some specific area of personality or habit or ethic is the perfect candidate for making a spirit stick. This opportunity might come about after a disciplinary encounter between student and teacher, but such a confrontation is not necessary to justify the use of a spirit stick. For a particularly challenging student, make the spirit stick yourself and offer it to him along with the explanation. The spirit stick will simply be a physical, visible tally of a specific behavior. Ask the student to consider a quality that he would like to eradicate from his personality. Or consider a quality that he does not possess but would like to own. He has the ability to do either, because humans possess the gift of *choice*.

It may not be true that anyone can be whatever he wants to be (not everyone can be a concert pianist or Olympic champion), but I contend that anyone can be whatever *way* he or she wants to be.

Making and Carrying a Spirit Stick

– Choose a firm, dead stick about pencil-size and shave away its bark. Near one end carve a groove around the stick

so that you can attach a thin bark rope to secure the stick to a belt loop or shirt button or wrist. In a straight line running down the stick, dab on 9 little spots of pigment – paint, dye, ink, etc. Wear this stick to raise your awareness of your quest, whatever it might be.

Here are some quest examples: to become less dependent on someone; to not surrender in a problematic situation; to be a quieter person; to be more understanding and less judgmental; to become more generous; etc. Each time an opportunity arises to test your conviction (you will be acutely aware of the arrival of such an opportunity because you are wearing the stick), if you successfully meet the challenge, carve away one spot of color from the stick.

Wear the stick until all the spots are gone. Never explain to anyone what you are doing, because your intent can be biased if you know that other eyes are watching for examples of your mission.

Here is an example of the whole scenario:

Perhaps you have spent enough time around someone you admire to learn that one of those qualities you respect in her is the ability to listen to others without interruption. When the time is right, you notice, she offers her comment on what was spoken to her, but she does it in a way that does not monopolize the conversation.

You realize that you are not like her in that way. You feel interruptive. You fear you talk too much. You want to change that about yourself.

Prepare the stick and wear it. During the day, someone approaches you and begins a conversation. Because you wear the stick, you are more aware of this situation as a test. Throughout the conversation, you consciously wait for your friend to complete his thoughts before you reply. Once – because of a ridiculous thing he says – you start to correct him, but you don't … you wait … you listen. When the time is right, you offer your suggestion.

If you maintain that mode of restraint and mindful response throughout the conversation, when he leaves, you can scrape away one spot of pigment on the spirit stick. If you had interrupted even just once, no spot should be erased.

Saving the Earth

Virtually every author who writes about the interaction of man in Nature has one underlying goal: to educate us to the point of changing our attitude about some aspect of the natural world. Writers and researchers harbor passions for their subjects, and they want to pass along some of that enthusiasm *for the sake of the subject.* Their hope is that an attitude change might bring about a behavioral change. Such an adjustment to our daily lives might have a positive effect on the welfare of a writer's subject, be it wolves, wildflowers, rivers, trees, or an endangered species of insect.

We're talking about conservation. "Conserving" means "saving." "*Save* the manatees!" "*Save* the spotted owl!" "*Save* the trees … go paperless!" "*Save* our neighborhood from a toxic dump!"

Each of these missions is but a fraction of the overarching aggregate of all quests: "Save the world!" But taking these quests one at a time is how we enter that arena.

I maintain that conservation cannot be fully taught by words alone. It must be self-realized after an important revelation occurs: *A person must have a reason to care about a subject before he will act on its behalf.* Actions require motivations. The reasons to care can be aesthetic, spiritual, pragmatic, scientific, or emotional. All of these rationales get their start in personal experience.

In other words, if we expect our new generations to embrace conservation, we've got to get them out there with the trees and rivers and wildlife. And in doing so we want to ensure that they have a positive first-experience so that they'll want to go back. If we can provide that fun experience in the wild, Nature will do the rest. We will see armies of converts take over the stewardship of the Earth.

To use the word "convert" says a lot about our time in history. Intimate relationships between humans and Nature once formed automatically. In the pre-Columbian days on this continent, the native tribes lived in a complete give-and-take arrangement with Nature that marked them as masters of survival skills and the apotheoses of gratitude. For Native Americans, knowing the fine details of plants, animals, water, weather, dirt, and stones was both necessary and commonplace. There was nothing esoteric about it. How could they not be grateful for what sustained them?

> *A person must have a reason to care about a subject before he will act on its behalf.*

In the ancient days even children wended their way through the "garden of plenty" as competently as the youth of today navigate the electronic pathways of a computer, cell phone, or video game. Once, appreciation for natural resources was instinctive and logical. The first consumers went to *sources* for their needs. Today, sources are separated from end-products and, therefore, hidden.

The facts of consumer statistics and the ecological ethics of certain philosophers can be inculcated into students' consciousness like multiplication tables, but true conservation requires tapping into the heart to release one's passions. For example, a student might read a report about the endangered status of a wood duck in a certain area, but only a person who has waded into a swamp to see the wood duck and her brood might develop a true sense of protectiveness toward them.

It is one thing to read sobering reports of city water pollution, but it could be argued that only a person who has hiked along, swum in, fished, or canoed a healthy stream might be moved to save a river in trouble. Only then might a person be interested enough to investigate our urban wastewater system and the impact humans have on natural waterways. A child who has seen only polluted waters is apt to accept sullied water as the norm.

Early in childhood, flushing a toilet becomes a mindless practice for most Americans. Young ones have seen family members send a just-killed spider down the toilet (with the aid of three to seven gallons of cleaned water). Rare is the child who gets educated about the water used in daily household life. Where does it come from? Where does it go? How does it get cleaned? Answering these questions with words might be compared to a boring sermon … unless the listener was already emotionally invested in water through his memorable experiences with a creek, river, or lake.

Once your students have experienced a stream through fun, adventure, and exploration – enough to fall under its spell – then it will be time to reveal all the ways that we impact that stream by our everyday habits. This same sequence of events is true for all other environmental subjects. People have to care about something in order to take care of it.

We have no shortage of subject matter: air pollution, water pollution, poor land management, erosion, over-harvest of trees, methods of mining, pesticides and herbicides, chemicals used in livestock sustenance, global warming, consumer ethical choices in the store, humanity toward animals, non-recyclable product packaging, population, and more. Once a student adopts a sense of stewardship toward the Earth, your lessons can branch out to any of these environmental areas known so well to the twenty-first century.

Most important in these lessons is that our work go beyond stating problems to include *finding solutions*. The wounds of the world can be overwhelming, so let us start with the home. If students can affect change in their daily family life, they can learn the confidence needed to take on a larger arena of problems. It is not the scope of this book to define every issue that has snowballed into the decline of our environment. I take it on faith that by picking up a book like this you are already well-informed on the ills of the environment. My hope is that the activities that follow will help you to make use of that information in a ceremony that can begin the reversal of these ills.

As hackneyed (and as preposterous) as the phrase may seem, "saving the world" is literally the goal of conservation. The trick is to attack it by spoonfuls with your students. Isolate one thing you can do … and then do it! Experience a success … and let that success inspire more successes. Rather than feeling defeated about how little you are doing, *be triumphant about what you **are** doing.*

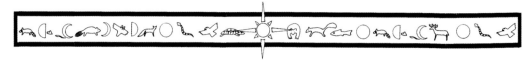

Here is just one example of a project for a class:

 ## *Air Pollution and the Greenhouse Effect* – Of the many contributors to this threat to our planet's well-being, one that involves all of us is: the excessive use of our motorized vehicles. As individuals, are there ways that we can lessen the carbon footprint spewed out by our cars?

First, have each student make a detailed list of every use of the family car(s) for the past three days. This will require a collaborative effort with parents. With that data in hand, your class can begin discussions about ways to reduce travel-time. You can kick-start these talks by mentioning ideas; such as: better planning for shopping trips, getting more done in a single trip as opposed to multiple trips for items that were accidentally left off the list. Talk about alternative transportations: like buses, walking, running, and bicycling.

Gives-to-the-Earth Ceremony

After each class research on some aspect of environmental woes and their solutions, use ceremony to affect a change. A Gives-to-the-Earth Ceremony provides an opportunity for commitment. Your students are now poised to begin the process of "saving the world," beginning at their homes. Because this ceremony includes multiple participants, you will need a respectful way to control how all talking is done. It is time to make a talking stick.

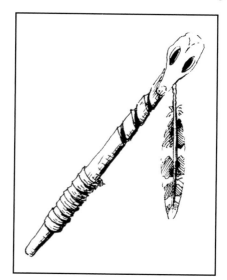

Making a Talking Stick – Carve and/or paint an interesting stick with any design that differentiates this stick from all others. Make the end product pleasing to the eye, perhaps something to elicit awe, by attaching a skull, feather, leather wrapping, or a string of beads. On the occasion of a ceremony, this piece of art will serve as permission to speak. Only a person holding the talking stick may speak around the fire. Any person has the right to step forward and take the stick from its resting-place, but as long as a person holds the stick, that person maintains center stage, and her words must be honored by respectful silence.

A Gives-To-The-Earth Ceremony – After many in-depth discussions about natural resources, consumerism, and conservation with your students, announce a Gives-to-the-Earth Ceremony to be held around a campfire in three days. This gathering will be an opportunity for courage and commitment … a time to make a promise to the Earth. Each student should bring to this event 1.) a specific commitment to the environment and 2.) a specially painted "promise stick."

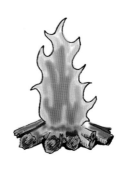

The *promise stick* should be painted with a symbol that relates to the subject matter of the coming oath. For example, air could be represented by a pictograph of wind: three undulating arrows of white. Water can be rendered by the same picture in blue. Wildlife by a simple silhouette of any animal. For plants, paint a tree.

On the night of the ceremony the teacher, with the talking stick in hand, begins by rising and standing in front of the campfire to face the students. She explains the environmental issue she has chosen to address, states her personal promise that explains how her interaction with this issue will make a change for the good, and then lays her promise stick in the fire to seal her commitment. Finally, she faces the others again and says, "I have spoken."

To continue the ceremony she passes the stick to a student. And so it goes.

Challenge your students to erase the word "try" from their promises. Instead of "I will try to …," make the promise "I will …" At the end of each declaration, the speaker says: "I have spoken!" as a way to let all know that the talking stick is available to another person … and as a way to show his earnestness in the promise.

Here are some examples of promises I have heard spoken proudly around the campfire during this ceremony:

"Wasted electricity calls for burning more coal, which pollutes the air. From this night on I will turn off all lights and appliances that I am not using. I will also teach my little brother to do this. My promise tonight is for the air. I have spoken!"

"Paper is made by cutting down trees. From this night I will write on both sides of a sheet of paper before recycling it. In this way I reduce my paper waste by fifty per cent. I will ask my teachers to honor this new habit. My promise is for the trees. I have spoken!"

"Our lands and oceans are tainted with garbage. I will treat all those locking plastic sandwich bags that I use for lunches just as I treat my socks. I will wash them and reuse them instead of throwing them away. My promise today is for our thrown-away things. I have spoken!"

"Our rivers have to carry so much waste water from our homes. Much of that comes from our washing machines. I will do one simple thing to reduce that pollution from my home by using my bathing towel many times before I send it to the dirty clothes hamper. I once thought that a towel was dirty after just one dry-off. I now realize how illogical that is. Each time I step from the shower, I am clean. I'm simply using the towel as a clean water transfer device. From me to the towel to the air. And I'm also trying to set a speed record each time I shower. So far my fastest shower (wet down, soap up, rinse off) is twenty-two seconds! My promise is for the rivers and streams. I have spoken!"

 ## *Gives-to-the-Earth Follow-up* – One month from the original ceremony, have all promisers return to the campfire for an evening of relating some experiences in fulfilling their promises. Let the talking stick pass to all.

 ## *The Nine Directions* – In a quiet circle in the woods, share with your students the idea of the nine directions by reading to them the text below. Then give to each a printed copy. Afterward, ask them to reveal how each direction carries a link to each of their lives.

Prayer to the Nine Directions

~To the East, where each day the sun is born, I turn to beginnings … of ideas, of commitments, of friendships … I turn to the path ahead.

~To the South, where in winter the sun swoops low to touch only the mountain's south face, I turn to clarity, art, honesty, observation, and detail.

~To the West, where each night the sun dies, I accept the gift of closure, the endings of old habits, paths I have trampled, time past and those parts of myself ready to be left behind. I acknowledge death.

~To the North, where winter's shadows shroud the mountain in dark mystery, I marvel at the beauty of that which I cannot understand, and I rejoice at the quickening of my heart to the unknown. In the dark of the north glows the smoldering ember of courage that I must breathe into a flame.

~To the Earth, my greatest tangible gift – through whose generous bounty I and all the beings of land, water, and air are nourished. The Earth is truly

the nine directions

our mother. At her four corners, the seasons mark her river of time from which I take a humble sip and strive to mark my own passage with a mindful step.

~To the Heavens, where perhaps in its vastness lies the home of the Maker of All Things to whom I give thanks for all that is. In the Heavens I turn to the Great Mystery ... the Creator.

~To the universe inside Myself, where my spirit abides ... where through choices I mold who I am ... I explore the strengths and weaknesses that balance who I can be. Here lies talent and conscience falling like stars into me from the Great Mystery. Here lies honor – validated by virtue of my own creation. Here lies the thinker, the poet, the listener, the warrior.

~To the bond of One-to-One, I look into the eye of my loved one, my blood brother, the fox, the hemlock, a stranger. We are connected.

~And One-to-the-All ... I acknowledge my place in the invisible web of life and strive not to overstep my boundary there but share the stature of the eagle and the spider as we turn together in the Great Circle of Life. I face all people and hope to understand that I am one of them ... that I am one of us. We are all connected.

The Giveaway

This traditional Lakota ceremony might fail to impress many modern non-native Americans, whose lives have become a narrative of amassing material things as a symbol of success. But the concept of this Give-Away rite is profound. When I first learned about it, the closest event to which I could compare it was giving the gift of charity. As a little boy, on those Sunday mornings before Christmas or Thanksgiving when my Sunday school had asked us to bring in donations for the poor, I opened the family pantry and looked over the shelves for a can of asparagus or beets or some other vegetable that was low on my list of palatable foods. Upon arriving at Sunday school, I dropped the canned goods into a cardboard box that would be carted off to a needy neighborhood.

I never saw anything in that box that I would have wanted to eat. We were taught to feel good about this giving. Indeed I was happy that I would not have to eat those beets or asparagus.

It is another concept altogether to give away things we truly want. Perhaps this is one of the profound differences between the first Americans and their conquerors. If giving away something of value does not come naturally to us, then it can become an opportunity to expand *who we want to be*. The giving can transcend from sacrifice to privilege. Such an act can bolster self-esteem and personal honor. You have to participate in a Giveaway in order to understand the depth of this ceremony.

Each time an article is passed from one hand to another in a Give-Away, it is a transforming moment for the giver, for the receiver, and even for the ones who stand by and watch. It is evident that some audience members feel some envy for those who receive a gift, but it is also clear to me that these same observers experience a similar envy toward the givers. Even as a receiver walks back to the crowd carrying his present, it is the givers who seem now to own something of greater importance.

 <u>Holding a Giveaway</u> – This ceremony works best, I believe, when held as a formal ending of a discrete session or gathering: the last week of school; the day that a summer camp ends; the final hours of a workshop. For a family wanting to create this experience, I suggest setting an age at which one may join in this ritual as a giver. In this way, a young one can anticipate the event in a later year and feel its importance pending during his growth toward maturity.

One way to implement a Giveaway is to honor a single person to be the sole giver. It should be a position that is earned. Bestow the privilege upon someone who in some way has earned a place of respect among the others by some deed that was done. Save the group Giveaway for a time in the future, after the ceremony has been established as one that honors the giver. In this way the students will want to be givers.

Early in the school year or camp session, explain to the children the concept of the Giveaway. Inform them that the privilege of being a giver will be awarded to someone who earns it by displaying character traits that contribute to others. This might be the camper who tries to ease the discomfort of a homesick loner ... or the student who speaks up with the truth when the truth is difficult to admit. This one who merits the title of "giver" will learn of a coming ceremony by finding a special symbol wrapped and waiting in a place where only she would find it.

This symbol should be something unique but familiar to all because you have revealed it to them: an unusual piece of jewelry; a found animal bone or distinctive piece of wood or stone with a pictograph etched on its surface; a turtle shell whose carapace plates are painted in various colors; a feather whose quill is wrapped in felt and leather; etc.

When the symbol is secretly delivered, include a date and time for the Giveaway. If this candidate accepts the offer, announce the date of the ceremony to your class and invite all to attend. The giver will bring however many items she wishes to present.

Begin the event by lighting a pyre or candle. At that point, the event belongs to the giver. Standing before her friends, she holds out a thing that she has cherished and then speaks about its history. Next, she speaks to the person to whom she presents the gift ... and why she has chosen that one. That chosen person then walks from the crowd to the giver and without words takes the item. If this giver has more to give away, she holds out the next gift and repeats the process with another recipient. When her giving is concluded, she joins the audience. To end the ceremony, snuff out the flame. The less said, the better.

Holding a Group Giveaway – When your class of students has achieved a mutual bond of camaraderie, announce a group giveaway in which all may take part. For this expanded version of the rite, make use of a talking stick. One giver presents his gift(s) and then passes the talking stick to another who takes his place. Repeat as needed.

The Closing Ceremony

Whenever a gathering is about to disband and its members poised to scatter to their respective homes, it is a good practice to recognize each person as an integral part of the experience. Of course, you, the teacher, could take on this project of praise yourself; but there is a better way that injects a feeling of intimacy as students wait to be assessed.

Closing the Gathering – With a group seated in a circle, ask each person to look at the person to his left to consider what that person contributed positively to the gathering. What social element might have been missing if that person had not been part of the group? You, the teacher, can begin the testimonials by speaking about the person to your left, and then after you have passed the talking stick, that person speaks about the next ... and so on.

Though a few might at first feel shy, awkward, embarrassed, or seemingly "above" this exposure of emotion in praising someone else, generally people of all ages seem to be hungry for this kind of intimacy. The way that you, the teacher, begin this ritual is important. You must keep it believable and sincere. Don't exaggerate.

If you are lucky, it will not be your testimonial that most inspires. When one of the participants shows the courage to speak openly, the ice is broken. That peer legitimizes the idea of expressing feelings about others. Often a chain reaction occurs, and this simple ceremony taps into powerful moments. Even if one member does not deliver as well as you might hope, you may see that he is secretly rapt within this circle of sharing, as others are in the spotlight. There are no losers in this experience.

"Remember the sacred word 'choose.' You can become any way that you want to be."

~ from the Ceremony of the Three Sticks

CHAPTER 13
Defining the Spirit
~ the naming ceremony ~

Long ago I was honored by a friend when he asked me to take the creative part in his naming. He had, he said, reached a plateau in his relationship with the natural world that fairly begged for some new definition of himself *in terms of the natural world*.

He knew that the Native Americans had derived names from Nature. He also knew that I had studied Native American history. A common friend had told him that I had carried such a "spirit name" for myself for some time, and that was why he approached me.

When he came to me about a name, I shared my spirit name with him. When he asked why I had chosen that particular name, I chose not to reveal the rationale for my name. I answered his question only in general terms. He too, I explained, would be just as protective of his "definition" once he had been given a name. He accepted this willingly, and later – after receiving his name – he understood the privacy of such matters.

The ceremony that resulted was a powerful chapter for both of us. He received a name that he came to cherish, and I began a service of dispensing spirit names. Since that day I have developed and formalized the naming ceremony, which I have used with thousands of people from fourth grade student, to corporate CEO, up to octogenarian retiree … and every walk of life in between.

The naming ritual reaches a place in the spirit where self-esteem lives, where inspiration thrives and guides us to follow our own personal codes of ethics and conduct. The spirit name represents the best of who we are … something we can-

> *The spirit name represents the best of who we are . . . something we cannot be all the time, perhaps, but can return to quickly if its symbol is close to our consciousness*

not be all the time, perhaps, but can return to quickly if its symbol is close to our consciousness.

The Native Americans were, in their naming, often poetic, always relevant, and trait-defining, even though the wording of the name might seem to be "in code." The substance of a name could evoke personal pride, strength, and courage for the name-bearer at critical times in his life.

Because native people lived intimately with Nature, they lived in awe of it – as anyone would who acknowledges the gifts of the Earth. So it should come as no surprise that these people drew their inspirations from the perceptive eye of Hawk, or the patience of Oak, or the economy of Worm. Early people craved this identification with the wild, not unlike some sports teams do today. Native names were constructed by the vocabulary of wildness – something that was misinterpreted by whites as paganism or Pantheism. (Consider the irony of the contemporary controversy over sports teams that use native names – Braves, Redskins, Utes, Seminoles, Illini, Blackhawks, Indians, etc.)

This desire to be associated with respected facets of Nature was powerful for the native people. The needs of some non-native people are no different. Those of us who recognize in Nature "the real world" have the same right to this connection. Anyone can take a spirit name. (I never refer to this appellation as an "Indian name," as so many people are wont to do.)

For many people who seek to better understand themselves and their place in this world, this naming practice from American Indian philosophy leaps from the pages of history books to their minds and hearts. I recognized its worth in my life and adopted its basic premise as naturally as I would turn to cool water to slake my thirst. Yet my naming ceremonies are not historically formulaic – not replications of any tribal ritual – for I am not a Native American. A historic, tribal formula would not be mine to use.

Anyone can respectfully borrow sound ideas from any culture in the making of their own ceremonies, ultimately making the rites their own. Need, creativity, and a little knowledge about the natural world are the necessary tools. Whatever ceremony you invent, its intent and content are as valid as any other rites developed by cultures throughout history all around the world.

At this point in my life, most of my close friends possess spirit names, and most of these people are non-native. The choice to obtain such a name is not "playing Indian." A self-made ceremony is as authentic as a marriage, christening, bar mitzvah, or school graduation … simply because we deem it so.

As namer, I treat the act of naming with sincerity, respect, and privacy. My part in the naming in no way manifests any power in me other than the gift of creativity and my respect for every individual's potential.

After I am asked to perform a naming, I present a naming candidate with three questions she must answer. She is instructed to write her answers on a piece of paper and mail them to me well before the ceremony. If there are to be multi-

> *A self-made ceremony is as authentic as a marriage, christening, bar mitzvah, or school graduation … simply because we deem it so.*

ple namings for a group (school class, circle of friends, summer camp, etc.), I set a deadline weeks before the event. It takes time to create something that is intended to last for many years.

My standard approach in naming is to work on a name until I myself would be excited about that name were I that person and it were given to me.

Here are the three questions:

1. Do you have an ineffable tie to a certain kind of wild animal native to our continent? This tie might be marked by an intense interest in that species, a feeling of "relating" to the animal, frequent dream confrontations, or an instinctive need or striving to observe the animal. If, at this moment, such an animal is not in the forefront of your mind, then you do not have such an animal. Omit this question. Do not try to conjure up one, as this would be a mistake. If you do have such an animal, name it.

2. We all have reputations among our friends. (I refer to positive traits only.) How are you known by the people who know you best? For example: Are you attentive to detail, a good listener, one who finishes what is started, strong of will, able to cope with disappointment, good at physical balance, one who rebounds from failure, fleet of foot, etc. What quality would be most often used to describe you by your friends?

3. What personal quality resides inside you – perhaps unknown to others – that embodies the essence of who you are? This trait defines the core of you, celebrating your uniqueness, a quality that you love dearly and know to protect. This question requires much more thought than the first two.

By answering these questions, the namee and namer enter into a partnership. The namee is, in effect, naming herself by providing the salient information, while the namer serves as an interpreter, getting the words into a natural order that is befitting of a name.

Once the name is bestowed and the choice of name explained in full, that explanation (of a spirit name) is seldom shared by the newly named one. (Of course, this explanation is never revealed to anyone else by the namer.) If the namee discloses this information too frequently, she might dilute the personal power inherent in the name – in the same way that bragging about a deed done tends to diminish the worth of the deed.

Since I, as namer, never divulge naming information about a namee to anyone else, I cannot share with you, the reader, an actual historical example of a naming. In its place I offer this hypothetical one to help you get started in the naming process.

A Naming

Let us say I have received the answers to these three questions from Mary, an office manager in a printing shop.

1. My animal is a coyote.

2. My friends think that I am a peacemaker – that I am good at helping people resolve their differences in a civil way.

3. I love to read. My favorite books are like friends. When I am reading I feel that I am transported to the place about which I am reading, as if I soak up the writer's words to the fullest extent.

As I begin my work in the naming I start with the image of a coyote and spend time thinking of this animal's lifestyle. What is it that a coyote does in reality that is similar to these personality traits? I consider both answers for a while and realize

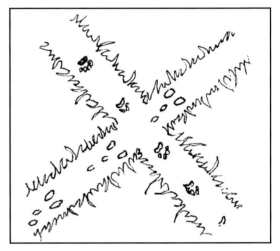

that a coyote does do some exemplary reading. It's called tracking. In fact, we often refer to examining a track as "reading a track." Even though the coyote reads mostly with its nose, the symbolism of "reading" is still valid. At this point I have advanced my image of the coyote to include the skill of following tracks. A tracking coyote is now at the center of my naming image. A picture rendering this animal can be as realistic or symbolic as you prefer.

How could a coyote promote a peacekeeping situation? At this point I exercise some poetic license. Imagine this tracker extraordinaire (the coyote) ascertaining those crossing points where a rabbit's daily run might intersect with a fox's hunting route, or where a snake's sinuous path might bisect the trail of a mouse.

To prevent the violent confrontation of predator and prey, coyote might seek out each crossing of paths and use this site as a place to howl (sing) and thereby discourage any animal from approaching that potential death site. One ancient symbol for singing is a line that loops from the mouth of the singer – like a lower case, cursive "e."

A poetic, long-version name emerges at this point:

<u>Coyote who follows the tracks and sings at their crossing</u>

A short-version name is then derived from this for conversational use:

<u>Cross Track Coyote</u>

This was a common Native American practice – to bestow a long formal name and a shorter conversational name. Another general rule was to bestow a "child-name," which was used until the time that the namee reached adulthood, at which time an "adult-name" was bestowed for a lifetime.

Of course, there are plenty of alternate options that would have worked for the short-name: "Singing Coyote" or "Tracking Coyote" or "Coyote Howling on the Trails." I much prefer those names that are filled with mystery, challenging a third person to wonder about the choice of words.

The image of a coyote creating a disturbance at an intersection of trails need not be logical or feasible or practical. It can be surreal. (In reality, coyotes do not attempt to foil the hunt for other animals.) What matters is that it symbolizes two important character traits. In fact, the more fabulous the idea, the more interesting. Taking this coyote out of the realm of realism adds a measure of mystery to the name. Everyone deserves mystery.

spirit name symbol

Next I draw a symbol – a picture that represents the long-name:

The symbol shows a coyote at the convergence of two trails. The swirl mark that loops back on itself is an historical stroke from early drawings that denotes singing. Varied tracks adorn the two paths to signify the egalitarian nature of peace-keeping.

These are the three gifts that a namee receives on the night of her naming: long-name, short-name, and symbol.

Matching Human Traits to Animal Lives – To get you started in
the naming process, let me help you practice your poetic license in the transference of human traits into symbolic animal behavior.

Consider these answers from a (fictional) student who has chosen to be named:

Animal: wolf
Reputation: good soccer player
Special talent: I'm good at drawing

First, let us consider all the facets of soccer and see if any one of them suggests some lupine activity. In soccer, an athlete:

1.) Runs while controlling an external object (the ball).

2.) Kicks or sends an external object to a comrade.

3.) Controls an external object with its feet.

4.) Sends an external object to a specific place for a reward (a goal).

5.) Guards a prized piece of ground (goal) and bars entry into it.

6.) Works while on the run and in harmony with a group of comrades.

7.) Performs on a special territory before onlookers.

Can you take one of these above features and assign it to a wolf? Let's look at some of the aspects in the life of a wolf.

A wolf:

A.) Digs a den for shelter and protection of newborn.

B.) Attends to the needs of family life (like bringing food to pups).

C.) Hunts in a pack, runs down prey by group maneuvering, and shares food.

D.) Achieves food harvest by either bringing down prey with its jaws and teeth or by pressing down smaller prey with its forepaws.

E.) Maintains a hunting territory that other predators must honor.

Here are some possibilities when you cross-reference the two lists:

1C, 1D, 2C, 3A, 3D, 4B, 5A, 5B, 5E, 6B, 6C, 7E

The process is manipulative – making one side of the list fit another – but, again, it is the symbolism that will be appreciated, remembered, and understood … not logic.

Now repeat the same exercise for these different animals offered as the answer to question 1: squirrel, snake, hawk, grasshopper, fish. The creative exercises required for naming will get easier as you learn more about animals.

The Spirit Symbol

There are four qualities that make a successful symbol:

1.) Ease in drawing. Hopefully the namee will want to make frequent use of the symbol as a mark of identification for personal property, signing a work of art, painting a spirit shirt, signing a letter to a friend. (Now that tattoos have become the rage, many of my students have chosen to mark themselves indelibly with their spirit symbols.) You'll want namees to be able to render the drawing fairly effortlessly. The more primitive the animal drawing, the better – like an ancient pictograph on a cave wall.

2.) Attractiveness. No one wants a symbol unpleasing to the eye. Each time I draw a symbol, one of my goals is that someone will later look at it and comment on its beauty and uniqueness.

3.) Uniqueness. Include fine details to represent every facet of the formal long name – details that only the namee understands.

4.) Mystery. This can be achieved by going beyond a realistic drawing with normal proportions, letting a dynamic part of the drawing dominate the scene, or using surreal colors for otherwise familiar objects.

To help you with your drawings, refer to books on Native Americans that show the pictographs they used in their rock paintings and winter counts (tribal annual records painted on a framed animal skin). You will get a feel for reducing an animal or other natural subject to its basic spare lines. One book that contains many such drawings is *Indian Sign Language* by William Tomkins, Dover Publications.

The Naming Ceremony

Adults

For adults, I write out all of the naming explanation on paper. Every rationale for name and symbol is described in detail. At the ceremony I hand out their papers (folded) and ask the namees to leave the fire circle with flashlight to wander out into the night to find a private place for their introduction to their spirit name. I strongly believe that adults should be alone at this moment, so that they are not burdened by other people's presence, questioning looks, reactions, or expectations.

I ask each adult namee to settle in comfortably before opening the folded paper. To allow several minutes of silence and stillness to prepare the mind for a special occasion. When he opens the folded paper, he should *look first at the bottom of the page to see all of the finalized material: the long- and short-names and symbol.* These three gifts should be studied before he reads any of the written explanation. Why? Because this is the one and only time in his life that he will be able to see and hear the mystery of his spirit name as others will – without benefit of interpretation. Once he has appreciated this blind exposure to his new name – and contemplated the possible connections to himself – only then does he read all the text I have written that explains his naming. At this point all the mysteries of the unexplained name and symbol become clear.

While the namees are scattered out in the dark reading their papers, those left at the fire circle (previously-named people) remain quiet. In our ceremony we beat a drum steadily – representing a heartbeat of the Earth – reminding all that this time is dedicated to and honoring those being named … and reminding all that the Earth is present at our ritual. This naming will tighten the bond between each namee and the Earth. After all, the new name uses the vocabulary of Nature.

Children

For younger namees, I have each child enter my tipi (any special spot with privacy would do: a candlelit stump on a hill; beneath a spreading grandfather oak; on the sandy bank of a creek; beside a boulder where spirit symbols are painted on rock; etc.) where I deliver the long and short names verbally and then hand to the child a piece of paper with those printed names and a drawing of the symbol. I give the namee about a minute to absorb the words and picture. Then I explain the details of every part of the new name and the symbol and answer any questions the child might have. This moment is a gratifying one for both namer and namee. It creates a memory never to be forgotten.

<u>Tea for the Naming Ceremony</u>

<u>**Tea for the Naming Ceremony**</u> – On the day of the night's naming event, describe to your group the detailed appearance of a tree, shrub or herb with which the group will make a ceremonial tea. Give each student one botanical characteristic of the plant to remember, so that finding and identifying the plant becomes a group effort. When the plant is found (and verified by you or a person knowledgeable about plants), form a circle around the plant and have each student reach out to contact the plant as you speak the Harvest Ceremony (see Chapter 11). Present to the plant a medicine bundle made by all. Dig for or cut off the part needed, carry it to a nearby creek for gentle washing, return to camp, and make the tea. (See *Secrets of the Forest, Volume 1* for an abundance of sources for teas.) Let it sit through the day. Some tea suggestions: black birch (twigs in summer, root in winter), sassafras root, loosestrife leaves, mint leaves, New Jersey tea leaves, pine or hemlock tree needles.

<u>*Black Birch as a Ceremonial Tea*</u> – In the mountains black birch (*Betula lenta*) offers a popular taste as a tea. Its wintergreen flavor seems to appeal to everyone. It is a perfect ceremonial tea, because it should not be drunk on a frequent basis. Used in moderation it is safe and delicious. It can be harvested quickly in any season with very little impact to the tree.

On the day of an evening naming ceremony, my dozen namees and I strike out just after lunch to find a birch for tea. Collectively we make a medicine bundle to leave on the tree, our way of showing gratitude and respect.

Before we leave our base camp we have a lesson on this special tree and assign to each student one descriptive trait that will help us to identify it. Once these clues are memorized, our group is armed with all the information needed to find the tree. The quest takes on the adventure of a treasure hunt.

Listed below are those features for you to use should you find yourself in either black or yellow birch country.

1. In my area black birch prefers to grow on cooler, north-facing slopes.

2. To assess number one, one of our group must understand the path of the sun for that season so that cardinal directions can be determined anywhere in the forest.

3. The tree is cautious about having its roots "drown" in very wet weather, and so it usually shows a lot of root exposure on the ground's surface.

4. Black birch bark shows random splotches of silver gray and dark gray. Yellow birch's (*Betula lutea*) more papery bark is golden with some gray.

5. Where the bark splits, it tries to scroll like a thick, crusty paper furling at the edges.

6. The bark shows lots of prominent, horizontal pores (lenticels) that look like dark, raised dash-marks.

7. Dark or rough stipule scars show on the trunk like inverted V's where present or former branches emerged.

8. Birches produce a great many dwarf twigs called "spurs," whose leaves might appear to be opposite because of the crowded nature of stunted twigs.

9. The leaves actually grow in an alternate pattern, as can be seen on larger limbs.

10. The leaves are double-serrate (double-toothed) with a cordate (heart-shaped), asymmetrical base and an acuminate tip (an S-shaped line-of-beauty curve).

11. Veins are pinnate, with the lateral veins very straight.

12. A scratched twig in spring/summer or root in fall/winter emits a distinctive wintergreen aroma. (This tree makes wintergreen oil or methyl salicylate.)

In the green seasons we harvest part of a living branch. In the cold months we dig for a root, follow it to a secondary root and cut a small end section. Never use the leaves, which work as a diuretic.

For a small pot of tea (one quart) we use a branch comparable to one #2 pencil … or a root half that size. Roots should be gently washed of dirt. Either source

In search of the black birch

needs to be scored before submerging into hot water to steep. This preparation (the making of the tea) is all part of the day's ceremony and performed by all.

<u>Holding a Naming Ceremony</u>

<u>*Holding a Naming Ceremony*</u> – This ceremony is always a much-anticipated event; after all, it is an occasion completely devoted to those doing the anticipating. The personal nature and promise of the ceremony creates its own formality. Watch the foreknowledge of the naming ceremony temper your students' behavior that day.

Prepare the tea and then choose a naming area that is within sight of the main campfire area. Almost any place can be made special by the inclusion of a lighted

harvest ceremony

candle or small fire. Your na-mees must know how to find this place easily from the main campfire.

Gather at dark around the main fire. (Have a pile of medi-um-sized sticks of firewood col-lected to ensure plenty of light for visibility.) Each person in the fire circle will need to see the faces of all the others. Let your tea warm again during the ceremony, but don't allow it to come to a boil.

Around the main camp-fire, talk about the concept of a name's pertinence and mys-tery. That is, no other individ-ual before or after the student will warrant such a long-name, because no other person is ex-actly like that student. Every name is a celebration of the best of who that person is. All who hear that name will wonder about its meaning, but none except the namee will be privy to its meaning.

I like to tell the story of the Lakota named "Man Afraid." He was renowned for his daring exploits in battle – crashing his warhorse into the horse of his enemy. His name held great mystery, for those who might know only his short-name were in for a tactical surprise. His long name was "Man Whose Horses the Enemy Are Afraid Of."

Explain how the naming will proceed. When you are ready to walk away from the campfire to the naming area, ask a veteran to begin the beating of a drum … as a reminder for all remaining at the fire to be quiet. (If a drum is not available, use two resonant sticks.) Each drummer can beat a slow cadence for an agreed time and then pass the instrument to another veteran. As long as the drum beats, all tongues at the fire are to be silent.

Walk away from the fire to the naming place, where you have another pyre or a candle set to be lighted. Lighting it is the signal for the first namee of the evening to walk from the fire circle to you at the naming place.

Sit in silence together for half a minute. Before you speak of naming explana-tions, tell the namee his long name. After another half-minute of silence, reveal the shortened version of his name. Then show him his symbol on the paper you have prepared. (This paper contains only the long name, short name, and symbol.)

Remind your namee that this time of being introduced to his name can never be repeated after this night. At this moment, he sees and hears his name as others always will hear and see it – without benefit of interpretation. Then explain in detail the meaning of the long name, how it represents all the facets of the namee's written qualities.

Encourage him not to reveal the meaning of his name to anyone for at least one year. Throughout his life, he might choose to share this information with a very few close friends or relatives or a spouse.

Give to this namee his paper and send him back to the fire circle, where he is to tap the shoulder of the next namee. That one will then leave the circle and come to you.

When it is done and all have returned to the fire, join them and take the drum and set it aside. Stand and hold the talking stick and explain that the group is going to share just once the formal long version of their names. Ask each namee to stand when he receives the talking stick. He should speak his new name with the volume and pride that reflects the special honor of possessing those unique gifts that contributed to his naming. (So as not to rush the saying of the names around the circle, ask that each speaker receive the talking stick, stand, and listen to his own heart beat nine times before speaking.) Once he has revealed his name, he passes along the talking stick and sits down.

If someone in the circle chooses not to participate in the naming or has never received a spirit name, do not exclude him. Have him stand at his turn and speak his full name as given by his parents.

With the mysterious long names still resonating in the circle, wait a few moments so as not to rush the ceremony. Then repeat the ritual for short-names – the names that shall be used openly on the next day. Do this three times to give all a chance to learn the names. On the fourth round, ask each namee to take the talking stick in his turn and then pause, giving the audience time to silently recall the name about to be spoken. When this one then speaks his name, each audience member can assess the accuracy of his memory.

On the fifth round, hold the talking stick and look across the fire at the person almost opposite you and say, "Across the fire I see my friend, Cross Track Coyote. Who calls your name?" (This demonstrates that you remember that person's short name.)

Though you still hold the talking stick, she recites your spirit name because you have requested it. If she cannot recall your name, help her. Then pass the stick to your left and ask that person to repeat the process with the person seated to Cross Track Coyote's left (your right).

(Note: If there is an odd number of people at the fire – including yourself – start with any person across the fire from you. If an even number, do not start with the person who bisects the group across from you … but start with either person to the bisecting person's side. In this way, when the talking stick reaches that bisecting person, the same name exchanges are not being repeated by the same two opposite people.)

Every name is a celebration of the best of who that person is. All who hear that name will wonder about its meaning, but none except the namee will be privy to its meaning.

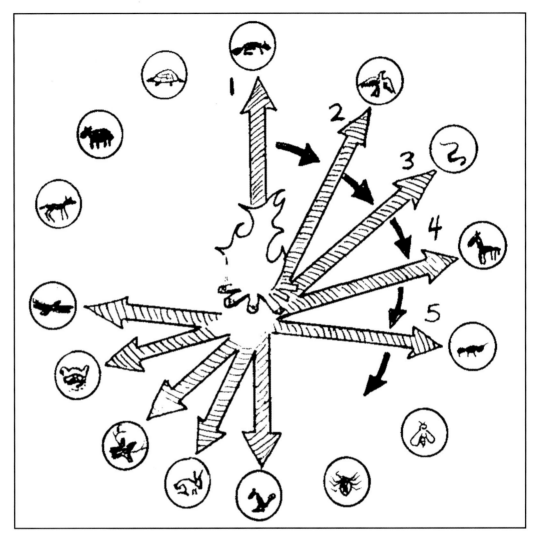

When this back-and-forth name recognition is complete and the talking stick returns to you, recite everyone's short name in the circle. Then ask for one female and one male to do the same. Usually, by this time, the names of all have been learned by everyone.

Now is the time to partake of the warmed tea. Together, toast your new connection to Nature and drink in the essence of the plant that provided the tea. Celebrate the collective honoring of each person's best traits. What better way to bond yourselves closer to Nature than to drink the lifeblood of a plant?

Finally, release your names to the night … by all shouting quickly (at a signal from you) their short-names. To hear that collective cry shatter the night, course through the valley and bounce off the mountains feels like the beginning of a journey of names that will encircle the planet.

The Ceremony of the Three Sticks

This ceremony has been a routine part of naming ceremonies at Medicine Bow. It is performed after the naming rounds. I record it separately here, because it stands well on its own. You may have a desire to use it for reasons other than consummating the naming ceremony. Basically, it is a self-improvement ritual held as a group but performed on a very private, individual level.

Performing the Ceremony of the Three Sticks – Each participant
should gather three dead sticks of pine, each thinner than a pencil. One stick's
length should match the distance from temple to temple on the skull. Another
matches the length of the mouth. The last is as long as the hand, from heel of the
thumb to fingertips. Early in the day, ask your students to bundle these sticks together using handmade bark rope. Each participant should carry his bundle on his
person until the ceremony.

On that night, after dark, when your campfire has settled to red coals, begin
the ceremony. Here is a suggested monologue for delivering the three challenges:

the stick of thought

"Take the stick that measures your skull and hold it in your right hand. This stick
represents the things that you think. In a few moments I am going to ask you to
make a decision about this stick. You must do one of two things with it: either lay
it on the coals to burn, or throw it behind you out of our circle. Listen carefully so
you will know how to make the decision of what to do with the stick.

"Inside the privacy of your own mind … that is the place where your absolute
honesty lives. Sometimes the true feelings that you allow in your thoughts are not
represented by your words or actions. Thoughts define your truths; therefore, your
mind is a sacred space, because it is the place that defines who you really are … as
opposed to the persona that you show to those around you. There may be aspects
of yourself that you are ashamed of … or disapprove of … or simply don't like …
traits that you cover up with contrary words. We all have these. But you are not
permanently saddled with those qualities, because you possess **choice**.

"If, for example, you feel difficulty in sharing your belongings … and if that
realization makes you feel small … then you can change that. All you have to
do is be aware of that tendency and, when the opportunity arises, defy it. Act on
your choice. Share something. Do this enough times and you will own the asset of
generosity. You will have earned it. But like any other skill, you must practice it in
order to be good at it.

"What if your thoughts were open to inspection by anyone? How would
you feel? Would you be embarrassed that others were privy to your most private thoughts? But is it not more important what **you** feel about your thoughts?
Shouldn't the highest level of personal dignity be about *how you are proud of what
goes on inside your own head*? The words we put out into the world do not always
reflect our true thoughts. Words can be manipulative and hypocritical. If your
thoughts – and I'm talking about the simplest thoughts you have in everyday life
– are of the highest order, you would never have need for a manipulative word or
an insincere act.

"The privacy of your mind is a sacred place. What better place to purify, to
honor? If you want to make changes about how to live your life, first you must
change what goes on inside your head.

"If you would now be willing to make a promise to turn to that private space
and improve it … to demand a higher quality of the thoughts that you allow to
take up time and space in your mind … if you would be willing to evict a petty

thought that is not worthy of taking up such space and time … then I ask you now to place your stick upon the coals. In this physical act you make a commitment. The memory of your stick releasing its energy through a flame becomes the permanent symbol for this quest of the mind. If you do not wish to make this promise, throw the stick behind you now."

If you, teacher, are willing to enter into this pact with yourself, step forward and set your stick upon the coals and watch it burn. Allow time for all to decide. Wait in silence and watch all the sticks burst into flames with the symbolism of everyone's promises.

the stick of talk

"In your right hand take the stick that is the length of your mouth. This stick represents the things that you say. Consider this question: Do the words that you say possess any power?"

Pause here to let all consider the potency of an individual voice.

"Another way to ask that question is this: Do your words have any influence on another person? To answer that let's consider your own experiences on the receiving end of words. Have you ever had someone speak to you in such a way that you felt small or wounded or even sick? Can you remember carrying that wounded feeling with you for an entire day or week or longer?" Pause again for memories to play out. "I believe the answer for all of us is 'yes' – we have all been hurt like this. But they were only words."

"What about the flip side of that incident? Has someone ever spoken to you in such a way that made you feel taller? Did you glow with pride? Did you become a better person for it? Yes, we have all experienced that, too. Yet, again, they were only words."

"Even though you may never have considered it, your words do carry great power. Whether you realize it or not, you have almost certainly and profoundly affected people with your words. All of us have made people feel small … and tall. We probably do it every day. With that in mind, how do you want to affect people with your words? To contribute or to hurt? What possible good can come of the latter, even if the person you are dealing with is someone you despise? Negative words would only make that person react in such a way as to become more unlikable.

"If you are willing to make a commitment right now to pause before speaking … to hold the words in your throat long enough to determine this: *Are my words going to contribute to this person or hurt her? Does this person need to hear my thoughts? Are my thoughts important enough to be made public?* If you will commit to this hesitation before speaking, this assessment of thoughts before they become words … then place your stick upon the coals and watch it shine with your promise. If you do not wish to make this commitment, throw your stick behind you now."

Allow a silent time to watch these sticks burn.

the stick of doing

"The last stick – the one that is the length of your hand – represents the things that you do. No one can read your thoughts. No one knows if your words are true. But people see what you *do*. They can believe their eyes. You define yourself to the world by your actions.

"Imagine that a friend of yours at school or at work is on the receiving end of mockery or criticism from others. If you think to yourself: *I don't like this. I'm going to do something about it … maybe talk to everyone about getting off my friend's back.* That's a fine thought. But that's all it is … a thought. It changes nothing.

"What if you told your closest friend about the dilemma and you expressed your desire to correct the problem by having an open discussion to clear the air. That's a fine thing to say … even inspiring. But they're just words. They change nothing.

"It's when you act on your beliefs that your ethic become real. Doing something – taking a stand – is stepping through that threshold that separates abstraction from reality. If you are willing to make this step, you run the risk of angering or disappointing others. But you also inspire and contribute. And you complete the circuit that runs from personal belief to tangible deed. You turn on the light above your spirit so that all can see who you truly are. You define your best self to the world.

"This stick of doing is also about fulfilling dreams … about doing those things we always say we will one day do. If you have a secret desire to dance, to be fluent in French, to shoot a bow well, to speak in front of a crowd, to learn how to survive in the woods, to write a book, to learn to play a violin, to hike the Appalachian Trail, to make a dulcimer, to build a log cabin, to weave cloth and make your own clothing … do it!

"If you are willing to make this promise to yourself: to act on your convictions … and to dust off one of those ignored dreams to make it happen, place this last stick on the coals and let it shine. If not, throw the stick behind you."

So ends the Ceremony of the Three Sticks.

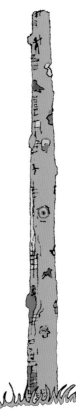

A Home for Symbols

At Medicine Bow I erected a totem in the center of the meadow. Painted in acrylics on this pole are hundreds of spirit symbols – each small enough to be covered by a hand. Symbols are painted on the totem the day after a night naming ceremony. The painting of symbols on the totem is a ceremony unto itself.

<u>*Establishing a Totem*</u> – Somewhere near your home or school or other place of gathering, create a space for publicly documenting the birth of a spirit name. Such a visible record becomes a place that attracts every eye with its mystery and attractiveness. At Medicine Bow this pole is a dead juniper tree, de-limbed and de-barked. Its 16"-thick base is buried four feet into the ground at the center of a meadow. It rises to a height of 12 feet, where it is 8 inches thick and cut on the perpendicular. Juniper is rot-resistant, as is locust. If such a tree cannot be found dead, you have other options: 1.) Harvest a live tree. Plan this harvest as a group event and before the tree speak of the sacrifice of the tree and your intent of its use. This Harvest Ceremony will never be forgotten by the participants. 2.) Buy a large pressure-treated post, rounded or squared. 3.) Use an existing boulder on which

to paint and establish its place in the woods as one private for your students. 4.) Hire a landscaper to deliver a boulder to your property. 5.) Erect a circle of sign posts in the forest. 6.) Create a circle of field stones like a mosaic wheel in forest or field. On each stone allow the painting of one symbol. 7.) Dedicate a wall of a building to record the symbols.

Each time a symbol is added, cover it with varnish to protect from weathering.

 Making a Spirit Shield – If a totem or wall is not feasible in your situation, consider chronicling spirit names on a skin or piece of canvas cloth. By referring to *Secrets of the Forest, Volume 3*, scrape a deer hide and sun-dry it to rawhide. Cut a straight green branch of hickory that measures 1" in thickness and 6' in length. Heat the stick by constantly moving it over a bed of hot coals until the wood is thoroughly and uniformly warm – so warm to the touch that the fingertips cannot linger on it. Using protective padding, bend the stick into a circle or oval and overlap the ends so that at least 10" of the hoop is double-thick. Carve the facets of the 10"-ends that touch so that they fit together, then bind this connection tightly with cordage.

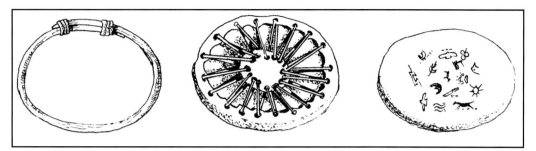

Lay the rawhide over the hoop and cut out the shield pattern so that it is 3" larger than the frame. Punch holes around the edge of the rawhide pattern 3/8" in from the margin and 2"-3" apart. From rawhide cut another smaller version of the pattern that measures about 5" across. Punch into its edge as many holes as you put into the shield pattern. This piece will serve as the nexus of lacing on the back of the shield.

Wet both rawhide circles (or ovals) by soaking in a creek overnight. On the next day stretch the larger flaccid rawhide over the frame and lace it to the smaller, starting loosely and then tightening as you go. Use lacing of wet rawhide strips or tanned leather strips. Once the holes are all laced, repeat the tightening process all around to get the front of the shield as taut as you can. As the wet rawhide dries it will shrink and harden, testing the strength of your hickory frame. Paints can be directly applied for colorful symbols. If you wish to keep the shield purely primitive, it's time to start learning about dyes.

Making Dyes for Painting

– Collect one root each from six different specimens of yellowroot, a sack of black walnuts still in their hulls, a small bag of ripe pokeweed berries, a cupful of inner bark from hemlock tree branches, and a bag of elderberry leaves. (See *Secrets of the Forest, Volume 1* for plant identification.)

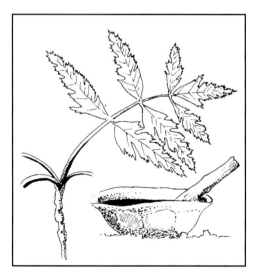

Yellow: Soak and crush 6 roots from yellowroot in a small amount of water. Let it stand overnight to extract as much pigment as possible for a brilliant dye.

Royal Brown: Soak a dozen black walnut hulls with just enough water to cover them. Let this stand overnight. For a richer brown crush and add more hulls.

Purple/magenta: Crush a cup of pokeweed berries in a small container. Add enough water to achieve the desired viscosity. No waiting necessary. Ready to paint.

Pink: Fill a small container with raw inner bark from hemlock and crush the bark. Let it soak in a small amount of water overnight.

Green: Cover 2 cups of elderberry leaves with water and crush vigorously. Let stand as long as needed for a desirable green.

Making a Paintbrush

– Carve the brush-end of any dead stick to give it a flat angled surface. Snip ¾"-long hairs from any mammal skin (yours?). Stack the hairs flush at one end and pinch that end between your fingers. Glue the other end to the flattened angle on the shaft with melted white pine glue (for manufacturing glue, see *Secrets of the Forest, Volume 1*).

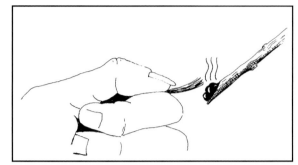

Symbol Uses

Symbols also become wonderful themes for homemade T-shirt designs, ownership painting on bows or other crafts, and signatures with which to sign letters. In short, the symbol is an emblem of pride. People of all ages seem to take the keenest pride in a piece of artwork that has been created just for them.

Making a Spirit Shirt

– As a group project, supply your named students with plain tee-shirts of a uniform color. White is a good choice because the spirit shirt is often worn in secret beneath another shirt. (There is a unique feeling of personal esteem experienced by those who wear the shirt without fanfare.) Use paints compatible with the fabric.

Making a Spirit Amulet

– A personal medallion showing one's spirit symbol can be made from a disk of wood, 2 pieces of handmade cordage, and painting supplies. Find and harvest a dead hardwood with a section of trunk about 2" in diameter. Dogwood (which the East is losing to anthrax infection) is an excellent choice for its density and light-colored wood. Using a carpenter saw, cut disks – one for each namee – 3/8" thick, with its cross-section of wood 1 ¾" wide (inside the bark.) Then use a drill to create a 3/16" hole near the rim, 3/16" from the bark.

Each namee paints his symbol on one side of the disk. As the picture dries, use strips of tulip tree inner bark to make a 3"-long, 1/8"-thick rope and a 2'-long, 1/4"-thick rope. (Cordage-making is covered in *Secrets of the Forest, Volume 1*.) Each finished rope can be cleaned of "whiskers" (and made more comfortable to wear as a necklace) by loosely wrapping it over the prongs of a forked stick and passing it (horizontally) at a steady rate through a candle or campfire flame 3 or 4 times.

Thread the short rope through the amulet hole and use its natural clasp (loop at one end, knot at the other) to form a closed circle. Send the longer rope through this circle and then wear as a necklace.

"Among the Lakota there were select warriors who took the Shirt-wearer's pledge. This man then wore a hair shirt to demonstrate his ability to cope with adversity. The tribe recognized the Shirtman as a living symbol of peace and, at the same time, a protective warrior."

~ S. Fox, *of the Medicine Bow nation*

CHAPTER 14
A Cloak of Pride and Proficiency

~ the honor shirt ~

Students who attend overnight workshops at Medicine Bow receive the gift of a Medicine Bow T-shirt. I often hear stories from students who were traveling – in Ireland or downtown Chicago or the Boundary Waters – and came upon a stranger wearing a Medicine Bow T-shirt. They were not strangers for long.

I designed another Medicine Bow shirt for a higher purpose. Acquiring this shirt is a reward for self-disciplined training and proficiency in one of three primitive skills. At the date of this writing – with Medicine Bow having been actively in session for over 40 years – there are 18 shirt-wearers scattered out in this world. These few are known collectively as "the Red Shirt Society."

The shirt is crimson with the Medicine Bow logo printed on the chest. It is called "the Honor Shirt." It recognizes a student who strove for and earned this garment through either plant usage, fire-making, or archery.

On each winter's solstice a celebration of the Red Shirt Society is held at Medicine Bow Lodge where a supper is provided, followed by a ceremony around the campfire in which new inductees – if any – are welcomed into the society.

In Medicine Bow Lodge there hangs a shield on one wall. Its rawhide cover is divided by a penciled-off grid of rectangles. Each time a student is inducted into the Red Shirt Society, she paints her symbol in the next available space.

Our sole purpose as members of this society is to pass on the teachings of the ancient ones and help others discover their ties to the real world. By wearing the Honor Shirt, a student is capable of teaching that skill by virtue of his adeptness.

Establishing an Honor Shirt – Talk to your students about the idea of a shirt of recognition. Decide what you would like the shirt to represent: the achievement of a positive character trait; accruing a certain number of years in membership; being voted "most _____" (helpful? improved in strength? Etc.); able to perform a germane skill.

Design an emblem to represent the subject matter of the Honor Shirt, select the colors, and print the shirts. Display on a wall one shirt and the requirements to win it clearly spelled out on a document.

Medicine Bow's Honor Shirt

Detailed below are Medicine Bow's requirements in each of the three subjects embraced by the honor shirt. You may want to borrow from these ideas or create your own.

Plant Identification and Usage

When a student feels ready, I lead him into a section of forest where he has not spent time. This must occur on a day when no plant instruction has been given to him. The challenge can be attempted only once in a day's time, but the number of attempts (on subsequent days) is limitless.

Over a 45 minute interval the student roams the woods, and I follow as his silent shadow. Within that time he must identify 10 trees or shrubs. Among those he must explain in detail how to use 3 for a food, medicine, or craft. He must also name 3 vines and explain how to use 2. Finally, he must identify 10 herbs and detail the uses of 3.

If an error is made, either in identification or usage, that day's attempt is aborted, and he must try again another day. This rule must be adhered to strictly, as making a mistake in the midst of a survival situation could prove costly … even fatal.

The explanation of a plant's usage must not be general. For example, it is not enough to say, "This plant can be used to cure a headache." The details of the preparation and how to administer it must be described.

All of the botanical information that you need to include this subject in your Honor Shirt program can be found in *Secrets of the Forest, Volume One*. *Part One* of that book takes you from beginner to practitioner in the use of plants.

Fire-Making

The fire challenger arrives at Medicine Bow with his own knife. Before he strikes out to meet the challenge, I hand him a 6"-long, 1"-thick, piece of dead wood. This is called the "ghost stick" and must be burned up in the fire-maker's pyre within 4

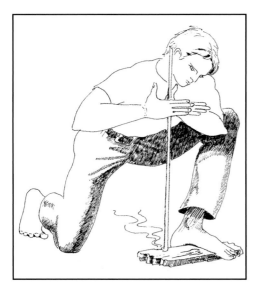

hours of starting the challenge. This ensures that the Honor Shirt challenger can not only create fire but also construct a successful pyre to sustain that fire.

If the challenger chooses to make a bow-drill kit to create fire, I provide her with a 4' length of store-bought rope. She wanders through an assigned area (where she has not previously visited) to gather materials for a fire kit, returns to base camp, creates the kit, builds a pyre, and attempts to create a fire that will consume the ghost stick. At the end of 4 hours, if the ghost stick has not yet burned, the attempt is a failure. Only one attempt at the shirt is allowed in one day's time.

Archery

There are 11 challenges in this trial of bow and arrow. All are performed in my two-acre meadow where targets are set up for testing the full spectrum of handling

a bow and arrow. If a challenger goes through the tests and misses only one challenge, she can repeat that single challenge at the end of the others and make it up to win the shirt. Only one attempt at the shirt is allowed in one day.

These challenges are detailed in *Secrets of the Forest, Volume 4* in the archery section.

(Note: On the Medicine Bow shirt logo there is a feather tied to the bow. Any time a member of the Red Shirt Society achieves the Honor Shirt <u>in an additional category</u>, that shirt-wearer paints another feather on the bow.)

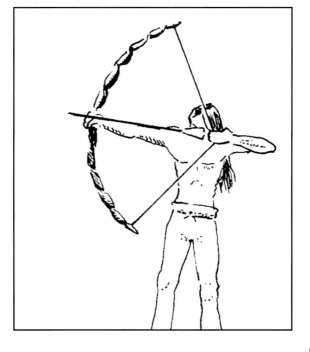

The Annual Honor Shirt Gathering — Each winter on the solstice, I

prepare a meal to honor the shirt-wearers. Our gathering is a quiet celebration. We hear of the year's accomplishments, the failures, the hardships endured, and the joys experienced. There are stories of sons and daughters born, careers changed, and school projects.

Throughout the evening, each participant visits a workbench where paints and brushes sit next to a ceremonial arrow. By the end of the meeting, each spirit symbol has been painted on the arrow and the date is recorded on the shaft.

Around the campfire and to the beat of a drum, new inductees create a dance that pantomimes the occasion of their winning the shirt. A new shirt-wearer might go through the motions of searching for, finding, and eating a plant. Another might act out loading an arrow and shooting. A fire-maker's dance might replicate seeking the wood from trees that swallowed fire, followed by spinning a drill and attaining a flame.

Finally, one veteran of our party loads the painted arrow to a bow, aims high into the sky in the direction of the many thousands of acres of forest that lie behind Medicine Bow. He releases and we listen to the arrow begin its journey to an unknown destination.

Finding the Solstice Arrow – Sometimes years go by before one of the ceremonial arrows is discovered. Leave

it in place. This becomes a landmark and an opportunity to talk to new students about the concept of the Honor Shirt and the society's annual celebration. Include each arrow on the map of your camp setting. Seeing that mysterious shaft on the map piques the interest of young students. Finding a colorful solstice arrow out in the forest is like stumbling upon a treasure. So begins the mystery that you would like to be associated with the Honor Shirt.

Making the Society Shield – Just as you did for the Spirit Shield in chapter 12, make another shield for the wearers of the Honor Shirt. Hang this work of art in a conspicuous place where all will see it. It will serve as an inspiration for those who would like to see their symbols added to its colorful collection of personal images.

"When you come to the end of your journey, how will you be remembered by the people who have known you? More importantly, before that time comes, how will you think of yourself?"

~ a shirt-wearer of Medicine Bow

CHAPTER 15
The Tracks of Time
~ the winter count and medicine pouch ~

Winter Count

Because pre-Columbian Native Americans did not have a written language, they used drawings called pictographs and ideographs as a means of graphic communication and record-keeping. Though symbols varied from tribe to tribe, much of it is easily recognizable, even by someone who has never studied this kind of art.

A deer, for example, was often represented by a simplistic line drawing of a four-legged with antlers, ensuring a clear identification of species. Other conceptual drawings might require explanation. *Famine* was depicted as an empty meat-drying rack outside a lodge. *Death* was sometimes shown as a darkened circle, denoting the circle of life was complete, filled in.

People all over the world have recognized the value of maintaining a continuity of progress by remembering their cultural roots. In a culture without a written language, storytelling was the primary means of passing along history. Usually this was accomplished orally. Some tribes assigned a person with artistic skills to make a tangible record that was handed down through generations of artists. This specialist painted a symbol that represented the most important event of the year for the tribe. (Sometimes there were two drawings per year.) Since the Plains tribes referred to years as "winters," the record itself is now called a "*winter count.*" Such annals were painted on animal skins laced to a wooden frame or rolled up like a blanket when not in use. Some winter counts still exist from the nineteenth century and earlier.

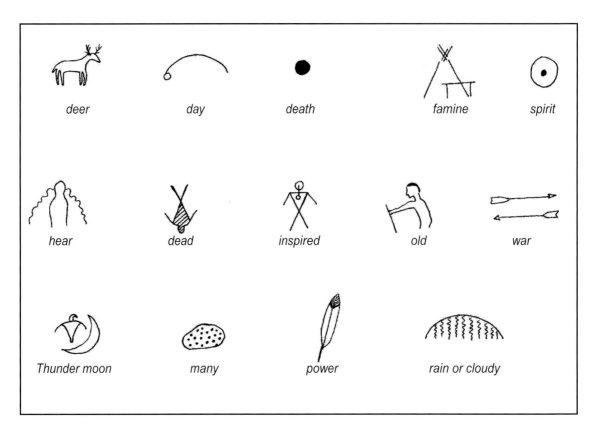

Winter counts were sometimes drawn in horizontal sequence like the words and lines of this page … and other times rendered in a spiral, starting at the center and working outward. Regardless of design, they provided an important grounding effect for the individual of any tribe. It helped him to understand who he was in the larger story of his people. There is an argument made by anthropologists that the disconnection of this legacy – like a modern American who knows nothing of his antecedents' association with slavery, or the Holocaust, or the civil rights movements – puts that American at a great disadvantage in taking his own constructive place in the world.

The same could be true on a smaller scale. Knowing about the early years of one's family life … or school … or summer camp … could have some bearing on the decisions one makes. Families have scrapbooks. Schools have yearbooks. Camps have all manner of photographs and memorabilia. But the amount of information can be overwhelming, denying the researcher an easy glimpse of the larger picture. The winter count provides just that.

 ### *Making a Winter Count* – Carve, shape, heat, and bend a hickory frame as you did in the last chapter for the Red Shirt Society shield. For a surface on which to paint the pictures, use any material that suits your fancy: denim, canvas, rawhide, tanned hide … virtually any fabric. Cut the material smaller than the frame so that the material can be laced inside the frame with the lacing showing as an added, aesthetic border.

For a spiral pattern, the first painting is rendered at the center of the canvas. Its size should be small enough to allow for the number of years you wish to record inside that frame. The next picture is drawn to its left and slightly lower – the top of each scene oriented toward the closest portion of the frame. The series of drawings continues counterclockwise. To view each drawing at the proper orientation, the viewer would have to rotate the frame in his hands as he followed consecutive drawings.

I once made a winter count using a portion of canvas from a retired tipi. By singeing the edges evenly over a flame, the final product took on an antique appearance. Another time I used yellowed, oiled paper … again singed for a dark border. I glued this to old canvas and ran the lacing through the double-layer of paper and canvas.

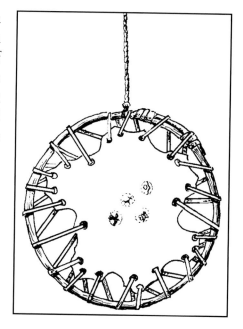

Variations on the Winter Count

– A pictorial calendar can be used in a number ways. Rather than representing years, each picture could display the prominent event in a given month. Such a craft could be called a *"moon count."* Or pictures could be added as weekly installments for a *"seven sunrises count."*

One industrious year I made a *"day count,"* adding a painting to the canvas each night. That calendar measured roughly 2 ½' across; and, after a year of paintings, both sides were completely filled with 365 symbolic pictures – each finished rendering the size of a large black walnut with its husk.

I chose to make the artwork anachronistic by omitting any drawing of modern technology. For automobiles I used horses. For trailers, travois. For telephone calls, smoke signals. For houses, tipis. That year is indelibly recorded. It will not be forgotten.

Such a "count" makes an unparalleled gift. Choose a friend, spouse, teacher, or relative for whom you will make a day, 7 sunrises, moon, or winter count and commit to it.

Camp, School or Family Winter Count

– Present to your students a group project of recording history by pictures. Decide upon the frequency of drawings and then the duration. From those calculations estimate the size calendar you will need to make as a group. Assign one person as "scribe" for a given length of time. It is the scribe's responsibility to decide which event is to be graphically memorialized. In private, she completes a painting. When her assigned recording-time comes to a close, the next scribe takes over. In this way, everyone plays a part in contributing to the work of art.

To achieve uniformity with the paintings, the areas to be painted along the spiral can be pre-outlined by using a template, marked by pencil, to show the current artist the boundaries of his work. Shared experiences, of course, make bonds. When the record keeping of those experiences is shared, the bond is all the tighter.

Naming the Moons

All the tribes of Native Americans created different names for the lunar divisions of the year that we call "months." These were often poetically descriptive and unique to the geography of a particular people's homeland. The Lakotas' Moon of the Popping Trees, for example, denoted that month (February) when the winter cold brought on hard freezes that caused live trees to rupture from the expansion of internal water. The Green Corn Moon (June) of the Cherokee honored the coming of maize. Other examples are:

Hopi – Moon of the Whispering Wind (March); Arapaho – Moon When the Ponies Shed (May); Shawnee – Pawpaw Moon (September); Omaha – Moon When the Deer Paw the Earth (September); Muskogee – Mulberry Moon (May); Choctaw – Moon of the Panther (November); Cheyenne – Moon When the Wolves Run Together (December).

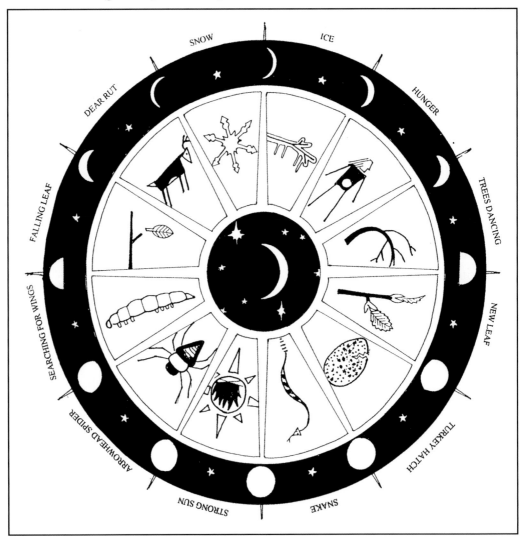

Each choice for the name of a moon tells us something about the events of the season as well as hints about what was important to the people who coined the phrase. By inventing your own monthly names, you can create a new awareness about your seasonal surroundings and create a new bond between your students and their environment.

On the facing page, as an example, is Medicine Bow's calendar of moons.

<u>*Naming the Moons*</u> – Create your own calendar over a year's time. Assign each month to a team of students to be named as each month arrives. These moons should reflect what goes on in Nature in your locale. At the end of a month, when a team has agreed upon the dominant, defining theme to be used, they must give that moon a name, design its symbol, and render it on the calendar of moons, which can be painted on a framed skin, canvas, or a paper scroll.

Medicine Pouch

Many Native Americans carried a medicine pouch filled with symbolic items that represented good fortune, stealth, wisdom, strength, courage, or any other quality conducive to success in life. It contained a person's spiritual "medicine." In other words, this was a psychological medicine that provided inspiration.

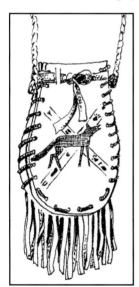

In battle, such secret paraphernalia might be meant to bestow upon the warrior the cunning of crow, the swiftness of falcon, the silence of stone. Each article was a symbol, a charm, an icon of a power that a man or woman would need. By these tokens the wearer was made craftier, faster, and stealthier, if only by association – as if these symbols were actual, potent medicines taken for specific needs.

A medicine pouch is a personal bag of items which represent important people, animals, places, and events in the life of the pouch-maker. It is a personal scrapbook of the most important experiences in a life and reminds the bearer of who she is, what she has done, what she can do at her best. The pouch holds no magic, only memories … mementos of days gone by in which she had fulfilled her highest expectations of herself. It differs from a medicine bag by being not an ephemeral gift bestowed to a place or being but a lasting chronicle of concepts of importance in one's life.

The owner of a medicine pouch does not reveal its contents. Keeping the items private protects them from being lessened in importance, much in the same way that the interpretation of a spirit name is not shared. Essentially, the pouch's items are "trophies" that represent events of courage, moments of honesty, stories of survival or sacrifice or strength, and bonds with intimates (people, animals, and places).

A medicine pouch can be worn by an attached strap or cord. It may lie loosely against the chest under a shirt, be carried openly on a belt, or be stored in a special place. It feels less like an amulet than a conduit to the heart. It celebrates a life and keeps its owner true and strong by evoking the best of one's spirit.

What Goes into the Medicine Pouch?

Since a person's medicine pouch cannot be emptied and explained to another, I will pose some hypothetical ideas for you to consider, so that you can get the feel for this satisfying method of creating an archive for your path through life.

1. At the actual spot where you stood when you made a stand against some adversity – a stand of which you are proud – pick up a stone or choose a flake of wood from a nearby tree and paint on it a symbol that depicts your cause. Place the item in your medicine pouch. The painted symbol will ensure that you remember the event that it represents when you review the pouch's contents down the years.

2. When you have striven for a goal with much dedication, sacrifice, and hard work – a college degree, a canoe race, a music recital, a soccer title, a correction of a misunderstanding – no matter the results, include in your pouch a piece of the printed program or a carved piece of wood (a tiny canoe) symbolizing the event or simply a name written on a scrap of paper.

3. A bundle of fur from the pet that made you a better person.

4. A piece of a spirit stick with a symbol painted on it.

5. Any small trinket owned by your most important friend. Ask her for it.

6. A piece of feather or bone or wood from a forest that has played an important part in your personal growth.

7. A fragment of a sports jersey.

 <u>Making a Medicine Pouch</u> – Cut two identical pear shapes out of supple leather or other material. If you would like to have fringe hang off the seam of the bag, cut the bulbous end of one pear oversized as shown in the illustration. Outline the other pear against it with a pencil. The excess outside the drawn line can be cut into thin strips that will hang from the pouch.

The stalk end of each pear should be cut straight across to serve as the opening for the pouch. One quarter-inch down from this cut, cut two pairs of vertical slits on each pear. These will serve as drawstring loops. The drawstring – a strip of leather or other cordage – will run through the loops to close the opening by tightening and tying.

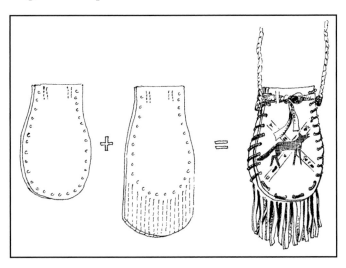

Sew the two pears together along the outline of the smaller pear with a spiral stitch, letting the spiral weave between strips of fringe. You'll want a long thin leather thong (a loop large enough to be worn around the neck) for a carrying strap. It should be sewn to the pouch during the joining of the halves. On the front of the pouch, paint (or bead) your spirit name symbol.

A Mindful Tradition

Once a year, in a private place, empty your pouch and review the milestones of your life. When a bag fills, it is time to hang it on the wall and make another medicine pouch.

Celebrating a Year – What is the beginning of a year? Our modern calendars give us one answer, but cultures throughout history and around the world have had reason to choose other times of the year to serve as one year's ending and another's beginning. Choose your own time to honor the passing of an old year and the entry into a new one. (If working with a school class, you will need to choose a year's end/beginning time during the school year.)

Your rationale for your chosen date is your personal decision. Perhaps autumn – because of its falling leaves and the cessation of photosynthesis for hardwoods – might signify an ending. To another person the onset of spring might represent a beginning. But there are many other ways to interpret the seasons. Perhaps summer represents the new year, because the sun returns to its highest arc over us. The decision is arbitrary.

Several weeks before the chosen celebration time, ask all your students to work individually and privately to determine the most important event of his or her past year. This event may have occurred in school, at home, or on a trip. It can relate to any part of life: sports, family, artwork, building a structure, wandering through woods, an accomplishment in music, personal relationship, a pet, interaction with a stranger, etc.

Once the event has been identified, each student must create a simple symbol that represents his experience. By using a reference book of ancient symbols, each artist can utilize authentic pictographs from history. Another option calls for the participants to invent their own renderings of symbols.

Choose a receptacle on which the group will, one at a time, paint these once-in-a-year events. The receptacle passes from one to the other in a relaxed way over a comfortable span of time until all have contributed their salient moment of the year. Consider using as this receptacle: a canvas stretched on a wooden hoop as we did with the winter count; a large bowl or vase; a scroll of paper; a slab of wood; an inside wall of a room; tiles that can be pieced together as a mosaic; a tapestry to be hung in the room.

Once the craft is completed, allow a passage of weeks in which all students can study the entire array of pictures. An element of mystery will surround these figures. If a student is willing to share the meaning of her symbol, ask her to draw a larger version on a drawing board, so that all the others can attempt to interpret its meaning. Once everyone has had a chance to interpret, she can reveal the true story.

"Maybe the people who are most afraid are the ones who can be most courageous."

~ *Niles Morgan*, The Lord of Fear

CHAPTER 16
The Fire Within
~ a warrior for our times ~

Who will decide the fate of our world? If we humans are the prominent threat to our environment, then, of course, we can be the remedy. But before that can happen, a majority of people must reconnect to the Earth. The definitive gifts of bark and wood, stone and animal, water and air, and medicinal leaf … all this must be valued before people have a reason to protect it. For these items to be valued, they must become integrated into daily life. To really know these gifts, people must have their hands on Nature's parts … seeing the details, feeling the textures, smelling the scents, tasting the flavors, while listening to the indigenous sounds of the forest.

Even the broader concepts of Nature must be rediscovered: photosynthesis, the water cycle, decomposition, and natural recycling, etc. Most Americans know the basic facts about these phenomena, but we don't behave as if we understand them. Human history shows a myopic trend. We tend to act on the short-term gain and ignore the long-term repercussions. And once entrenched in the day to day, old habits are hard to break.

It seems paradoxical to say that complaisance has a powerful momentum, but I believe it does. Having worked in the area of conservation with people of all ages, I am convinced that our best chance to reverse the fouling of our nest comes from our children.

If our children have the opportunity to immerse themselves into Nature under the guidance of an enthusiastic teacher, then they will have reason to value it. (In a nut shell, this is the primary mission statement of the four volumes of *Secrets*

of the Forest.) They need to make rope from the bark of a dead tulip tree … to ease a stomach ache with the root of yellowroot … to fend off chigger bites with the scent of pawpaw leaves… to fill a hole in the stomach with cooked tubers of wapato … to stalk a deer and observe a chapter of its life in the wild. When these experiences are a part of the formative years, the children have reason to become stewards of the land, water, air, and their inhabitants. They can become citizens of the real world

What finer gift could be handed down from teacher to student or parent to child? If a young one better connects to his home (the Earth) … and to all who came before him to live in this same world … in time he will want to pass this on to the generation that will follow.

Forming a Warrior Society – With your students, examine every facet of our modern lives that continues to put a strain of the welfare of the Earth. The subjects are numerous:

Electricity overuse	Paper waste	Lack of Physical Fitness/Nutrition
Fossil fuel overuse	Erosion	Water waste
Water pollution	The Homeless	Waste Water
Air pollution	The Starving	Alternative Energy underuse
Recycling inconvenience	Toxic Waste	Loss of Wildlife Habitat
Lack of Consumer Wisdom	Animal Cruelty	Ill-Conceived River Damming
Drinking Water Treatment	Litter	Population control
Invasive, Non-Native Plants	Toxic Products	Lack of Laws to Protect Nature
Noise Pollution	Urban Deprivation	Lack of Enforcement

Naturally, such discussions are apt to elicit complaint, outrage, blame, and condemnation; but never let a session end without exploring solutions to problems, for in the solutions lie a future.

When your class research has covered a wide spectrum of environmental problems, ask for a show of hands from those who would be willing to act on solutions. When enough show a willingness to be active as conservationists, announce that your class will form a society of warriors who will commit to peaceably acting on behalf of the Earth.

In attacking a subject, go farther than the typical poster-making that every child has taken part in at school. (*Don't Litter!* or *Save the Whales!*) Get your teeth into a quest. Make a commitment. Once challenges are set, make them public. Let the newspapers know of your missions. Let the minister and rabbi know, so that these projects can be talked about in public gatherings.

Where do you start? Here is one example:

One of the many sources of water pollution is the family washing machine. No matter where that gray water goes – backyard, sump hole, septic tank, or sewage treatment plant – it adds to the Earth's problems.

Attacking a Water Pollution Problem – Have your students do a detailed study of the types of articles washed weekly inside their homes. What better way to do this than have the student-warrior take over laundry responsibilities in his home? This is ideal for creating a hands-on experience full of relevance and accountability.

This project presents an opportunity for a mathematics assignment. (Projects like this one belong in every taught subject in school – math, English, economics, science, etc.) A pie chart or graph can be made that depicts the percentages of sheets vs. socks vs. sports uniforms, etc. Percentages of item-types must take into consideration item-bulk. For example, six towels might fill up a washer, while it might take forty articles of underwear to do the same. Therefore, six towels carries a lot more weight than six pairs of underwear.

If towels are discovered to be one of the main culprits in filling the laundry load, then it's time to investigate towel-use in the household. Interviews are in order. How many times does Dad use a towel before dropping it in the clothes hamper? What about a brother or sister? How often and for what reason do family members bathe or wash up? Enlist the family to keep a record to help in the research.

When these findings are complete, it's time for a group meeting of the society to discuss solutions. There is a *revealing* (what's going on at home) and then a *revelation* (an idea about changing what's going on at home). But for that change to take hold, there has to be a reason for the family to embrace it. They have to care.

A student-warrior cannot force caring upon someone, nor can he create it at will. The caring must eventually come from within the family (unless Mother or Father is willing to enforce a new edict). Orchestrating this caring is the hardest part of environmental education.

Offering a Solution

– A towel is nothing more than a convenient way to remove water quickly from the body. It makes perfect sense to use one. To let water evaporate slowly off the skin after a bath or shower – especially in winter – has its health liabilities. So let's see how a towel works.

A person steps into a shower because of a need to clean the skin. There are other reasons, too, and these should be examined … like the morning attempt to be "sprayed awake" by emptying the hot water heater … like a morning washing of already clean hair for the purpose of achieving the desired "look" for that day.

If a person scrubs with soap and rinses, he gets clean. He steps out of the shower clean … but wet. The towel serves to transfer the water – first from body to cloth, then from cloth to air. A towel is nothing more than a *water transfer device*. By the definition of "washing," the water transferred is clean.

How many showers can one towel accommodate? How can such a test be made? Probably the best gauge to employ is smell. If the repeat performance of a towel gets up to, say, thirty (which is this author's average), then how much water pollution does that represent as being eliminated by fewer washing loads?

More math and water measuring with a washing machine are in order. If the water in question is city water with a price tag on it, what is this cost? Look at a broader picture. How much water-use would this represent with a thousand families of four? What is your town's population? Figure the volume of water saved if everyone conserved water with repeated towel use alone. And remember, the water saved is also an equal amount of polluted water not returned to the Earth.

Now, what to do with the findings? Publish the study. Get it in the newspaper. Get it on TV, on the local news. Challenge your classmates to get their parents en-

listed in the mission. Challenge other classrooms to join the campaign. Challenge other schools. Challenge your town.

Advertise a time period when the class or school or town should employ the conservation solutions you have published. Now it's time to make posters about the action that's being done. Challenge the reader of the poster to join the mission. Include a tear-off tab for the reader to fill out and send in. Publish the names of these new environmental warriors in the newspaper.

And what about that "caring" factor? How do you get the public-at-large to participate? Now you've made the challenge a matter of public pride. You've made the issue known. You've educated. Most importantly, you've offered a solution to a problem.

All this … just about towels. We have only begun.

Courage lies at the heart of this chapter. A student-warrior must be willing to speak in the presence of strangers, to edify and show the way without seeming judgmental. The warrior's actions are her loudest words. She must have the courage to be an example in the face of those who would belittle.

Arguably, ceremony has faded in most households of the modern American culture. Outside of a few religious rites, the closest events to coming-of-age rituals in our society might be said to be: 1.) getting a driver's license; 2.) graduating from high school or college; 3.) legal purchase of alcoholic beverages; and 4.) voting. Only one of these "coming-of-age" milestones (school completion) is actually earned; the rest are simply ascribed by an accumulation of years. If these are considered ceremonies of our times, they are rather unrecognizable. The school-journey is spread out over years. (Though the graduation ceremony does indeed encapsulate the protracted studies into a memorable moment.) The other milestones might be said to be empty or out of balance, since no effort was required beyond living out a certain number of years.

By introducing ceremonies of substance to your students, you bestow upon them a series of gifts that can change lives and improve the health of the Earth. Introducing a warrior society can inspire youth toward self-improvement, courage, and deliberation. Teach them well. Good luck

"He piled on sticks until the flames rose like a mirror to the burning in his soul. Raising his arms again he took in the heat on his skin like the lashes of a whip meant to awaken him. He looked up at the night sky ... at the sparks racing upward. Those sparks might have been nascent stars racing to their assigned places in the heavens. He imagined his spirit ascending in a like manner ... seeking a higher place."

~ *Russell Storms*, Song of the Horseman

CHAPTER 17
The Sequester and the Song
~ a journey within ~

In various cultures throughout history, there was a *going-out* trial that a youth would face at the coming-of-age time. He walked into wilderness alone to contemplate, to better learn himself, and to endure. This lasted for days. According to some tribes' oral traditions – as in the aboriginal "Walkabout" – this rite was practiced by males only. In this book we shall rightfully include both genders, but due to the inherent risks – both perceived and unpredictable – this journey should be undertaken only by adults old enough to assume any risks for themselves.

One Native American version of this rite was called the "Vision Quest." Simply put, a young man left his village for a sacred place (often a mountain overlook with an impressive view), where he spent three days and nights fasting. His lone possession was a blanket. During this sequester he prayed for and earnestly awaited a sign, or message, or answer to the question of his life's purpose now that he was becoming a man. On the fourth day an assigned helper came to him with broth and escorted him back to his people.

As a coming-of-age ceremony the Vision Quest was available to a youth usually around his thirteenth winter (year) ... whenever he was deemed mature enough to be called "a man." This honored event was probably anticipated with varying degrees of trepidation, eagerness, and adventure; for it can arguably be said that, universally, the young have always wanted to be older ... but at the same time unsure of their ability to step into the responsibilities of adulthood.

The historic Vision Quest of the Native Americans was also employed at later ages as well, when the quester was in need of spiritual guidance. Such a quest

could result from one's need to answer a pressing question, to resolve a problem, to renew a dedication, to ground oneself after troubling times, to express gratitude, to acquire a new name … or to deal with any number of personal or tribal issues.

The historic Vision Quester engaged an internal search for a pertinent revelation. But it was not all internal. A quester hoped for an intervention – a message from outside himself. This might be expected to come from the Creator, from an animal, from the weather, from a dream, or from a combination of these sources.

I am not Native American; and, therefore, I offer no historical replication of any tribe's going-out ritual. But I do understand the value of this concept: isolating oneself with purpose and dedication. It marks a person's arrival at an important threshold. It is the time when one wishes to reach for a new awareness of self … and what it means to be a participant in this world for the brief time that he or she is here on the Earth. And so, in this chapter I offer a variation of such a rite, which I call simply the "Aerie."

It is doubtful that a modern American thirteen year-old youth would be equipped for three or four days without food or drink in the unfamiliar environs of wilderness. Because of the state of our high-tech/Nature-alienated culture, such an ordeal would be daunting and perhaps dangerous. This is why a contemporary version of the going-out ritual would be best suited for someone who meets these three criteria: college-age or older, comfortable and experienced in wilderness settings, and so eager to fulfill the ritual that he or she initiates the process.

The concept of the Aerie ought not be presented to an audience like an announcement of trying out for a sports team or signing up for a club. The students' exposure to the ceremony should be indirect. Make available to mature students an array of books that contain stories of Native American Vision Quests, Aboriginal Walkabouts, or some other cultural rite that practiced a "going-out." A few examples are: *Black Elk* by Joe Jackson (Farrar, Strauss & Giroux, 2016), *Crazy Horse, the Strange Man of the Oglalas* by Mari Sandoz (Bison Book, 1992), and *Hanta Yo* by Ruth Hill (Doubleday, 1979).

Once the ritual has become a subject of conversation within a group, questions usually follow: Who should undertake such a quest? Why do it? At what point in life should one consider it? What happens to someone on it?

The best answer to the first is probably this: A candidate is one who wants to embrace an enhanced probe into Self … and an advanced intimacy with Nature.

There are many answers for the second question. Here are two: transition and reflection. During the Aerie, time slows down. There are no distractions. The head clears and one's innate paleo patience (which has been suppressed by the pace of the modern American lifestyle) naturally surfaces. The dedication of spending time alone inspires penetrating and concise thinking about whatever direction, understanding, or revelation one hopes to achieve.

The answer to the third question begs another question: Do you consider yourself an adult? Some say that adulthood arrives with the right to drive a car or to vote or to legally drink alcohol. But, truthfully, these are arbitrary rights,

merited only by age. I have known thirteen-year-old students who, in my opinion, were adults; but I have known men and women in their thirties and forties whom I suspected were not. Perhaps no person can truly assign the term to another. One must make the decision for himself or herself.

The fourth question is made difficult by the fact that people who have experienced a going-out like the Aerie seldom, if ever, talk about it. In this way, it is similar to the rationale for a naming. The experience is too precious to be exposed in conversation.

Many participants generally describe a going-out as a spiritual experience. Some may have expected to hear a mystical voice ... or to see a misty image emerge from the fringes of hallucination. Maybe this does happen. I cannot speak for others. The Aerie is probably as varied in its content as the human race is varied in its personalities. There can be no comparisons between two individuals' experiences.

> *When one comes of age, he carries his home with him .... no matter where he may go.*

Initiating the Aerie should begin with a potential quester approaching the teacher. At that point, the teacher must make an important decision: Is this person mentally, emotionally, and physically suited to the occasion? The Aerie is a solo experience. Before entering into it, one must not be a stranger to solitude. Perhaps a student who asks for your guidance in the Aerie first needs a few assignments that will help to familiarize him/her with the meaning of aloneness.

By formalizing this ceremony, by dedicating a place and time for it, by anticipating it and entering into it with deliberation ... we give weight to the Aerie. Once it has been carried out, its memory may last as one of the most important pivotal points in one's life.

When the going-out is completed, we are much the same as we were before the journey, and yet on some level we are forever changed. We know more than we did going into it, and yet we may know nothing new that might be of value to another person. We are lost from time for four days, and we come to own the world and our place in it. The real world holds us in its hands for a few days, and when finally we stand to go "back," we realize there is no "back." When one comes of age, he carries his home with him ... no matter where he may go.

The Aerie is what it needs to be. Perhaps we should not define it more than that.

There may come a time when you, the teacher, are approached about assisting someone through the process. What follows is the information that can help you do that. These guidelines offer a template, which you may decide to personalize with your own modifications.

<u>Overseeing the Aerie</u>

– If you decide to accept a request for assistance in the Aerie, let safety be your primary contribution. Since we are not following any tribe's formulaic rituals, there are no set rules that must be met. However, parameters are sometimes in order.

The quests that I have overseen have all varied according to the student's age, demeanor, and intent. Today I would rarely suggest that a thirteen-year-old spend a three-night experience alone. Nor would I send him out in winter. Or without

water. A fully-grown man whose body is soft and unaccustomed to physical hardships would not fare well without some food and water. If a journeyman-to-be has a medical history that precludes participation in an event that requires endurance, he should consider a modified format that better matches his physical state. Perhaps a two-day sequester in isolation would serve better than no journey at all?

The student and teacher must agree upon a reasonable schedule for duration and sustenance. As to purpose? That is a private affair that belongs to the student. But it is proper for the teacher to join into a discussion about the intent of the occasion, if the student so desires. The teacher is not expected to have absolute answers. The teacher can guide and illuminate and suggest and turn questions back on the student.

Duration, food/water supply, accouterments to be carried, and location must all be decided. In preparing for the ceremony, periods of silence are advised, as are periods of aloneness. Together create an agenda of preparation, but gear the conversations toward letting the quester take control of the ceremony. Help the journeyman to make the experience *his own*.

The journeyman should make every effort in the weeks leading up to the quest to avoid conflict. He should be unequivocally honest with anyone he encounters. Embrace peace and quietness. Carry no negative "baggage" into the ceremony. Give the mind a vacation from strife.

The chosen site should be remote, ensuring that the journeyman will feel completely isolated and risk no intersection with any other human. Traditionally, such a place would afford a dramatic view with minimal signs of civilization: a cliff overlooking an expanse of land; the edge of an open meadow; or the bank of a river. But, ultimately, the chosen area is the student's prerogative. Some personalities might prefer a cave or a cathedral of deep forest. Find out what the student values. Let the journeyman's search for the site (a process that might take weeks or months) be a part of the training in solitude and the anticipation of the rite. No one should accompany him or her. The quester needs to feel full ownership of the place he or she chooses.

Once the terms of the ritual have been agreed upon, the teacher's main consideration is safety. In order that the teacher can monitor the well-being of a student during the journey, that student must decide upon a "signal post" that lies within 100 yards of the sequester site. During the preparation time before the ceremony date, the student must draw a detailed map that shows the way from signal post to sequester site.

On the day that the ceremony begins, the journeyman guides the teacher to the signal post. Now the map is given to the teacher so that, should an emergency arise, teacher can find student. At the signal post on the morning of day-one, they separate, the student retreating to his/her chosen sequester site and the teacher returning home.

At this post the journeyman will leave a daily semaphore that shows he or she is having no problems. This post must be visible from a distance so that the monitoring teacher does not have to invade the student's territory each day. If

the post is a sapling, the journeyman simply ties a new, brightly colored strip of cloth around the tree trunk each morning after sunrise. The first cloth is tied in the presence of the teacher on day-one. On day-two and day-three the teacher approaches at noon to count the cloth bands from a distance. If a cloth strip is missing, the teacher must follow the hand-drawn map and get to the student. In such a case, the Aerie is aborted until another time.

Decide together the terms of what will be carried on the journey: no food or limited food (if so, precisely what food?) ... no water, limited water, or lots of water ... blanket (traditional) or sleeping bag. Because the quester is about to enter a fast, a good steppingstone toward abstinence might include a tapering off of quantity and an elimination of extravagant foods for the week preceding the sequester. During the allotted days on the Aerie, the only walking that the quester does will be the morning stroll to the signal post and to a nearby hand-dug latrine. On the final day at an appointed time, the monitor should meet the quester at the signal post and escort him or her out.

Entering into the Aerie is, for most participants, a holy act. The simplicity of the rite – of stripping down to the bare essentials of body, blanket, and a place to sit – gives the quester no other place to look than at the Creation and at Self. In isolation, the journeyman has a chance to see his or her place in a bigger picture. There is time to study oneself as never before.

The journey is mistakenly thought by some to be a controlling force that completely takes over the destiny of the quester, as if the ceremony comes with a guarantee. In reality, the quest holds no absolute promise. Just as it is up to the quester to prepare for the event, it is also his or her responsibility to enter the ceremony with humility and reverence as well as strength and deliberation. Then, when it is done, it is the participant who must interpret its message and its worth. This may take years.

A Song of Dying

The Aerie provides a perfect setting for a quester to compose a sacred song that is meant to be sung (to oneself, to the world, to the Creator) at the time of death (provided, of course, one is granted the time and grace to perform it). This concept is foreign to most Americans, yet it was a common practice among some Native American tribes, who called this song a "Death Chant." It is a most personal act – this composing and, of course, the singing. It can be sung throughout the Aerie so that it is embedded in memory. Later, in alone times, it is a song that can be sung to the forest in order to keep the melody alive and safely stored away in the mind.

This song is designed to help one meet his death while having some say in the matter. Death will not be such a stranger. The occasion of dying can be less a shock to the chanter, because he or she has rehearsed it with every singing. The chant may enable a person to one day meet death with a grace and courage that, perhaps, was not previously available.

 <u>Creating a Song of Dying</u> – Privately compose a melody to represent your life, your personality, your spirit. One need not be a musician to do this. If there are words to accompany it, write these lyrics on a tiny scroll of paper and secure it inside your medicine pouch.

SUGGESTED READING

History, Myths, & Sacred Formulas of the Cherokees, James Mooney, Historical Images 1992

Hanta Yo, Ruth Beebe Hill, Doubleday 1979

Crazy Horse, the Strange Man of the Oglalas, Mari Sandoz, Bison Book 1992

Bury My Heart at Wounded Knee, Dee Brown, Henry Holt 1970

Black Elk, Joe Jackson, Farrar, Straus & Giroux 2016

The Indian Sign Language, W.P. Clark, Bison Book 1982

Indian Sign Language, William Tomkins, Dover Publications 1969

Indian Signals & Sign Language, G. Fronval & D. DuBois, Wings Books 1994

The Southeastern Indians, Charles Hudson, University of Tennessee 1976

American Indian Trickster Tales, R. Erdoes and A. Ortiz, Viking 199

INDEX
Numbers in bold indicate photographs/illustrations.

Gourdy Old Style on 100gsm (70#) matte artpaper
Case 14pt. C1S with gloss film lamination – Flexi-Bind
Type and design by Karen Paul Stone